To Kirsten, for being the most beautiful, wonderful, patient and awesome girl I have ever met. My Love for you knows no bounds.

To Missi, for the mantra, the guided tour of Midian, and endless support. Love you, Monster Sister,

To Grimm, for the constant inspiration and motivation.

To my sister and Core-dog, my Mom and Dad, for being awesome.

To Chris for the ads. Your audio work blows me away every time

And to Anthony, Ray, Tori, John and Missi - The Horror Vision - for always talking Horror!

DECLARATION OF INTENT

The moon hangs low in the sky, its three-quarters face obscured by the Autumn clouds. The night this time of year in Sundown Hills is loud. Bugs, wind and the occasional bat infest its knowing calm with forced intervention. In the distance, the sound of a tractor-trailer's hydraulic brakes hiss and lock. A car on the highway that connects the town to the state beyond squeals its tires as a collision is narrowly avoided. A murder of crows starts at the commotion and takes to the air in panicked flight. They pass before the smoldering moon, marring its visage before striking out to the East. On the road below, the truck begins to move again, turns off I40 onto Samson Bradley Parkway and travels the half mile to the gate that still reads Peppermill Pharmaceuticals. This place, abandoned for so long, has seen great changes over the previous month. Construction crews come and go, landscapers cut back the forest that once served as a border to prying eyes, now overgrown and claiming half the land.

Farther up is the main campus, comprised of five warehouses. A flashlight beam guides a lone figure between buildings. They pause at a door marked with the alchemical symbol for Earth. Through this, past row after row of plants until another doorway opens onto an iron staircase that spirals down into stygian darkness. The figure begins its descent, the rhythmic clang of boots on metal fading as they disappear into the Earth. Down here are tunnels.

Many, many tunnels.

Sundown Hills was once an oil town, digging a given. The traveler does not stop in these man-made warrens. Instead, they venture further into this underground world, where town founder Samson Bradley unearthed subterranean passages that predate man's impetus to steal the Earth's lifeblood. A veritable labyrinth unconnected to the upper world, its purpose and origin unknown. A place that was old when humanity was young...

The traveler emerges from the final Earthen corridor into an ancient room. The walls, floor and ceiling are beyond black. The ground is spongy, as though sodden. In the center, the dim light of a single torch reveals several similarly hooded figures, all gathered around a raised dais. Upon this, an altar of obsidian stone holds the prone figure of a young man, no more than seventeen years old. Long, dirty blonde hair hangs in clumps over an unshaven face. His body is covered in bruises, his arms in track marks.

Before the altar is a small aperture in the floor within which a viscous red liquid gently laps, as though alive. Whispers can be heard buried softly within the liquid's susurrations.

"Mammon...Mammon...Eiah... Eiah..."

The newly arrived participant slips past the congregation and up a small copse of stairs, mounting the altar and coming to rest behind an octagonal table covered by black cloth.

Upon this cloth rests a single, sharpened blade. The participant grasps this blade by the hilt, raises it above their head and begins to chant:

"Eiah Eiah Olumtwoo Hollum! Eiah Eiah! Eiah Eiah!"

A shimmer passes over the world. The walls flex and breathe as faces slowly push out through the deep black walls, masks so life-like they present a chilling sentience, inanimate objects temporarily made flesh again. These are the faces of those who made this place, who traveled from far away to open the doors hewn into this land long ago, an unholy pact that forever left a mark on the town. The Wilhelm Egregore - a focused culmination of fear, hatred and greed, pressurized into a blade that could cut a door between worlds.

"Eiah Eiah Olumtwoo Hollum! Eiah Eiah! Eiah Eiah!"

Amidst the rhythm of this escalating mantra, the faces on the walls stir, their hollow eyes and flat features return to life, if only to observe the ritual they once initiated. The participant plunges the blade into the body of the unconscious man and all around the room, dark red blood begins to flow from the ceiling down the walls. As the liquid reaches the stone floor, it moves toward the aperture, slowly draining into the excited pool, raising its volume until the tide line rests just below the edges.

"The game has begun."

Abruptly, the mantra stops, and the figures file from the room. This was but a declaration of intent; they possess all the required elements except a receptacle for the blade.

All is quiet and the liquid is still.

PROLOGUE

Saturday, June 27, 2015

"Didn't some kids get killed by Satanists here back in the 90s?"

Six teenagers duck beneath the fence that reads *Peppermill Pharmaceuticals - Private Property,* quickly slipping into the trees as headlights drift by on the road behind them. They find the trail quickly, collapsing into a single file line, fighting back brush on a path that leads deeper into the woods. Everyone is buzzed; the night feels electric, charged with a potential only available to the young. To five of them, what lay ahead feels epic. To the sixth, going through the motions is about the extent he can muster.

"That Satanic shit's just town folklore, Sue. My brother said Peppermill made all that crap up to keep kids from partying here."

"Didn't fucking work, did it?"

They walk on in silence for a time, the balm of dismissal

failing to quell anyone's nerves. They are alone in the woods at night. Woods where bad things are said to have happened.

The path ends abruptly; the trees and brush open onto a large, circular clearing that reveals their destination: the Fire Pit. Surrounded by ad hoc log benches pieced together before any of this current group were born, this secluded spot represents a local teenage rite of passage, a place for revelry and intoxication hidden from the eyes of their elders. Located just over a mile inside the fence surrounding the old Peppermill property, local police don't have access, and since the Pharmaceutical giant closed in the late 90s, the site is derelict. Or so it has been until recently when new owners began construction to make this place... something more. Something, thus far at least, shrouded in mystery.

A sound stops them; branches snap in the immediate distance, just down the path. The group holds its collective breath. When nothing appears, they resume their journey, mindful that with revitalization comes the likelihood of security. These woods are thick, though. The chestnut, spruce and hackberry trees that grow here surround the pit, virtually guaranteeing the partiers are left to their own devices.

Teenagers are made of devices.

That sixth, forlorn adventurer, Bill Brouwer, let his teammates Brian Panosian and Marty O'Donnell talk him into accompanying them this evening, even though he'd rather have stayed home. On the losing end of a recent break-up, Bill was still licking his wounds. He'd figured there would be girls; he had not anticipated Angela Walters, the cheerleader he'd carried a torch for until he met Lisa McCready.

Clearly, Marty and Brian wanted to convince him to move on, but Bill didn't care; Angela's power over him paled in comparison to what he felt for Lisa. Bill was in no mood for a hook-up. His friends' hearts were in the right place, but he refused to believe things between Lisa and him were over.

"Those stories? About the kids that got killed? Totally true," Marty says, his cadence mocking Vincent Price.

"Oh, come on."

"Swear. Couple dudes brought their chicks out here trying to impress them; the demon got all of 'em!"

"The demon?" Angela asked, naively saddling up to Bill. He knew she knew the story. Everyone did.

"Pfft. Right." Cindy Charles was Angela's best friend and, like Angela, one of the 'elite' girls of the incoming Senior Class. Cindy's parents owned a trendy, ultra-chic restaurant five hours away in Nashville. Cindy's straight A's meant they left her alone on the weekend. Little did mom and dad know about their daughter's penchant for 151 Rum and cocaine. Bill wondered if it was the booze and drugs that made Cindy a bitch; he doubted it. Most likely, it was the money.

"I don't know. I've heard that story like, a hundred times, and every time, it's always spot-on the same." Sue Contreras, on the other hand, was a looker *and* a sweetheart. A lot less maintenance than Angela, who'd been making eyes at Bill all night. Still, none of these girls held a candle to Lisa.

The girls sat while Bill lit the fire. It wasn't easy; heavy Summer rains the last few days had left the area damp, so it took a little bit of that old Eagle Scout know-how, something neither Brian nor Marty possessed.

"Wow. You're sure good with lighting fires," Angela said, and Bill almost laughed. He supposed her routine might seem hot to other guys. To him, the word that came to mind was 'cringe.'

Bill didn't regret coming along to hang out with his friends, but even three beers in the first half hour hadn't ousted Lisa from his mind. Six months into the best relationship of his life and school gossip fucked everything up! Ever since the baseball team's away game last weekend, word was Bill and Johnson City Cobra's head Cheerleader Regan McAllister hooked up in the girl's locker room. Lisa heard Misty Bradley and her friends talking about this and she confronted him. Bill explained that, yes, Regan had made a pass at him, but he ignored her.

Lisa didn't believe him.

What Bill wanted to tell her, what he was sure would convince Lisa of his innocence, was that he'd spent the last few months building the courage to confess his love for her. Lisa's reluctance to believe him about something as trivial as a rumor meant someone was feeding her lies. The two most likely candidates were Angela Walters and her scummy chum, Misty.

Before Lisa, Bill would have dropped any girl who called him a liar. Recently, though, something changed. Maybe it was the threshold of Senior year and, beyond that, the real world. Or the knowledge that, as good as he was at high school football, baseball and track, Bill knew he would never be good enough to go pro. Either way, Lisa McCready had come to mean a lot to him, and when Bill found her unwilling to believe his side of the story, he nearly went mad. He couldn't even imagine sleeping with anyone else; try as he might to put her out of his mind, Lisa was the only girl he wanted.

The night dragged on, the injustice of his situation running laps around the inside of his head; finally, after his fifth beer, Bill became motivated.

"Be right back," he said, standing up and heading into the trees.

"Where you going, dude?"

"Piss," Bill lied, his phone already dialing Lisa, not realizing he had it on speaker.

"Hey, if you're going to take a leak, someone here might wanna help!"

Bill didn't respond; he heard their talk recede as he

entered the woods. The path they'd come in on led him back about one hundred feet to where he'd spotted a fallen tree earlier; Bill swiped the screen open on his phone. As he did, the annoying ringtone for FaceTime chimed. It was Lisa.

"Hey!" he said, excited. Lisa's image froze instantly, and her words glitched with that weird, broken-robot effect.

"Whzzz yzzz..."

"You're breaking up, babe."

"Whzzz yzzz..."

"Babe?"

He stepped into the light of a small clearing and the signal shot to full strength.

"I was just thinking about you."

"What? You're all garbled," Lisa raised the phone closer to her face as if studying the screen. "Are you in the woods?"

"Ah, yeah. Just hanging out with Brian and Marty and–"

Panosian appeared out of nowhere, snagged the phone from Bill's hand and took off down the path toward the pit.

"Angela Walters is SO gonna fuck Bill's brains out tonight, Lisa Lisa!"

Caught off-guard, Bill was a full five steps behind until Brian accidentally veered off the path into a thorn bush.

"Ow!"

"DUDE!" Bill slammed Brian double-handed in the chest, and the second-string wannabe toppled into the spiky branches.

"What the fuck, bro? Can't take a joke?!" Brian whipped the phone at Bill, who caught it easily.

"I'm not gonna tell you again: Nothing happened with me and Regan, okay? I love Lisa! Now leave me the fuck alone!"

"Sorry, bro. I just thought–"

Brian's apology broke off when one of the girls began to scream.

Brian might have been a mediocre athlete, an annoying

practical joker, and a burgeoning alcoholic, but he was no coward. Panosian was up and out of the thorns, racing by Bill's side toward the pit. When they burst from the trees into the clearing, they stopped short at the sight before them: a figure in a black ski mask brandished a large machete at their friends.

With no hesitation, Panosian threw himself at the menacing shape, coming down hard on the back of their neck with a double fist hammerlock; the would-be attacker crumbled. Brian ripped the mask off, and a gasp went up as the Sundown Hills Devils' starting quarterback and all-around jack-ass Gary Sherman lay revealed before them.

"Hahaha, got you fuckers!"

"Fuck you, Gary!" Cindy whipped an empty bottle of Zima at Gary's face, spraying lukewarm malt beverage on everyone in the vicinity.

"You guys are dicks!"

That was it for Bill.

"I'm out."

"Hey, Bill! Bro!"

Bill ignored Gary, brought his phone back up and was surprised to see Lisa was still connected.

"What the hellzzzts' going onnnzzzz?"

"Sorry, babe. Look, I had to talk to you. I mean-" As he spoke, Bill stepped back out onto the path. Only, this time, the path wasn't there.

"What the hell?"

He looked around for a minute, then reluctantly returned to the clearing and tried to reconnoiter.

"Whazzzt are you doing?"

"Back so soon?"

"Fuck off," Bill said and leveled his gaze at Brian. "Isn't this where the path was a minute ago?"

"How should I know?" Brian said, picking brambles from the flesh on his forearm. "I'm drunk. You lost?"

Bill shook his head in disbelief, crossing to another spot where the trees thinned to form a natural exit. Same thing: no path.

Bill stepped into the trees anyway, wading through thick burr bushes.

"What the f-"

"Bill? Whzzzy are youzzz-"

Behind him, another scream.

"Jesus Fucking Christ, guys!"

"Billzzz?"

Bill stepped back into the clearing just in time to see a large figure bury a hatchet in Cindy's head, opening a geyser of blood that would have been right at home in one of the Evil Dead movies. It looked totally fake.

"Gary! Enough!" Bill said, walking toward the pit. After three steps, he tripped on something and fell to the ground.

"Huh?"

Bill's feet were entwined with Gary Sherman's camou-flaged legs, but everything above Gary's belt line was missing; the limbs terminated at the hip joint in ragged and bloody scraps of flesh and camouflage. Large intestines lay strewn about the dirt and leaves, some of them snaking into the flames. The hideous smell of burning offal filled the space.

"Billzzzz?"

"Call your father!" Bill screamed into the phone on instinct as a thick, red cloud of terror suddenly engulfed him. He turned his head and saw Gary's top half arc through the air and land next to his entrails, the resulting black smoke not enough to obscure the agony on the prankster's face as his life drained from him in greedy gulps. Was it Bill's imagina-tion, or was the ground suddenly open below the corpse, drinking Gary's blood straight from the wound?

"FUUUAAHHHCCKKK!"

Amidst the slaughter, Bill jumped back up and ran toward the trees. No more hero left in him at the sight of such bodily destruction. To his right, a machete took off most of the right side of Marty O'Donnell's face. To his left, Sue slipped into that gaping maw in the Earth; it slammed shut on her bare midriff; Sue screamed, vital organs bursting from her mouth, high into the night sky like some horrible, bloody geyser.

Bill sensed movement and snaked to his left just in time to see a hatchet come down on Cindy's head, splitting her skull into two pieces that flopped down on either side of her petite frame.

"Whazzzzt? Bill, whazzzzzt the hell dozzzzes my dad have to do withzzzz-"

Lisa's voice disintegrated as Bill cut left again and slammed face-first into a tree. Upon impact, the phone flew from his hand and clattered to the ground. Dazed, Bill watched the killer's boot grind the device into the dirt, a loud SNAP signaling the moment the screen shattered. The sound reactivated the stalled teenager, igniting in him the purest purpose he'd known in his short, eighteen-year-old life of privilege and frivolity:

Survival.

Bill ran as hard as he could, refusing to slow down even as he navigated the slaughter and burst back through the wall of trees into the woods.

He'd only made it about ten feet when he felt the first wincing shock of the blade pierce his shoulder; nearly collapsing under the gargantuan weight of pain, Bill managed to dodge a second blow and, squinting through the agony, ran on. He plowed through the woods and finally, mercifully, reached the path again. No sooner did salvation present itself than it was torn away when, impossibly, his attacker reappeared before him and drove a six-foot steel pole through Bill's sternum.

"Help!" someone yelled behind him, but Bill was sinking, sliding down a tree trunk and settling into a pool of vital juices. He felt light as air. Pieces were missing, some tangible essence flaking off like rust in soda, flittering up toward the sky, dissipating into a natural order that opened its arms and welcomed him home, away from the pain, away from the image of the figure before him, raising one giant, steel-toed boot over his head. The treads on the boot were new, a branding logo sculpted into their center: a horse with wings. Bill thought that was nice, the idea of a flying horse. He imagined Lisa sitting on its back, climbing from the soft grassy knolls of Sundown Hills to the pink clouds in the sky. It brought a smile to Bill's face an instant before the boot came down and caved his head in like a rotting pumpkin. Behind where he lay dead, the screams from the clearing had stopped. The night was silent in all its crimson glory.

BLACK GLOVES & BROKEN HEARTS

Shawn C. Baker

NOW HE WANTS TO KILL YOU

CHAPTER ONE

Sunday, August 30: Mather's Sanitarium, est. 1937

Twelve hours.

In twelve hours, Lisa will go home and her life will begin anew. It will be a different life; the one that ended two months ago in blood and horror washed away her old existence and ushered in one birthed from pain, paranoia and madness.

Twelve hours.

The sound of footsteps roused Lisa from her despondent reverie. A tremor shot through her spine, turned to a full-on case of shivers. Twelve hours, but first, she had to make it through one more night, one more visit from Philip. Lisa wanted what Philip would bring her, but more than that, she wanted to be out of Mather's, away from the soft white walls and harrowing screams that echo from the room down the hall, the one where the patients who misbehave went.

Because there were always patients who misbehaved.

Lisa's anxiety increased as the footsteps grew closer. She

knew the sound well - the steel-toe boots had ingrained themselves in her mind as a harbinger of imminent threat.

Clik-Clop

Clik-Clop

Lisa knew Philip swindled this route from Jerry, the less creepy orderly. She knew he did this because Philip liked her. She knew that when he looked at her, Philip was looking *through* her clothes, thinking about her body and what he wanted to do to it. Had he ever been inappropriate with a patient? Lisa was sure the answer was yes based on the incident last week. Nurse Landing had walked into her room just as Philip cornered her, his hand on his belt buckle.

She shook harder when the memory merged with the sound of the encroaching footsteps.

Clik-Clop

Clik-Clop

Philip had scurried off at the sight of his superior, but despite what she witnessed, Nurse Landing refused to acknowledge this precipice of impropriety. Heather Landing was a family friend, but as the head nurse, she looked the other way on a great many things at Mather's; it made her job easier.

Not for Lisa, though. Not for any of the girls at Mather's.

The door opened, and Philip stood at the threshold, limned by the sodium vapors in the corridor outside.

"Lisa Lisa. Time for your meds, baby."

Lisa practically cowered in the corner as Philip sauntered in and shut the door behind him. Right arm outstretched, the orderly cradled her favorite purple pills in the shallow cup of his tattooed palm. She hated that Philip held such power over her, hated that she'd begun to dream about the creepy black stars tattooed from his hands all the way up to where his skinny arms disappeared into the short sleeves of his scrubs. Dreams where she saw those stars as they descended over her eyes, wrapped around her throat, pulled at her nightgown...

Philip offered Lisa the pills, his smile a jagged scar cut into his pock-marked face, exposing rotted teeth. He could smell her fear.

"Take your pills, Lisa Lisa, or you'll end up just like your little friend Onya. You don't wanna end up crazy, do ya? I mean, it's good for me cuz nobody believes what crazy girls say, ya know? Maybe not so good for you, though, eh? Madness is a scary thing, baby. You know where we put the crazies, right?"

"The third floor?" Lisa said, tears choking her voice.

Built in the late thirties, Mather's Sanitarium stood three stories high. However, the top floor had remained closed for the past fifty-something years. The popular explanation was the expense of keeping an unused floor heated. Among the residents and some of the staff, however, rumors abounded of more nefarious reasons. Illegal experiments, torture and even human trafficking. Philip was always only too happy to pontificate on these ideas, as the fear the rumors created helped him get what he wanted from the residents.

Lisa moved to accept the pills, and Philip reneged. The smile on his face was the same one from her nightmares, an image she felt certain she would see every night for the rest of her life. As if he understood his effect on her, Philip pinched the pill from his palm and held it out to her, a priest offering communion.

"Uh-ah. Allow me. Open wide, baby..."

Disgusted to the point of tears, Lisa accepted the situation and opened her mouth. Instead of relinquishing the pill quickly, Philip reached in and set it on her tongue, moving his fingers around the inside of her cheeks and across the roof of her mouth. His flesh tasted of bleach.

"Such a pretty mouth. You know who likes a pretty

mouth? The Devil. Hahaha. Now be good and maybe I'll come back to read you a bedtime story when everyone else goes to sleep."

When he closed the door, Lisa began to cry. Eventually, she dozed off and only woke when Nurse Landing came in with the sun to ready her for release. She had no idea what god she should thank for preventing Philip's return, so she offered a prayer to them all.

———

"Today's the day, my dear. Excited?"

Lisa nodded.

"How are we feeling?"

"Kinda like my old self again," Lisa lied. Her old self was dead, never coming back.

"I'm so happy to hear that, hon."

Did Nurse Landing believe her? Or was this all a game they played for one another?

There was a time not so long ago when Lisa could not have imagined leaving Mather's, let alone returning to school. But as the shadows traveled across the walls from left to right, day in and day out, a need for stability had returned to her life. Having spent the better part of her convalescence in what the doctor called a "fugue state," Lisa's mind finally began to repair itself a little over a week ago; her recognition and reactions to the people around her changed from foggy ambivalence to a perfunctory social veneer. The doctors called it a 'psychological reconstruction based on social demand,' which was apparently an excellent sign. It meant she was returning to the world, remembering how to adapt and assimilate to social structures. Based on this, Lisa's orders for discharge had come through yesterday, and today, Philip be damned; she meant to leave this dreadful place for good.

"Are we still having thoughts about Bill? About... death?"

"None," Lisa lied again, this time with an exaggerated smile. Her initial reaction to Bill's murder in what the media had dubbed the "Peppermill Woods Massacre" was one of terror. It was the kind of reaction one might expect from an eighteen-year-old whose formerly benign reality suddenly reared back and coughed out the mutilated corpses of half a dozen high school friends.

Well, calling most of those who died that night friends was a bit much, but in the wake of an event such as this, social malfeasance seemed an insignificant slight indeed.

Before that night, Sundown Hills had been a safely guarded oasis from the ocean of chaos the twenty-four-hour news cycle reported on a machine gun basis. Terrorist attacks? University shootings? Megalomaniacal politicians out to end the world? Lisa studied all of it the way a biologist studies cancer cells in a petri dish - from a safe, occluded distance. In eighteen years, the only thing that had come close to those headlines in Sundown Hills was Annie Harrison's death. Even that had seemed a distant tragedy, partially because, although once best friends, the girls had grown apart shortly before Annie's death and partially because the crime was eventually attributed to her erratic stepmother, a foregone conclusion based on the drama that haunted Annie for much of her teenage years. The night of Bill's death, however, cleaved Lisa's world in half. The resultant psychological fugue was, the doctor said, a natural reaction to losing someone she loved and the parameters of her existence all in one fell swoop.

Nurse Landing busied herself tidying the room and then made to leave.

"Your father will be here soon; be sure to look pretty for him."

"Nurse Landing?"

"Yes?"

"Am I crazy?"

Nurse Landing stopped what she was doing and turned to address Lisa in a staunchly sympathetic manner.

"Why, of course not, dear! Look," she sat on the bed, patting the mattress beside her. "What happened to you - to your friends - was horrible. You just needed time to recover."

"Are the pills the only thing keeping me from... from..."

"Regressing? No. They help, though, so we want you to continue to take them. It won't be forever, but for now, while you're facing school and life outside these walls, they will help take the edge off. Okay?"

"Okay. It's just that..."

"Lisa, if you don't feel up to leaving just yet, I can talk to Dr. Caldwell..."

"My dad would be furious."

"You have to take your time with these things. You've been through a lot. If you want to stay another week, I don't think your father would be angry."

"Then you don't know my dad."

"Of course I know him; Gerald has been the Sheriff for almost as long as I've been a nurse."

"My father views all weakness as a disappointment. My mom's death? Disappointment. My breakdown? Disappointment. Ashely's attack-"

"Lisa! My goodness, girl. Gerald *does not* think like that. For god's sake, your mother died bringing you into this world; how could anyone view that as anything but the ultimate sacrifice for love?"

"How do you know what he thinks?"

"Well, because... because it just wouldn't be right. It wouldn't be true." Nurse Landing leaned into Lisa and put her arm around her. It was a comforting gesture that Lisa cherished, knowing she would not receive the same delicate treatment from her father.

"I think it's this room. Too many bad memories. Why don't we wait for the Sheriff in the rec room?"

"Sure," Lisa agreed, feeling small and more than a little helpless. They sat like that for a while, nurse and patient bonding over the challenge of recovery. When Nurse Landing led Lisa to the elevator, Lisa watched her push the button for the first floor. She opened her mouth to ask about the button for the third floor, why it lit up as though the car had descended from above, but she didn't get a chance. That was the same moment the screaming began.

———

Nurse Landing ran from the elevator so quickly she didn't realize Lisa was at her heels. In the corridor, a throng of staff and patients converged into a mob, everyone clamoring for a look at the disaster that was Onya O'Sullivan. Incidents like this were not uncommon with Onya, but it'd been weeks since the previous one. Onya herself was harmless; the chaos her outbursts created was not.

When she first heard the screams, Lisa felt certain this wasn't the usual Onya drama. She imagined rounding the corner to find Philip in mid-assault. The thrill of this potential revelation made Lisa feel equally exhilarated and terrible. Terrible for her willingness to sacrifice her friend for an opportunity to destroy the guy who had made her life a living hell these last few weeks.

Philip wasn't there, only tiny, blonde, thirty-two-year-old Onya. Lisa and Onya had become friends despite the woman's occasional violent fits and spooky prophecies. Another girl, Trini Hollbrook, previously told Lisa that just before she arrived at Mather's, Onya had predicted the massacre at the fire pit. Lisa eventually mustered the courage to ask Onya about this, but she often didn't remember the predictions made while in one of her 'states.' It bothered Lisa that she would never know the veracity of Trini's statement, but thus was life.

"Get away from me!"

Shrieking in the hallway outside the lunch room, blood clung to the front of Onya's gown and matted her hair against her face. She looked like something from a Horror movie - one where the final girl ended up smothered in blood. The image sent a primal shock through Lisa; the heightened state of awareness it ignited remained even after the realization the mess was the Cherry Cobbler served with lunch, not precious bodily fluids.

Two orderlies attempted to restrain Onya, but at a whopping five-foot-three, one hundred pounds soaking wet, she threw them off her like paper dolls. Diagnosed with acute schizophrenia after an attack when she was younger, Onya's episodes often involved impossible bouts of strength. Sure she could help, Lisa side-stepped Nurse Landing and ran to her friend, getting close enough to lay a reassuring hand on her shoulder.

"It's okay, Onya. You're okay."

Onya moved like she was about to toss Lisa next, but when they made eye contact, she stopped cold. Everyone else - the nurses, orderlies and onlookers alike - stood motionless as Lisa took charge of the situation. She heard Nurse Landing instruct Nurse Ritter to quietly go find Onya's stuffed turtle, Arturo.

"It's okay, Onya. No one wants to hurt you."

"Not true! Not true! They tried. He killed my mother and now he wants to kill me! Kill me!"

Lisa's hands went up before her face, and Onya flinched violently backward directly into Philip's waiting grasp.

"Got you!"

Lisa watched in horror as Philip maneuvered Onya into a full nelson.

"Don't do that! She's fine. Let her go!"

Onya began to buck and kick.

"Lisa! Get back and let us help that girl!" Nurse Landing ordered.

"She doesn't need your help!"

Furious at the intervention, Lisa turned her anger on Philip and lashed out with a fist to his right temple.

"Don't touch her!"

Before Lisa could do anything more, another orderly caught her by the arms and pulled her away.

"No!"

Lisa kicked and screamed as she watched Nurse Landing administer a syringe full of sedatives to Onya's right arm.

"Stop! She's fine! She was going to be okay!"

Nurse Landing stared at Lisa with open disappointment.

"Andre, take Ms. McCready to the lobby to wait for her father. If she gives you any trouble, handcuff her to the visitor's bench, please."

Andre dragged Lisa kicking and screaming through the security doors and promptly handcuffed her to the bench. Simultaneously, Nurse Ritter returned with Onya's turtle; Onya hugged Arturo tight to her chest with the last moments of her ebbing consciousness.

Andre double-checked the cuff and, thinking the problem solved, returned to the fracas. He neglected to shut the security door completely, and as soon as he turned his back, Lisa performed a trick her father had taught her and slipped from her restraints. Andre heard the sound of the cuffs hitting the floor and turned just in time to catch both Lisa's fists in his chest. Before he even hit the floor, she was through the double doors and back into the fray, which was mostly over now that Onya had been drugged. She lay on a stained cot, writhing in slow motion, leather restraints pinning her arms to her side, Arturo discarded on the floor.

Nurse Landing had yet to notice Lisa's return; her attention was focused on dispersing the crowd. Lisa moved in close to Onya and took her hand. Lisa knew this woman had been through so much; she hated seeing her treated so poorly. Onya stirred when Lisa's skin touched hers, rousing briefly from the chemical slumber that weighed her down into a malleable state.

"It's okay, Onya. I know you didn't mean any harm. I'll help you. I'm not sure how, but I'll find a way."

"He killed her. Killed my mother; now he wants to kill you..."

Whispered like a confessional, Onya's mantra chilled Lisa even before she realized the subject of the premonition had shifted to her.

"Wait? Onya? What did you-"

"Lisa!" Nurse Landing screamed, her anger downright frightening.

"How did you get back in here? Andre! This is your ass, boy!"

"He wants to kill you!" Onya shrieked.

"You can't treat her this way! She's hurt! She's been through too much already and -"

"Lisa!"

Grainy and worn like the wood in the old fence surrounding their house, her father's voice stopped Lisa cold.

"What the hell is going on here?"

———

Things went from bad to worse. Lisa knew her father was already disappointed in her inability to deal with the tragedies of everyday life - a given to someone who'd worked law enforcement as long as he had. She'd been unprepared for him to refuse her side of the fracas in the hospital altogether, which is precisely what he did. Lisa knew Gerald McCready's professional relationship with Helen Landing went back nearly three decades; what she didn't realize, however, was that Landing was Gerald McCready's liaison in all cases involving mentally unsound individuals. Thus, the two compatriots enjoyed not only the nostalgic bond of shared memories but also a level of professional respect that made them thick as thieves. When Lisa accused Landing of mistreating another patient, and that patient turned out to be Onya O'Sullivan, daughter of local ne'er-do-well Frank O'Sullivan, Gerald immediately shut down. Witnessing his daughter's erratic behavior didn't help; Gerald rejected Lisa's side of the story without a second thought. Wielding only a disappointed look and an upturned eyebrow, Lisa's father remanded her to sit quietly while he filled out the necessary paperwork and caught up with his colleague. Mentally and emotionally traumatized by the entire ordeal, Lisa accepted defeat. She sat quietly for the better part of an hour, a television droning away before her.

On the screen, large yellow font promised LOCAL MYSTERY SOLVED. Lisa hitched in a breath and prepared to learn the identity of the killer, only to be disappointed a moment later as local news reporter Ted Owens spoke excitedly:

"Michael Bradley has revealed that not only is he the mysterious purchaser of the Peppermill Pharmaceutical Property, but that he is currently in the process of introducing a bill to next month's ballot that would make Marijuana *legal*. That's right, in an exclusive interview with Channel Five, Bradley outlined his plans to, quote, "bring Sundown Hills out of the past."

On the screen, Michael Bradley appeared before city hall. His brown hair, perfectly quaffed into an athletic smattering of spikes, balanced the golden tan he'd honed during his years on the West Coast. He wore a cream-colored blazer over an off-white polo. He looked friendly and professional but not corporate.

"My father knew what big oil was doing to this town. No disrespect to my great-grandfather Samson, but times have changed. The world needed oil to get us where we are today, but we don't need it for tomorrow. In fact, I think it's high time the human race left fossil fuels behind altogether. One need only look at the problems plaguing our town to understand I'm right. Oil drilling is why we had a rash of fires that took nearly two decades to extinguish. It's why our wildlife population has diminished, and it's eaten into our beautiful forests."

"And how exactly does legalized Marijuana help?"

"I never said it did, Ted. What legalized Marijuana does is reduce alcoholism and create a taxable crop that I will use to bring new technology to Sundown Hills. First up - electric automobiles."

Lisa's disappointment disappeared as she listened to Bradley outline an ambitious plan to turn the Peppermill land into a state-of-the-art Pot Farm, then use that money to begin converting the town's fossil fuel footprint to Solar and Electric. In spite of herself, she smiled at the thought of her father's inevitable response to this new turn of events. For Sheriff Gerald McCready, the ends would not justify the means.

Lisa herself wasn't quite sure where she stood on legal weed, but she trusted Michael Bradley. She'd worked for him on a nonprofit her Sophomore year, and in the limited interactions that position provided, she'd grown to think of him as "one of the good guys," the complete antithesis to his brother David, who only seemed to care about one thing: Money.

As one half of the infamous Bradley Brothers, heirs to the Inner Earth Oil fortune, Michael did not see eye to eye with his younger brother, David, on their family's legacy. Their great-grandfather, Samson Bradley, was one of the town's original settlers. A farmer whose fields perpetually failed, Samson became one of the wealthiest men in the state almost overnight when he abruptly switched to mining oil. Each generation of Bradleys since expanded the business, gobbling up land until Michael and David's father Roland nearly bankrupted the company in the 70s and sold part of their land to Peppermill Pharmaceuticals. Roland was forcibly removed and disappeared shortly after that.

After a rebellious streak as a teenager, Michael Bradley left town at eighteen and his younger brother David hit the fast track to take over the company. Business and David didn't mix at first, though, and it wasn't until the late 90s that the board felt confident bringing him in as CEO. Once aboard, his aggressive fracking policies saw Inner Earth begin to recoup its losses. Then the media exploded with environmental reports about the dangers of fracking and the company stalled again. Peppermill began pumping exorbitant amounts of money into propaganda the town had no choice but to buy into. Even when a large part of the drinking water took to catching fire, people looked the other way.

Sinkholes? Unrelated.

Wildlife devastation? Nope. Nothing to do with drilling for oil.

Sundown Hills' entire history was rooted in oil production; without it, how could they survive, let alone prosper?

It boiled down to fear of change, and upon his return, Michael Bradley started to proselytize the dangers of his family's company. Thus began the feud that simmered to this very day.

On the screen, Ted Owens asked Michael to comment on David's recent anti-marijuana ad campaign.

"The day after the press release about your plans for the Peppermill land, your brother went on record blaming Marijuana for the murders that occurred here back in August. What do you have to say to those allegations, Michael?"

"My brother's comments are not just asinine; they are disrespectful to the victims and the families of those victims. Marijuana did not kill those children; a madman with a machete did."

"Let's go," her father's booming voice interrupted the tv. Lisa didn't need to be asked twice.

———

Gerald piloted his Police cruiser Northwest on I24, his daughter in the passenger seat, staring out the window at a world that somehow seemed... different. Having been in Mather's for nearly two months, Lisa sensed Sundown Hills had changed. The graying fields that isolated the Asylum from the rest of the town seemed to have spread their monochromatic influence in all directions; the homes and lawns that once sparkled now dull and tired. Was it the end of summer or something more malevolent?

A convoy of semi trucks passed them as they exited the Interstate and breached the town's limits.

"What's with all these damn trailers?"

"The mystery's over. Michael Bradley bought the Peppermill land from Craig Walters."

"I heard. Something about legalized weed."

"Not while I draw breath."

"I thought Michael was the 'good' brother?"

"The Bradleys and I have never seen eye-to-eye on anything."

The trucks passed, five total. Lisa knew her father didn't trust David Bradley. His upcoming bid for Mayor had recently become a certainty now that his only opponent, Craig Walters, had stepped down following his daughter Angela's death. Lisa suspected Gerald was more concerned with this development than his own daughter's mental health.

"If Mr. Walters isn't running, why don't you?"

"That a joke?"

"No."

"Lisa, a lot of people in town aren't happy with me."

She knew he wouldn't say it, but the dangling thread of a murderer on the loose wasn't doing the Sheriff's approval rating any favors.

Just another symptom that had thrown Lisa's entire teenage world out of whack; try as she might, this didn't feel like the town she'd grown up in any longer. Her doctor said this was natural after an event as traumatic as the murders, but Lisa felt her disorientation ran deeper. She felt a bit like Alice: she'd gone through a magic door inside Mather's Sanitarium and come out in a world that looked like her old one, smelled like her old one, but was in some fundamental way different.

The man sitting next to her, though, was the same as he had always been.

"Just a thought."

"Yeah, well, a few more spectacles like the one you caused today and-"

"I didn't cause anything that happened today."

"Lisa..."

"Look, you're the one who taught me to stand up for people who can't stand up for themselves."

"Helen says that girl was near to causing a riot that you basically tried to help her."

"Dad! You know Onya O'Sullivan couldn't start a riot if she tried. I'm telling you, she's being abused in there. I think a lot of girls are."

"Were you?"

"Well, no. Never directly. But, I could tell the orderly, Philip, I could tell he-"

"Let me just stop you right there, honey. These are serious accusations you're making. If you haven't experienced this firsthand - lord knows, I pray you haven't - and you haven't actually witnessed anyone else being abused, then you need to be careful about accusing people. That's a tough job those folks have. I'll give you they're not always up on their social graces; some of 'em are downright assholes. But that's a far cry from abuse."

"But -"

"No, Lisa, listen to me. You're right, I do know Onya. I'm the one who brought her to Mather's in the first place after we found her in the woods that night all those years ago. She's not well. What's more, this 'abuse scenario' you're talking about isn't that different from the accusations she made against her father at the time. Lotta talk that Frank had abused her, that he was the one that tried to kill her."

"She still says that."

"Well, I listened at the time, and I almost lost my job. Take my word for it; trouble finds that girl."

"Jesus Christ, Dad, I can't believe I'm listening to you blame the victim of a horrible crime. Do you seriously hear yourself? 'Trouble finds her?' What if people said that about Ashley?"

"People don't say that about Ashley because her father's not a drunken lout."

"Jesus."

"Enough with that, okay? Now, let's forget Onya O'Sullivan and focus on getting Lisa McCready back in school and acting like a normal teenage girl again; how's that?"

Lisa said nothing.

'Purple is the only normal now,' a new voice in her head chimed. She pictured her pills in Philip's hand, would have once again accepted his fingers into her mouth just to have that sweet release...

"How do you feel?"

Still nothing.

"Answer me, Lisa."

"Normal. That's what you want to hear, right?"

Not normal until Purple.

"Well, I'd imagine so, wouldn't you?"

More like what *you* want, Lisa thought.

They drove on in silence until they passed Christmas Park; in the distance, just beyond the Gazebo, Lisa could see the distinctive dark green gabled roof where James Harrison had lived alone since his daughter Annie died.

"You talked to Mr. Harrison lately?"

Gerald hesitated before answering.

"No. I hear he's not doing so well. You can see it in him now, the cancer. Like he's starting to disappear inside his clothes."

Lisa didn't respond. She missed Mr. Harrison, had thought about visiting him hundreds of times, but nothing moved that needle. Since Annie's death, it seemed the last person Lisa wanted to find herself face to face with was James Harrison.

"Probably won't last the winter."

The air between them soured; Gerald awkwardly changed the subject.

"Doc says to get you back in school, soon as possible. What do you think about tomorrow?"

"Are you being serious right now?"

"What?"

"Well, I was kinda hoping maybe I could have a week or two. Maybe we could, um, go somewhere?"

"Go somewhere? What the hell does that mean?"

"I thought we could go visit Ashley. You know, just the two of us on the drive, maybe see if I can stay in that extra room her sorority has, and you could get one at that nice little bed and breakfast down the road."

"Sure, Lisa. And did you even stop to think who would look after the town while I was gone?"

"Well, Matt's pretty good, right?"

"I'm in the middle of investigating multiple goddamn homicides, there's an election coming up, and to top it all off, Michael Bradley wants to legalize drugs; I can't just go running off to visit your sister at college just 'cuz you -"

Gerald caught himself.

"Just 'cuz I what?"

"Nothing."

"Dad, are you ashamed of what happened to me?"

"Now what the hell kind'a question is that?"

"A pretty goddamn simple one if you think about it."

"That's it, missy. Look, I'm sorry your friends got killed the way they did, but me running off ain't gonna catch whoever did it, and you spending your senior year acting like a zombie won't help anyone either."

"Jesus Christ, Dad! My boyfriend was brutally murdered less than two months ago. Is it okay if I grieve?"

"This ain't grief; it's lethargy. Look, I don't want to sound insensitive-"

"Too late."

"Lisa, I was there, remember? I saw what happened to those kids, to Bill."

"You never liked Bill."

"That doesn't mean I wanted to see something like that happen to him."

Purple

"I heard Angela's body was never found."

"You know I can't talk about an ongoing investigation."

Thinking of Angela's dead body tangled somewhere in the woods surrounding Peppermill, Lisa's eyes stung with salty tears, and her cheeks flushed warm. This was the change she'd sensed: Lisa no longer felt safe in Sundown Hills. What's more, she was pretty confident her father didn't feel safe *for her.* She studied him in the dimming afternoon light and saw a weariness she didn't recognize. Lisa knew this man as a force of unbending will, a stalwart old-schooler with calloused hands and unshakeable resolve. To see him like this now, dark circles under his eyes and hesitation in his responses, she wondered if the unflappable Sheriff McCready was out of his league.

"Who did it?"

"Well, now Lisa, I don't know yet. That's why I can't run off to college town with you. Okay?"

"Fine."

Part of Lisa actually wished she could help somehow. The other part wished she could leave and never look back. Ashley had been gone the better part of two years, and she hadn't come back once, not even for Christmas or her birthday. Graduation was a long way away, though, so Lisa was trapped. As for helping her father, she could barely help herself; the thought of being without her little purple pills lodged in her throat, made her suddenly feel like she was going to vomit.

"You okay, honey?"

A massive sense of exhaustion settled over her, like the blow from a hammer. The sensation chased away her sudden nausea, and a moment later, Lisa regained her composure.

"We need to stop at the pharmacy. For my prescription."

"I told Helen you don't need any more of her pills."

"What?" Lisa's voice croaked, her throat seized by pure terror.

"You don't need that horseshit, honey. Believe me."

"But -"

"Look. I'll take a swing by Vern's on the way home, grab a couple of burgers and we'll sit outside and eat. How's that sound?"

Lisa said it sounded good, but in her head, all she could hear was the sound of her nails scratching the plastic molding on the inside of the car door.

CHAPTER TWO

Monday, August 31

"Oh my god! Lisa, tell us everything!!!"

In her daydream, no sooner did Lisa step inside Sundown Hills High than her friends from Honors Bio and Debate Club rushed to join her, laughing and teary-eyed and ready to welcome Lisa back to the life she had left behind for two months of isolation and silence. In the fantasy, that first day went by in a kaleidoscope of welcoming embraces and smiles. It was the first good dream she'd had in months and the only one that didn't feature Bill being ripped to pieces by a faceless apparition. Nice as it was, this fantasy ended up bearing absolutely no resemblance to reality. Even Lisa's two closest friends, Cynthia MacMaster and Beth Grobe kept their distance from her. It was as if she had some communicable disease.

If madness is catchy, you caught a full dose while you were inside, toots.

The new voice again. The purple voice.

After arguing all night, Lisa lost the battle with her father. She ended up crying herself to sleep in the wee hours, only to be woken at 7:00 AM by his call to arms.

"Lisa! Up and at 'em, honey!"

He'd prepared a perfunctory breakfast, which they ate in silence. Afterward, Gerald instructed Lisa to go straight to her Guidance Counselor's office. No one came to greet her when she walked through the school doors. No one even batted an eye.

Ms. Galdykas was a wonderfully kind woman, and she welcomed Lisa into her office with a comforting smile and a box of tissue. She respected Lisa's initial silence, explaining that she would be on hand to help her return to a regular routine in any way she might need. For Lisa's part in the performance, she smiled politely and said the things she had learned the adults in her life wanted to hear. This was the routine now, the undercurrent of that strange doppelgänger world she first glimpsed through the passenger window in her father's cruiser, a world defined by constant worry and anxiety of those around her, as if they were all waiting for Lisa to collapse again. Without those pills, it was anyone's guess when that collapse would come.

A good student and nothing close to a troublemaker, Lisa had first been sent to talk to Ms. Galdykas after Annie's death. Now, it felt like this woman might be Lisa's only friend. She liked Ms. Galdykas very much, but this realization made Lisa decide she would die before letting another adult see the weakness inside her. She answered all the counselor's questions precisely the way she knew they should be answered, nodded when cued to, and said nothing of the pitch-black storm that threatened to consume her insides. She also said nothing of the longing for those little, purple pills or that without them, all bets were off.

"Call your father..."

Bill's voice, a raving phantom in her head. Why hadn't she realized he was in trouble, was asking for her help? If she had called her father, would he still be alive? The questions were insistent, the ramifications staggering.

Shortly before Second Period, Ms. Galdykas released Lisa so she could use the restroom. Lisa walked the empty halls alone and ducked into the Girls' room in C Building, where the classes were populated mainly by boys: shop, auto, etc. She hoped to have a few moments to steady herself.

She would not get them.

———

Jillian Maskowski entered the girls' room at a run. A Senior in high school and captain of the girls' volleyball and basketball teams, Jillian - or "J" as her friends called her - already stood so tall she had to duck beneath the low-hanging door jamb.

"Holy shit, ladies, Sheena apparently just saw Lisa McCready leaving the Gilded Dyke's office!"

"You mean they released that psycho from the nuthouse? Wow, I feel safe."

Jenna Roberts took a long drag from her vape pen and exhaled a sweet-smelling cloud into the room as she spoke. Jenna was short - 5'2" to be exact - and the only team she was captain of was Misty Bradley's fan club; ever since reading the cliff notes for King Arthur, Jenna learned to take great pride in considering herself the most popular girl in school's Merlin.

"Excuse me? Can we get back to business, or should I count you both out for Thursday?"

"Sorry, Misty."

Lisa sat motionless inside the stall, her feet pulled up against her backside, heels resting precariously on the edges of the seat. She'd been trying to compose herself when she heard the pack of jackals enter, the tell-tale cloud from their vapes instantly clouding the room, followed by a deep snorting that most likely signaled Misty's breakfast bump. As the sexual sidekick to town drug dealer Vic Lamb, Misty Bradley was a seventeen-year-old coke head. Fearing ridicule or worse, Lisa limited her breathing and went into stasis. She didn't want to be late for second period, but more than that, she didn't want to end up at the mercy of ruthless Misty Bradley and her posse.

"I can only take one girl with me, and so far, I'm not even close to convinced it should be either of you."

"You promised to take me, Misty!"

It sounded like Jillian whining.

"You're always at Slo Motion, J. What the fuck?"

"Um, excuse me? I've never been to one of the after-hour parties."

"Look. Slo Motion's management is very cautious, ya know? They trust I'll only refer the most mature girls for their parties. Right now, you both sound about as mature as a couple of preschoolers."

When Lisa was twelve and she and Annie were still best friends, they used to look at Misty Bradley's life and dream about what it would be like to be that rich. Then high school hit, and neither girl could stand the spoiled socialite train wreck that Misty became. Later, when the girls reached their Sophomore year and Annie returned from a month at camp with the body of a twenty-two-year-old, Annie and Lisa's friendship all but ended as Annie was absorbed into the 'popular crowd.' As far as Lisa was concerned, that was Misty's doing.

Annie began to ditch debate team and tutoring, reveling in the fact that her looks had started to turn the heads of older boys. This made it easy for her to be absorbed into the school's ruling class, which made it inescapable that she would become Misty Bradley's friend, even as she stopped being Lisa's. Annie went from watching movies with Lisa on Saturday nights to dating football players and, as she had once confessed to Lisa during a brief revival of their friendship just before her death, attending a party with Misty that had opened her eyes to the heavy, dark bottom that festered at the heart of Sundown Hills. Annie never offered specifics, but Lisa felt reasonably sure that Misty and her friends were mixed up in prostitution and drugs. Misty practically proved that now, as Slo Motion was a notorious truck stop and lounge on the outskirts of town that men patronized. The kind of place truckers used as overnight parking, surrounded as it was by a two-acre parking lot and minimal lighting.

"Look, no offense to Jillian, but I've got two tabs of Molly I've been saving; you take me, Misty, and the second one's yours."

"Oh, please. We've all had your brother's Molly, Jenna; it's, like, two-thirds heroin. I don't want to sleep through the good stuff."

Inside the stall, Lisa's disdain grew. It sickened her that someone like Bill died so terribly while Misty and her friends went about life at ninety miles an hour, not caring what it did to them. Bill had a future; he might have been turned down for a football scholarship, but his family was wealthy and had connections in the business world. He'd recently been pre-selected to test for both Harvard and Yale. Conversely, these three took everything for granted by dancing with the devil nightly.

"Look, Vic can get me anything I want, so don't try and bribe me with drugs, okay? I still haven't forgiven you after the godawful mess you almost made with my guy."

Lisa had no idea what they were talking about but couldn't help listening anyway.

"That wasn't my fault! I didn't realize she was his daughter. At least I wasn't the one who actually set up the deal that night."

This sounded like Jillian, almost in tears, seeking Misty's approval. Something terrible must have happened; Lisa grew more intrigued.

"Wait a minute! Who my brother sells to isn't my problem, okay? Sorry if he and Vic are in competition or whatever, but that's got nothing to do with me. Besides, after that party, Brian's scared to shit. He won't be selling in town anymore, guaranteed."

Party? Were they talking about the fire pit? And who was this 'my guy' Misty referred to? Vic didn't have kids.

"The point is you brought it up, bitch!"

"That tears it, I'm not taking either of you stupid bitches!"

The two sycophants exploded at this, all 'whys' and 'pleases' and 'I'll do anythings.' Lisa felt like vomiting. Unable to sit still for even a moment longer, she slipped her feet to the floor, flushed the toilet and exited the stall. As she did, she stepped directly into a massive discharge from Jillian's vape pen.

"Whoah, you spying on us, psycho?"

Lisa looked directly into Jenna's face, "Get over yourself, bitch. What do I care what you whores do?"

Two hands planted fast and hard on her back, and Lisa stumbled forward. She caught herself on the edge of the sink, but her right pinky hit at an odd angle and a hollow, reverberating pain shot through her wrist. Her first impulse was to retaliate, but Lisa had never been much of a fighter. With three of them present, there was no chance it would be a fair fight.

"You know your boyfriend died because of your dad, right bitch? First Annie and now the Fire Pit Massacre!"

"What the fuck did you just say?" Lisa stepped into

Misty's space and sized her up eye to eye. Misty did not flinch.

"You heard me. First Annie and now-"

"Annie was killed by her stepmom."

"Did your dad ever prove that? No? Wanna know why? Because it's not. Fucking. True."

"You didn't know Annie. I knew Annie!"

Tears began to fall down Lisa's cheeks; behind her, Jenna began to chant:

"Look at the wittle baby cwy! Cwy baby! Cwy!"

Jillian joined in as Lisa stepped close enough that their breasts touched.

The J's in unison: "Cwy Baby Cwy! Cwy Baby Cwy! Cwy Baby Cwy!"

Misty: "Correction, Lisa Lisa, you knew the *old* Annie. We knew grown-up Annie: no time for dolls, no time for Lisa. And since you obviously don't know your ass from a hole in the ground, I'll tell you this, too: Annie was killed by a couple guys from Slo Motion. She used to party there with me sometimes, and I guess the wrong guys took a liking to her. The reason no one talks about that? Because your dad covered it up to protect his own interests. He hid evidence and made up that stupid story about her stepmom!"

"You fucking liar!"

"You're calling me a liar? Oh brother, that's messed up. You're the liar, Lisa Lisa. You lie to yourself so you don't have to admit what a pathetic piece of shit your daddy is!"

Without anticipating it, Lisa drove her fist straight into Misty's mouth. It happened so fast that the two J's didn't have a chance to react. Never having hit anyone in the face before, the pain from the impact startled her; lightning shot through Lisa's knuckles, and it took her a second to recover. When she did, she saw bloody gouges across her knuckles from where Misty's teeth dug grooves into the tight, white flesh. The pain didn't stop her, though; Lisa pounced on top of Misty Bradley and started taking her apart when the first of the Deans came bursting through the door.

———

Clutching a blood-soaked rag to her knuckles, Lisa sat staring at the name professionally stenciled on the opaque glass of the office door across from her. Dean Laramie - A.K.A., the most feared faculty member at Sundown High. Lisa read the name repeatedly, trying to figure out what she would say when it was her turn in the hot seat. She imagined being questioned by the Dean, the fearsome woman's eyes probing Lisa's face for the slightest hint of a lie, or worse, the enjoyment Lisa knew she would be unable to hide if asked to explain why she had beaten the living shit out of Misty Bradley. No, waiting for her turn at the wheel of punishment, Lisa knew she was screwed. Especially when her father arrived.

The Purple would help

Students called the waiting area outside the Dean's office "The Square." This is where the teachers sent anyone whose misbehavior could result in criminal charges. Mr. Belvins, the Theatre teacher transplant from Ireland, had coined the term, and it stuck. "Away tew The Square with ye!" he'd shout when he caught kids smoking pot in the back of the Little Theatre, or worse, grinding on one another in the rafters. It was an almost comical way to be sent off to die, and it wasn't long before all the teachers followed suit. None of the three Deans or even Principal Severin had an office with a waiting area as legendary as The Square because, realistically, none of them dealt with the kind of disturbances Dean Laramie did. Sundown High was a pretty laid-back school before Annie's death; afterward, things changed, and the biggest of those changes was the addition of Laramie to the staff.

Patricia Laramie had obtained her Master's in education before she served in Afghanistan and Iraq. One of three sisters, the Dean's father believed the good lord had sent him a son and Mother Nature simply mixed up the order. Wounded in Kandahar and again in Fallujah, Patricia returned to the States and took a position at a high school in her hometown of Yonkers, NY. Shortly after that, for reasons unknown, she relocated to Sundown Hills, where her reputation grew by the day.

Lisa wasn't used to sitting in the Dean's office, let alone committing an offense of this magnitude. Fighting was a big deal here; she knew she'd be lucky to make it out without suspension.

Her dad was indeed going to kill her.

Purple.

A loud THUD interrupted Lisa's morose reverie. She looked up and saw Vic Lamb, tongue pressed against the glass like a squashed slug. Behind him, Freddy Snow pretended to strangle himself. Lisa had never spoken to either boy, and the fact that Vic was Misty's boyfriend made her wonder if she should take the display as a threat. Her concern died when both burst into laughter. A second later, Vic walked in and sat down next to her.

"How's it going?"

Lisa looked over each shoulder, perplexed that Vic was talking to her.

"Ah, okay, I guess."

"You really kicked Misty's ass!"

Lisa recoiled at Vic's smile when he said this; their eyes met, and a tiny fire started at the base of Lisa's spine. Awkward: Lisa's knuckles were still bleeding from where they had split on Vic's girlfriend's teeth.

"I guess I'm public enemy number one around here."

"It's okay, way I hear it from her two shithead friends, Misty had it coming. You been outta Mather's what, a day and a half? I always tell that girl, she thinks her looks make her untouchable, but looks don't stop a punch. Well, maybe they do, but not in the way she thinks, right?"

"I..." Lisa had no idea how to answer, no idea how to even talk to Vic. As the boyfriend of her most hated peer, she found it disconcerting that her guard disappeared so completely in his presence. Befuddled and still charged with emotion from the fight, Lisa began to cry. Mortified, she tried to turn away, but in a move she would never have anticipated, Vic put an arm around her shoulder.

"It's okay, you've been through some really fucked up shit. Your pops ain't gonna be too hard on you, is he?"

The door to the Dean's office opened, and Vic stopped talking as Laramie's battle-hardened face corkscrewed with fury. When she spoke, Laramie's deceivingly feminine voice reached a volume that swapped Lisa's tears for shivers.

"Mr. Lamb! What are you doing in my office?"

"Here to pick up Misty."

"Misty will be leaving with her father."

From inside the office, Lisa heard Misty say, "Hello-ohwa! I already told you, my dad isn't coming to get me; he doesn't give a shit about me. If I can't leave with Vic, I'll be walking home."

The Dean ignored Misty and doubled down on Vic.

"Mr. Lamb, if you would be so kind as to move to one of the chairs across the room, I will sort this out presently."

Vic immediately complied and Lisa smiled at the realization that even the school badass feared the Dean. Her smile receded, however, when the Dean's attention turned to her.

"Miss McCready. Your father is currently not answering his telephone, and I am afraid the receptionist at the Sheriff's

Station cannot raise him, so it looks as though you are stuck with me for the foreseeable future. I beseech thee; do not use our time together to make me more upset with you than I already am. Now, I will be finished with Miss Bradley shortly. After that, we will talk."

The Dean returned to Misty, closing the door behind her. When Lisa finally looked up, Vic's smile beamed at her from across the room.

"What'a bitch, eh?" he laughed, and Lisa found it hard not to follow suit. Soon, they were both snickering like old friends sharing a joke.

"I'm... I'm sorry I wrecked your girlfriend's face."

Vic laughed out loud.

"Ha, well, like I said, sounds like she deserved it. How do *you* feel? I think this town is full of sadists or something, ya know? It's only been two months since the Fire Pit Massacre and, what? Laramie's gonna lace into you over a fight? I mean, shit man, can they cut some fucking slack around here or what?"

"Please don't call it that."

"Huh? What? Oh, the Massacre? My bad. Sorry."

"It's okay; it's not like they don't plug away at it on the news every night."

"Yeah. Man, that's shitty. I guess I hadn't really thought about it. You want me to kick Ted Owens's ass for you?"

Lisa laughed again. She'd begun to feel better, all thanks to Vic.

"It's okay, it's just that, well, I don't know. I feel like calling it that makes the whole thing less real, like it's something that happened on tv and not, you know, here."

"Sure. Hey, you look like shit."

"Now I know what Misty sees in you, Mr. Smooth Talker."

"I just mean–"

"I know what you mean."

"Did they give you a prescription?"

"Huh? Who?"

"Your doctors at Mather's? They didn't, did they?"

"They tried."

"What did they have you on? I can tell from the way you're shaking they didn't have the decency to give you a doggy bag."

"Not sure. Little purple pill."

"This?" Vic extended his open palm toward Lisa; inside it was a business card and several of the pills she had come to rely so heavily on during her sabbatical.

PURPLE.

"Oh my god yes!"

"Here. Take 'em. If you want more, I have tons. Well, not tons, but more than I'll ever use. You can call me if you want more."

Lisa hesitated, the word 'please' on the tip of her tongue. Before she could make the acquiescence, though, the sound of Dean Laramie's office door opening incited a fresh wave of panic. Without thinking, Lisa snatched the pills from Vic's hand and stuffed one of them into her mouth. The rest followed the business card into her back pocket. To cover her movements, Lisa stood and went to the water cooler across the room, pulled one of the little paper cups from the sleeve and poured enough water to swallow the pill. The cooler made a deep gurgle when she tapped the blue handle, and by the time she finished, her father's hand landed on her shoulder.

"C'mon Lisa, you can talk to the Dean tomorrow. Right now, we're going home," Sheriff McCready addressed his daughter, his voice distant as he stared at Vic over his shoulder, the frown on his face a direct message for Vic:

Stay away.

CHAPTER THREE

Lisa knew her father was mad; it hurt knowing she had disappointed him, but to add insult to injury, he made her ride home in the back of his police cruiser like a criminal. His warning after the incident at Mather's had been a non-negotiable command with harsh consequences. This wasn't new; Lisa's straight-and-narrow path was a direct result of an overly strict parent who worked in law enforcement. She often envied her sister's early departure for college. She sought to replicate it merely to be free to make a mistake or two. After a somewhat reckless beginning to her teenage years, Ashley McCready used a frightening reality check to re-focus her energies away from being a rebellious kid. Subsequently, Lisa's older sister plowed through High School, graduating a full year early and leaving Sundown Hills behind shortly after. From everything she'd told Lisa since, college was a life-changing event, filled with boys and parties and all kinds of glorious trouble to offset the hard work it took to maintain the type of grades the McCready girls were known for. By comparison, Lisa's existence was frightfully dull.

Until the massacre.

"Now I'm calling it that," she said under her breath with a sniffle. The pill had begun to smooth out her anxiety, washing her in a wave of

Purple.

"What?"

"Nothing. Dad, could you pull over and let me ride up front? You know, so the locals don't think I've lost my shit again?"

The Sheriff didn't answer his daughter at first, his silence a poignant expression of his displeasure. Gerald had paid a lot of money to have Lisa 'fixed.' He wouldn't forgive having to collect her from the Dean's office on her first day back.

"You just had to pick a fight with the David Bradley's goddamn daughter, didn't you? This is shit I do not need right now, Lisa."

"She said terrible things about you."

"I don't need my teenage daughter to defend me from her classmates."

"Misty said you covered up the truth about Annie's death!"

"I don't care what Misty Bradley thinks about me or Annie's death. Got that?"

"Obviously, but how could I stand by and listen to someone say that about you?"

"There are people saying a lot worse."

"Why don't you stop them?"

"It's a free country."

"It might be a free country, but I'm pretty sure a lot of what people are saying constitutes liable."

"I'm a public official. Also, they're not wrong - I don't know who murdered Bill and those other kids. Do you know how that makes me feel? I'm useless, and it's not helping that

I'm treading water in this town. Then you go and attack my main detractor's daughter; that doesn't make me look any better."

"But why would Misty say something like that about you?"

"Get a clue, Lisa. She said it to hurt you because whether she realizes it or not, she's taking her father's side and trying to help him, hurting me by hurting you. That's what this town is coming down to: David Bradley and me."

"But you're the Sheriff!"

"It goes deeper than that."

"How? Please, explain this to me."

"I don't have to explain anything to you."

A far-away look came into Gerald's eyes. Lisa watched him, recognizing for the first time a great and terrible pain he held inside. Had it been there all along, and she just failed to notice? Or was this something new, something more immediate, crushing him beneath its heel?

"Maybe my detractors are right. Maybe people want legal dope and a narcissist as their Mayor."

Hearing her Gerald McCready express such incredible doubt chilled Lisa, made her eyes sting with terrible, salty tears. They were little girl tears that rallied against the idea that her father wasn't the man, the hero she'd always believed him to be. What's more, this self-doubt wasn't like him at all; he was weakening because of public opinion. Worse yet was the idea that, deep down, Lisa wasn't sure that the accusations against him were unfounded. She couldn't help but feel there was something she was missing, something her dad wasn't telling her.

Annie and Lisa had been best friends from the age of five to thirteen; in all that time, Lisa never even heard Annie talk about her real mom, who, like Lisa's mom, died during childbirth. Mr. Harrison remarried a few years before Lisa and

Annie became friends, so her stepmother Ruth was the only mom Lisa knew for Annie. Not that Ruth acted much like one. The woman carried with her a whole host of problems, chief among them a closet drug habit that eventually consumed her completely.

It nearly consumed Annie's dad as well.

A divorce followed. A nasty one. This was just as Lisa and Annie were becoming young adults, but Lisa remembered a little of it in a vague, little-kid-feeling-threatened sort of way. By the time the girls were in Junior High, the Harrison household was just Annie and her dad. It was with Mr. Harrison that the girls had come of age; he made them popcorn and let them watch scary movies when Lisa stayed the night. He took them to the mall to get their ears pierced and even out to dinner at the Mexican restaurant in the food court a couple of times. The idea that Annie's stepmother, a woman who had only known her for a few years, would return to harm her never made much sense to Lisa. But then, Lisa had grown up a little girl in a man's house, and even though she knew her dad loved her, he'd never allowed her to be anything other than a kid in his eyes.

Hence their trouble now, as Lisa prepared to finish high school and leave for college.

Gerald McCready had already relinquished one daughter to an out-of-state school: Ashley was five years Lisa's senior, and this head start on adolescence strengthened her independence. Theirs was a battle of wills, Ashley and their father. In the end, Ashley earned herself a full ride at the school of her choice. That was something not even the Sheriff could contest. With her older sister out of the picture, Gerald quickly became the dominant figure in Lisa's life. Through the pangs of high school, she had finally begun to outgrow the need for daddy's influence. Daddy, however, had not experienced the same transformation.

"Sheriff?" Bridget Johnson's voice crackled over the walkie-talkie. The Sheriff's long-time secretary and receptionist, Bridget always seemed a bit off to Lisa. "Sheriff, we've got a problem."

Gerald grasped the talkie and stretched the coiled cord taut from the dash as he brought it to his lips.

"What's up, Brig?"

Static first, then: "Trouble at the Red Lion, Sheriff, and I'll give you one guess who's causing it."

The Sheriff turned to his daughter, his brow furrowed.

"Hold on."

"What?"

Sheriff McCready placed the whirling red light on top of the truck, clicked on his sirens and pushed the gas pedal to the floor.

———

In no uncertain terms did Dean Laramie explain to Vic that he would have to wait for Misty elsewhere. A quick text to Freddy and Vic walked out to the small patch of woods that bordered the school's track. Freddy was already waiting, a fresh bag of weed in one hand, his trusty metal bowl with the anarchy symbol scratched into it in the other.

"So, is your girlfriend's face all fucked up?"

"Yeah. Ha. It's kinda funny."

"Yeah," Freddy said, packing a massive, red-haired bud into the pipe. Vic pulled a small Blue Tooth speaker out of his bag and used his phone to fire up some old-school Danzig. The opening chords of "Mother" kicked in, and both friends took a moment to croon along with the lyrics. Five minutes later, Vic and Freddy were stoned out of their gourds.

"Good shit, bro," Vic said, staring at the Interstate in the distance. A caravan of trucks sailed by carrying dirt and foliage from Peppermill.

"Better be. Bought it from you."

They laughed.

"Surprised you're hitting it this early; ain't you got work?"

"Yeah, but I'm still training. It'll be a minute before your dad lets me near any of the dangerous equipment and shit."

"Papa Lambe taking care of you?"

"Definitely. Hey, you got Danzig three on there?"

"Never leave home without the first four, bro."

"Speaking of Metal, you get the tattoo you told me about?"

Vic raised his right leg, catching it by the ankle. He turned it slightly to show off his new ink - Iron Maiden's mascot, Eddie, from the cover of 1981's *Killers*.

"Awesome! I totally thought you would'a got ol' Vic Rattlehead. Ya know, cuz'a your name."

"Nah. They've got, like, two albums I like. Fucking Mustaine's still cryin' over getting kicked out of his first band."

They laughed as Vic clicked over a couple albums and played the first two tracks from *How the Gods Kill* while they watched the girls' track team run a couple laps.

"Man, that Jenna Roberts has an ass, right?"

"Yes she does. You know who else does?"

"Who?"

"Lisa McCready."

"Boom! Sheriff's daughter? You gonna do it, man? Dump Misty? That'd be a pretty big coup, ya know?" Freddy pronounced this 'coop.'

"Girl like Lisa'd never go for me."

"Aw, c'mon man. You're waaaay better-lookin' than Bill - especially with that hatchet buried in his face and all, am I right?"

Vic laughed. Freddy's sick sense of humor was one of his most endearing qualities.

"Naw, I mean, her father and I are basically business rivals, ya know?" Vic held up the pipe to demonstrate.

His phone buzzed. It was Misty, finally released from Laramie's office.

"Time to grab the girl, do some boyfriend shit to make her feel better about her face. 'You're so beautiful,' and all that crap."

"Man, I don't know Misty half as good as you, but I know all she's gonna talk about is Lisa."

"Yeah, well, then I'll give her something else to do with her mouth, right?"

Vic gave Freddy another pound, shut down his speaker and headed back to school. He surprised himself by thinking about Lisa McCready the entire time. When he arrived at the parking lot, Misty was waiting for him by his truck. The scowl on her face only enhanced the damage Lisa had done to her; the swelling was still pretty intense, and the bandages over the cuts on her left cheek and forehead were pink and sweaty.

"What the fuck, Vic? You leave me standing out here, looking like this?"

"Sorry babe, had to break away."

"Fucking stoner."

"Don't be like that," he said cooly, handing Misty a joint once they were inside his truck. She hit it twice in a row, holding the smoke in as long as possible. A moment later, she relaxed accordingly. Vic threw some of the stupid pop music she liked on the radio, and by the time they pulled into his driveway ten minutes later, she was so stoned she could barely talk.

Vic gave himself a mental high five.

———

The Red Lion was a small restaurant and bar near the center of town. During the afternoon, it was common for local businessmen to lunch on the patio, sipping cappuccinos and eating the Lion's famous Sundown Salad - a modified Waldorf with pears and raisins instead of apples and grapes. Along about quitting time, however, the clientele shifted drastically. The white shirts headed home to their families and a decidedly different population set in, mostly occupying the bar inside. These were the working class of Sundown Hills; many would kill a few drinks and a burger before heading home for the night, others hit the Lion as pre-game for more serious debauchery at Slo Motion.

Craig Walters was one of the few men in town who could straddle this class divide, lunching with the executives, wining and dining new prospects for the commercial side of the real estate business that funded his non-profit Project Pegasus, and knocking back beers with the salt of the Earth as the sun went down. After all, many of those men worked on construction projects overseen by Pegasus, which currently oversaw two rather large projects: the ongoing modernization of the Peppermill land for its new owner's high-tech pot farm and the continued expansion of the upper-crust subdivisions Michael and Craig had partnered up on: *Artisan's Ridge: Modern Living for the Modern Family*.

Craig always said, "Altruism might be the goal, but it doesn't pay the bills."

Needless to say, the evolution of Project Pegasus had, in recent months, garnered nearly as much blowback from many of the locals as Michael's prospective marijuana business.

Since his daughter's murder, however, Craig's demeanor had shifted; now, when he showed up at the Lion, he did so already hammered. No longer prone to handing out business cards, Craig hunted for trouble, prowling for altercations, a fist in the face or a knuckle duster that left him battered and senseless, just as his daughter's murder had done. Any opponent would do, but everyone in town knew who Craig was really gunning for: Sheriff Gerald McCready, the man who let Angela's murderer disappear into the wind. This would be Craig's third incident in twice as many days, and although Lisa didn't know that as they pulled into the parking lot, she could sense the anger simmering in her father.

To tell the truth, the Sheriff didn't begrudge Craig his pain; he knew from experience that anguish and frustration were a natural part of the grieving process. On more than one occasion, McCready had wondered how he would cope if Lisa had been at that party with her boyfriend. As Sheriff, though, what he did take issue with was the streak of public intoxication, vandalism and broken noses Craig left in his wake.

Gerald brought the cruiser to a stop with a squeal on the blacktop to the left of the Lion's entrance. As he did, Walters and David Bradley stumbled through the restaurant's double doors. Walters connected with a right, then a left and David went down.

"Craig! Stop right there and back away!"

Walters either didn't hear the Sheriff or didn't care; he drove a wingtip into Bradley's ribs. The man on the ground was clearly at a disadvantage, and the one rearing back for another cheap shot was in the mood for trouble, so...

McCready leaped from the car and fired a round into the sky. Even from the back of the cruiser, the sound proved deafening to Lisa, nothing like those times she'd accompanied her father to the range. Shooting at a target in the Station's basement, those big, ear-sealing headphones added a degree of removal to the experience. Lisa had never stopped to consider what a gun fired in a 'real world' situation would sound like or how that might differ from the isolated environment of the range.

Boy, did it differ.

It wasn't just her; Lisa saw how the weapon's belligerence affected the entire mob gathered in the parking lot to watch the fight. Angela's father nearly fell to his knees, and David recoiled as if struck by the bullet. Smart enough to use this momentary reset to his advantage, Lisa watched her father take charge. That's what Gerald McCready did best - assert control.

"Put your hands behind your head, Craig. I'm not going to tell you again."

"Fuck you, Sheriff! Why you defending trash like this while my daughter's killer is still on the loose? You even questioned O'Sullivan yet? Or he just gets a free pass again?"

"Final warning - back away from David and put your hands behind your head."

"You see that everybody? The Sheriff can't solve any of the real crimes in Sundown Hills, can't find the person who butchered my daughter, can't tell us why a grown man was found dead with those kids. Fact is, way I hear it, may be a reason he don't want the killers found-"

Grown man found with the others? This was the first Lisa heard of this, but the information barely had time to register before she recoiled at the sight of her father cracking the rabble-rouser in the head. Walters went straight to the ground, landing face-down beside Bradley.

"Nice one, Sheriff," David said as he picked himself up and uselessly tried to brush the dirt stains from his clothes. "Thanks for the assist."

Lisa noticed a funny look pass between them. David's brother Michael stepped from the crowd and offered him a hand, which David waved away.

"You pressing charges?"

"Goddamn right, I'm pressing charges."

"See you at the station, then."

"I'm busy. I'll send Inoue."

"Whatever."

"I can go," Michael Bradley said, falling in step behind Gerald.

"His lawyer's fine, Michael."

"Anything I can do to be of assistance," Michael waited until his brother was out of earshot before continuing. "Sheriff, I must apologize on David's behalf. If there's anything I can do to help Craig. Anything at all."

"Way you two go at it on the news, I keep expecting to find one of you beaten bloody."

"It won't get physical with us. We're brothers. David doesn't appreciate what I want to do for the family, but he will. Eventually."

"Yeah, well, if you can make sure he gets home okay, that'd be help enough."

"Consider it done, Sheriff."

McCready carried the unconscious Craig to the cruiser's back seat, ushered his daughter out and deposited his prize.

Lisa hadn't seen Craig Walters since before his daughter's death. Since Angela and she hadn't exactly been friends, it was a rare occasion that Walters and Lisa would occupy the same space. Despite this, Lisa had a relatively sharp image of the man as he used to appear: short, well-maintained salt-and-pepper hair, impeccable clothing of the casual business variety, and not a trace of facial hair. Seeing him now, in a state of maximum dishevelment, Lisa barely recognized him. His hair had grown out in uneven patches, his baby blue oxford shirt hung untucked from his dirt-stained Khakis, and a dirty, scraggly beard undid the tender eyes and father's brow that surely helped him become a respected civic leader. This person before her now was, simply stated, a disaster. In light of such an unexpected transformation, Lisa found it difficult not to turn and stare as he lay unconscious on the seat.

"Tough position to be in, this one."

Lisa turned to find Michael Bradley standing behind her, smiling.

"For you or my dad?"

"For all of us, Lisa. How are you? I mean, since..."

"You mean since I got out of the looney bin? I'm okay. I might be better if your family wasn't out to ruin my dad."

"I wouldn't have said it quite like that, but believe it or not, I was worried about you. Kids in this town have gone through some terrible stuff in the last few years, you more than most. I know it's not your dad's fault; it's just this place. It's trapped in the past, so how could we ever hope to bury it?"

"Lisa!" Gerald hollered from behind the wheel. He possessed a way of wielding her name like a command.

Lisa blushed as she acquiesced, nodding goodbye as she climbed into the front passenger seat. Once she closed the door, she could sense the question before her father asked it.

"What the hell you talking to him about?"

"I worked with him. Remember?"

Gerald didn't respond, just slipped the truck in gear and headed out of the Red Lion's parking lot. They drove for a bit before Lisa asked.

"How are Michael and his brother so different?"

"Michael got out. He saw what his family was, how money corrupts them from almost from birth. It's a tough lesson, and I, for one, never expected him to succeed on his own. Happy to say he proved me wrong. Still don't trust 'em."

"Because of the Marijuana thing?"

"What'd you think?"

McCready gave his daughter a sly smile; it was their first

good moment since her release. A moment later, all hell broke loose in the back of the cruiser.

————

Craig Walters came to and began to kick against the bulletproof glass that separated the back of the cruiser from the front. Non-verbal howls turned to pitch-black threats of violence, the words eventually melting back into ominous sobs.

"Goddamnit Gerald! Find my daughter's killer! Why won't you find my daughter's killer?"

What proved especially agonizing for Lisa was how the man's fury remained undercut with a current of raw anguish; Walters howled in tears as much as he hurled threats. When they finally arrived at the station, Gerald dragged his prisoner inside, leaving Lisa to wait in the truck while he processed the man into holding. It was a long ten-minute ride and a longer twenty minutes waiting in the failing daylight, no music, windows up while her father performed his civic duty. When he finally returned, Lisa noticed the knuckles on his right hand were caked in blood; she wondered if he'd struck Walters.

"Okay, we're going home and putting this goddamn day behind us once and for all."

"Sure."

It should have been only another ten minutes home from the station, but Gerald chose to drive the edge of town, slowing down as they passed Peppermill. It was Walters who sold the land to Michael Bradley. The history proved some-what incestuous, but in a nutshell, Craig came into the land after his mother Nancy purchased the hundred-acre plot from Roland Bradley near the end of his tenure at Inner Earth. As CEO of Peppermill Pharmaceuticals, Nancy's shrewd maneuvering made her family rich until the Federal Government charged her with supplying local drug manufacturers with Methylamine, a key ingredient in the street drug crystal meth. Unable to convict her, the property avoided going to the state. However, when Nancy disappeared and left it to Craig, it lay dormant until Michael returned and purchased it.

"I thought we were going home?"

Focused, Gerald didn't answer. The woods behind the massive fence were dense, and only the gated access road farther North offered a clear view past their obfuscation.

"You're looking for Frank O'Sullivan, aren't you?"

Still no response, but at the intonation of Frank's name, Onya's prophetic mantra resounded in Lisa's head:

He killed my mother; now he wants to kill you!

"Dad, how did Onya's mom die?"

"Childbirth. Just like-"

"Mom. Did you arrest Frank when Onya was attacked just because of what she said? Or was there something else? Something about him that made you think-"

"I'm only going to say this once, Lisa. Stay the hell away from that O'Sullivan girl; you read me?"

"Well, unless you plan on putting me back in Mather's..."

"Lisa!"

"Loud and clear."

"Good."

———

The sound of the front door's lock cracked like thunder as Gerald let the chill evening air into their modest ranch bungalow. The light from the lamp at the foot of the driveway spilled into the darkened front room, and for just a moment, Lisa felt afraid to enter her own home. Nothing else in town felt safe; why should the house she'd been raised in?

"Inside, Lisa. You're letting the cold air in."

Gerald shut the door behind them with a growing sense of impatience that carried over from the incident with Walters. Lisa swallowed the inexplicable lump in her throat and obeyed, holding onto the slow-motion waves of purple that lapped at her thoughts, turned them into pretty little pictures in her mind.

The McCready house sat one mile inside Sundown Hills's Eastern border, surrounded by trees on two sides. To the right was the Western edge of Phil Harlow's farm, across the street was Margaret Laderman's cottage, three years into the decline that had followed its owner's death. The area was practically as far from Artisan's Ridge and the 'nice part of town' as one could get without stepping into the low-income area known as Olde Creek. Walters had offered the Sheriff one of the first homes built in Artisan's, but his partnership with Michael Bradley prompted her father's stubborn refusal to accept.

"Dad! You're not listening to me!"

"Yes, I am Lisa. I'm simply choosing to ignore your accusations."

"I'm not accusing you of anything; I just want you to help me understand why Annie's stepmom would have come back into her life after barely ever being in it in the first place. To kill her, no less. I mean-"

"Enough."

"Dad!"

"Enough!" Gerald hollered so loud his anger seemed to shake the house. "Go to your room. We can talk more tomorrow. Right now, I've got a headache and want a beer."

"What about dinner?"

"I'll think of something. And Lisa..."

She stopped and turned to face her father again.

"I don't want you leaving this house for a while, okay?"

"So now I'm grounded?"

"You're not grounded. This isn't punishment. I'm *trying* to protect you."

"From what?"

When he didn't answer, Lisa turned and stormed up the stairs to her room and slammed the door.

———

Lisa sat cross-legged on her bed, thinking about the scene at the Red Lion, Craig Walters coming apart at the seams, and her father's hatred for the Bradley family.

She felt stuck in the middle of something, but she wasn't sure what. Her mind wandered and her eyes trained on the mirror across from her. The vanity attached to the back of the dresser was a hand-me-down from Ashley, who'd given Lisa most of her stuff when she left for school. By the look on her reflection's face, Lisa wondered if she would ever get the chance to leave Sundown Hills. The thought of being stuck here like Craig Walters, Helen Landing and her father suddenly terrified her. Guys like Vic Lamb and Freddy Snow were the next generation of captives; Freddy was already in the work release program at school; he left every day at noon to work with Vic's dad, the foreman at Inner Earth. Vic was a drug dealer. What kind of life was it to never leave the place you were born? To take the first easy answer that happened along?

As Lisa focused on the mirror, her reflection split into fractured narratives. One part wanted to help her father, wanted to help Craig Walters and Mr. Harrison and all of the horribly scarred men in the town. It seemed Sundown Hills worked to destroy them, killing off the women early, stranding those who were left in the wax and wane of testos-terone-fueled power struggles. Then there was the part that thought about Vic and what she was pretty sure Misty did with older men at Slo Motion. This part of Lisa wanted to surrender her delicate flower bullshit and use all the gnarly survival skills her dad had taught her to escape Sundown Hills, hit the road and never look back.

Escape seemed impossible, though. There was a gravity to this place. A gravity amplified by the nightly reenactment of Bill's murder. When Lisa closed her eyes, her thoughts put her there, front and center.

"Call your father..."

She would no doubt spend the hours before dawn imagining Bill's death over and over - the damage to his face and body had been so catastrophic his family chose to have a closed casket. She needed another pill; her only escape from that startling precipice she'd learned bordered not just her life but *all* life. That was the *real* existential crisis - the fact that *everyone* was this fucked up, that chaos was never more than a moment away in any direction.

She took another of the pills and waited for the soft, fuzzy arms of prescription soma to muddle her terror. She lay still for close to forty minutes before dozing. On the cusp of a dream, a tiny 'ping' startled her awake. She picked up her phone off the nightstand beside her and saw a new email notification. Reading it, Lisa smiled at the fact that, as things with her father continued to fall apart, someone out there cared enough to offer her a way out.

———

Lisa,

I wanted to say that despite how it may look, I have a great deal of respect for both you and your father. I know it's been difficult, especially with all the horrible things happening in Sundown Hills of late; however, if you're interested, I have an opportunity for you with my company. Specifically, my Seattle office. I would love to talk to you about this; drop me a line or, better still, stop by my office at your convenience and we'll chat over lattes. My treat.

Best,

Michael R. Bradley

······················

CHAPTER FOUR

······················

Tuesday, September 1

Zak Geller's twenties had not been easy. Hailing from the Gulf of Mexico - what people from Florida said when they didn't want to tell you they were from Florida - Zak never really found his niche after high school. Not an athlete, not very smart, Zak was good at two things: drugs and girls. These things had given him a somewhat lofty existence in school, but the day he graduated the twelfth grade, Zak realized his life was, essentially, over.

He knocked up his girlfriend at nineteen; he didn't even really like the girl, and he definitely didn't like their offspring. Too bad a judge said he didn't have to like them, just support them. So, at twenty-two, Zak took a job in the oil industry because his cousin told him he could make good money. He did indeed make good money, and Zak hadn't looked back since.

Except oil labor work proved sporadic at best. Unless you

were prepared to move. Which Zak definitely was. The further away he was when he mailed those checks, the better.

At twenty-three, Zak headed into North Dakota for the first big fracking run the media jumped on. Never mind that this type of drilling had been around for decades; the news always needed something new to yell about. As far as Zak was concerned, that's all the media did - stirred up shit better left forgotten. This worked to his benefit more often than not, and in the case of North Dakota, Zak made a lot of money. He lived high on the hog, so to speak, for a good year and a half. Then, his child got sick, and the court ordered him to pay the hospital bills. On Zak's twenty-fourth birthday, he bought a brand new Escalade; six months later, he defaulted on the payments, lost his ride and began catching the bus to work. Zak's mood worsened, and when a protestor got in his face one day on his way to the job site, Zak lost it. A week later, he was out of a job and on the road, unsure where his next paycheck would come from.

One of the guys Zak had worked with in ND sent him a text about a town called Sundown Hills. He'd heard there was significant money in this backwater burg, and the camp owner had good, low-rent housing available for his employees. Even offered three squares if you got involved in some local chapter of their Masons/Shriners equivalent. Zak figured he'd probably skip that - he liked to spend his free time at the bar - but the place was so far off the radar, and with housing cheap and utilities free, Zak figured he might just be able to dodge out on sending any more money to his ex.

Everything went according to his plan for a few months.

———

Burke Lamb had worked for Inner Earth's operation for almost four decades. He came on under Roland Bradley when the company was still thriving. Burke made foreman right about the time Roland had the breakdown that turned him into a born-again Christian. Burke watched the company suffer one bad turn after another, culminating with Roland selling a large parcel of their family land to the Peppermill Pharmaceutical company. After that, the board took care of Roland. There were some lean years, but Burke made do. Eventually, his seniority paid off, and things really picked up when David Bradley took over as CEO. Burke and David bonded over similar appetites, and eventually, David had his foreman hire an assistant so he could take over the back end of his other business venture.

Slo Motion.

Burke got along with David fine, even if the man was a pompous ass. Michael was a different story altogether. Especially with all this crap about making pot legal. Burke had a few things he'd like to tell Michael Bradley. Most of them required a machete.

At ten after three, Burke was called into the Inner Earth office to reprimand his newest employee, who had been spotted smoking pot on the job by some of the other guys. Freddy was Vic's friend, so Burke's initial fears that the kid might think he was untouchable had indeed come to pass. This pissed him off; Burke didn't like nepotism. On his boat, everybody rowed equally. Everybody, except him.

"See Freddy, I like to show the new guys - especially ones as young and stupid as you - what they're getting into when they come work for me. I don't want no Nancy boys hiring on under false pretenses, thinking they're gonna make a lotta money without lifting a finger. Uh-ah. I'm gonna work your ass off. Believe me."

"Sorry, Mr. Lamb."

"That's another thing: just 'cuz you're friends with my kid, don't expect no special treatment. Got it? You wanna do your pot, fine. Not on my time. You get in an accident and piss hot, it comes to light I was lenient on you today, I'm in just as much shit as you. Capiche?"

"Sorry, Mr. Lamb. It won't happen again."

"Hey, Burke!"

Zak Geller ran at them from out of the lower level. He looked upset.

"Can't you see I'm in the middle a' sumpthin', genius?"

"I think we got a problem."

Burke studied the younger man. Geller was still relatively new. Couple months since he hired on, maybe? An out-of-towner and, by the look of it, a recovered drug addict. He had those meth teeth. Burke hated that.

"What is it, Geller?"

"Well, ah, I think you'd better see for yourself."

Exhaling loudly to emphasize his irritation, Burke stepped out after Geller and motioned for Freddy to follow. Whatever this was, it'd do the new kid good to see it firsthand. It'd also do him good to see what happens to a fuck-up like Geller, who Burke suspected he might finally be able to send packing.

The three men traversed a small corridor that dead-ended at a service ladder. With Geller in the lead, they descended to where a host of hoses fed H2O to a giant, water-cooled drill. Because this area was peppered with so many underground tunnels, it was common for little tributary oil pools to pop up here and there. It was to one of these that Geller led Burke to now, Freddy still in tow.

"All right, Geller, what the fuck you bring us all the way down here for?"

Geller pointed at the small oil pool.

"That? This shit happens all the time, ain't you figured that out yet?."

"No. Inside the pool."

"Huh?"

Something caught Burke's eye. He moved closer, realized what he was looking at.

"Holy shit! Is that a hand?" Freddy Snow shrieked.

Burke Lamb's joy at the realization he would soon be rid of Zak Geller once and for all was only slightly dampened by the fact that Freddy Snow had also seen the hand.

"Shit. Well, that just sucks."

"What's that, Mr. Lamb?"

"Nothing, Freddy. All right, guys, it's been a long day, and you've both had a traumatic experience. I'll call the Sheriff and put my boys on this. Meantime, what say I drive us over to the Lion, lunch and beers on me?"

"Hell yeah, that'd be awesome!"

Burke Lamb's face cracked in a cold, unfeeling smile.

———

When Lisa woke the next day, she was surprised that she'd slept through to early afternoon. Her suspension for fighting would, at the very least, grant her a bit of a buffer before she had to return to Sundown High again.

"Good."

Vestiges of a dream lingered in the form of a great lethargy that initially made it difficult for Lisa to do anything but lay on her back and stare at the ceiling. The pattern of sunlight through her blinds triggered a recollection or revelation, but try as she might, she couldn't quite decipher it. After a time, it left her, and she passed back in and out of sleep for the better part of an hour.

Eventually, Lisa crawled from bed. She plodded through a shower and a small breakfast, thinking about Michael Bradley's job offer the entire time. She still couldn't believe it, and though sidestepping her father felt a little creepy, it wasn't enough to prevent her excitement. Lisa finally had what she wanted more than anything else:

An out.

Tantalized by the enormity of the situation, she stepped onto the front porch and sat in her mother's old rocking chair. She opened the email app on her phone and re-read the letter. Below the signature were three contact numbers: office, home, and cell. Feeling somewhat treasonous, she dialed the office, which seemed the least intrusive of the three. When Michael's secretary answered, she informed Lisa that Michael had been expecting her call and Lisa's heart fluttered; 'this is really happening,' a voice from inside her said. The secretary put Lisa on hold, returning a moment later to ask if she could call Michael on his cell. Lisa hung up and did just that.

"Michael Bradley."

He even answered the phone with confidence.

"Um, hi. Mr. Bradley? It's Lisa McCready."

"Lisa! So good to hear from you. I hoped my email wouldn't be too presumptuous."

"Oh no, not at all! I mean, you're totally right in assuming I'm counting the days until I graduate. I want to get out of Sundown Hills so bad."

"Follow in big sister's footsteps, eh? Nothing wrong with that. Look, the situation I mentioned in my email is more urgent than I let on."

"Come again?"

"The opportunity would require you to leave town now. By the end of the week, to be exact."

Lisa was stunned. This, she had not anticipated.

"Oh. Well, that's... that's really soon. I mean, I have to finish school and everything."

"Look, I hope I'm not overstepping my bounds here, but school was an obvious concern when I thought of you for this position. I... well, this is the presumptuous part. I spoke to your counselor, Ms. Galdykas."

"You did?"

"After the... incident with my niece, Tracy - that's Ms. Galdykas - couldn't get a hold of my brother, so she called me in on Misty's behalf. When I heard you were involved, I was shocked. I knew you'd been going through a rough patch, and I expressed my concern. Tracy soothed my apprehensions."

"She did?"

"Very much so. She was very optimistic about your standing at graduation."

"She was?" Lisa covered her mouth with both hands, suddenly mortified that she sounded like a broken record. The shock was disorienting. Bradley laughed reassuringly.

"Do you doubt your success? Lisa, you're in the top five percent of the senior class. I'm sure you know this, but you already have more than enough credits to graduate."

"Yeah, I knew that. I mean, I know. I mean... I still have to complete Gym, and I made a *huge* commitment to the class Sociology Project."

"Lisa, the opportunity I have with my Seattle office, I don't want to sound brazen, but it's immediate. Big things are happening, and my secretary had to resign to take care of her daughter. Hit and run. Poor girl's in a coma."

"Oh my god. I'm so sorry."

"Thank you. This is a difficult time, and I saw you yesterday and thought, I've known since you helped launch Pegasus with that Children's Hospital Project that you have what it takes. My Seattle office, well, it's in shambles. I truly believe if I put you in there, you would excel. So I spoke to Ms. Galdykas and the Dean, and they both agreed that whatever credits you're shy of can be waived or earned through a work-release program through me. Lisa, everyone knows what you've been through, first with Annie and now this tragedy with Bill and his friends. The Dean and your counselor agree that this fight with Misty and your time in Mather's are both symptoms of a larger problem. You need to get away from the place where all these bad things happened. You're so far ahead in school that you're bored. There's nothing in Sundown Hills to help you work through your trauma."

Lisa's head spun. The whole thing was unbelievable! Even the particles of air around her seemed to move at high speed as Michael Bradley went on and on about how great she was, how smart, how he could use her help. It was overwhelming, and Lisa realized that no matter how hard he pressed her, she would just not be able to make this decision over the phone.

"Mr. Bradley, this is amazing, and I'm so... I don't even have the words. If it's okay, though, I need to take some time to think about this?"

"Of course, Lisa. I wouldn't dream of demanding an answer this very moment." The way he said this made Lisa think that was precisely what he'd been hoping for. But this minor social transgression wasn't enough to sour the moment; if Michael respected her as much as he said, he would respect her need for the time to think it over.

"Just don't take too long, okay? That office in Seattle really needs someone by next week at the latest."

———

After Lisa hung up, she sat and stared into space for what felt like an eternity. She needed to talk to someone about this. The recent conflicts with her father made her question whether they were in a place to come to any decisions about her future. Especially when this decision meant Lisa might leave the state to work for Michael Bradley.

Completely overwhelmed, she spent the remaining afternoon light in the chair on the porch, gently rocking herself into and out of the kind of deep teenage introspection that resulted in blueprints for the inevitable segue to adulthood; for Lisa, though, these thoughts were tinged with painful memories; the scars the town would leave on her. Chief among these scars, Annie Harrison returned to the forefront of her mind.

The day Lisa learned of Annie's death, her entire life changed. She and Annie had drifted apart by then, but that didn't alter the fact that Annie had been Lisa's first real friend and, thus, occupied a perpetual place in her heart. When Lisa watched a Horror movie, she often wondered if Annie would find it scary. When it rained, she sometimes thought about Annie's almost paralyzing fear of lightning. When Bill was murdered, her instinct to call her friend for comfort was instinctual, even after all this time. Annie Harrison's friendship had come and gone at the most developmentally important time in Lisa's life and, as such, she would never entirely get over the split that marred their relationship and, inadvertently or not, led to Annie's death.

The reunion the two girls experienced just weeks before Annie's death was far from all-encompassing; however, the two evenings they'd spent together had been enough to remind them both what their friendship meant. When Annie died, the pain Lisa experienced was considerably worse than it would have been a month or two before that reconciliation. The idea that Lisa's father might be covering for Annie's killer seemed catastrophic. She felt like a traitor thinking this way, but there was so much her dad kept from her, how was she not going to entertain suspicions? Mainly due to this maddening cognitive dissonance, Lisa craved escape, and the idea of leaving town by the end of the week - while terrifying - also felt exhilarating. Before she could decide, however, she knew there was one loose end that required her attention, one person Lisa felt she owed an explanation and a goodbye.

So, with the wind still in her sails, Lisa hopped off the swing and began the short walk to the Harrison residence at five minutes to six.

As Lisa walked, she noticed how signs on almost every lawn she passed advertised views on the subject of Proposition 72, attesting to just how divided Sundown Hills was on the topic of legalizing marijuana. She still wasn't sure where she weighed in on the issue, but after her encounters with Michael Bradley, Lisa felt more inclined to believe he had the community's well-being in mind than his brother. Why wasn't Michael running for Mayor?

Lisa brightened at the idea of hearing what Mr. Harrison thought about all this. As outgoing Mayor, she suspected he would have a more impartial insight than her father. Plus, during his previous career as a lawyer, James Harrison handled the Bradley account for Geist-Wilhelm. A German law firm that maintained a branch office in Sundown Hills because of Inner Earth, Harrison knew Michael well, had helped him relocate and briefly ran the company while David was fast-tracked.

There was another aspect of Harrison's experience Lisa hoped to draw upon. When her father arrested Frank O'Sullivan for the attempted murder of his daughter, Harrison stepped in to represent the man. During one of their heart-to-hearts at Mather's, Onya mentioned Harrison's kindness toward her. Because of this, Lisa felt like maybe Onya's situation might be something Harrison could help with.

"He killed my mother; now he wants to kill you!"

Onya's late-onset mental illness made her an unreliable witness. Maybe Mr. Harrison knew something that might prove useful in tracking down Bill's killer. Surely, there had to be some connection between the crimes, despite the interim. Especially when she considered that Onya's attacker had never been caught.

"He killed my mother; now he wants to kill you!"

Of course, hearing Onya's premonitions shift to include her gave Lisa chills. Doubly so, when she remembered the route to Harrison's, as it brought her close to the southern edge of the Peppermill land. If Lisa cut through, she could shave a considerable amount of time off her walk, and while she usually wouldn't take that shortcut for any reason, she knew she was already pressing her luck just by leaving the house. Her dad's instructions had not come with any caveats.

The faster she got to Jim Harrison's, the better the chance she had at making it back home before her father.

Lisa veered toward Peppermill's fence.

Since long before the recent murders or Onya's attack, local lore pegged Peppermill as haunted. The legends began shortly after the Methylamine scandal, when several people went missing in the woods that bordered the property. The disappearances led to accusations that Craig Walters' mother, Nancy, was a Satan Worshipper, that she abducted people for ritualistic human sacrifice to try and coerce the Devil to help her avoid prosecution. This was Sundown Hills' ultimate urban legend, locally on par with Slender Man or the Jersey Devil, and it had haunted the town ever since. After Onya's attack, the legend returned with a vengeance, and the recent murders would only further reignite teenage talk that demons stalked Peppermill's Woods, hungry for anyone engaged in drinking, drug use, or pre-martial sex for yet another generation.

"Just cutting through, not here to party."

She followed the ten-foot-tall chain link fence until she came to the yawning mouth of the first of several large drainage pipes that poked through on all sides of the land.

Hand on the pipe's lip, Lisa pulled her head up over the edge, the hairs on her arms and neck prickling with anticipatory fear as a figure emerged from the shadows and acknowledged her: Frank O'Sullivan.

As the property's lone security after Peppermill's closure, Frank had spent years breaking up teenage parties at the fire pit. Gerald had initially arrested him due to Onya's accusations and Frank's *access*. Eventually, he was acquitted based on an alibi. Frank's social reputation - what little of it there was - could not survive the damage, and he disappeared from the public eye. Despite this, it still proved a common occurrence for late-night partiers to report seeing Frank in the woods.

An apparition in filth, Frank stared at Lisa as though sifting through shattered memories.

"You're the Sheriff's daughter, aren't'che?"

Now he wants to kill you

"Yes," Lisa responded, dropping back onto her feet and moving away from the tunnel. Frank followed right up to the edge, so he stood looking down at her.

"You were there, yes?"

Lisa didn't answer, and Frank hopped out of the tunnel and followed her.

"You were there, yes?"

In a failed attempt at fearlessness, Lisa stopped abruptly and dug in to meet Frank's accusatory stare.

"What do you want?"

"Mather's, yes? You were there. Did you see my Onya? Did you? Tell me!"

Lisa didn't answer. Instead, she ran.

"Wait! Please! I just want to know about Onya!"

"I'm sorry," Lisa said under her breath as she ran, the apparition's cries echoing in her ears, tears streaming from her face.

———

When she felt certain Frank O'Sullivan was not following her, Lisa stopped to catch her breath. After a few moments, she started moving again, and the Harrison residence came into view shortly thereafter.

Upon seeing the single-story, red-brick house she'd all but grown up in, Lisa's fears disappeared in a deluge of memories:

Her and Annie's first sleepover; the broken wrist she suffered in the driveway (roller skates); Mr. Harrison inventing the Ultimate Grilled Cheese (Cheddar, PepperJack and fresh Mozzarella); writing her first letter to a boy (Marshal Delacroix - moved away in seventh grade).

The flood almost proved too much to bear, and Lisa's tears returned. How had so much time passed? How were things so different now?

A snapped twig behind her made Lisa turn in alarm. Instead of Frank, James Harrison's smile blinded her. It was the same smile he'd welcomed her into his home with so many times before.

"Lisa? Is that you?"

She almost didn't recognize the skeleton before her. A ghost wrapped in flannel and denim, seeing this once great man so defeated, Lisa's tears turned to sobs.

"Oh dear, please. Don't cry. It's so nice to see you," Harrison opened his arms and Lisa stepped into a hug she'd missed more than she realized.

"I was thinking of things, of you, and..."

"You were thinking of Annie."

The embrace lasted a few moments; when it broke, Mr. Harrison reached out and caught a single tear from Lisa's cheek.

"How 'bout that?"

Embarrassed by her show of emotion, Lisa turned away

and smiled when she noted the large white sign with the words "YES ON 72" at the edge of the driveway. Five minutes later, she was seated in the Harrison living room, drying her eyes on his handkerchief. The house still smelled of Annie, or maybe, Lisa thought for the first time, Annie had simply smelled of the house.

"I'll admit, when you didn't come to see me after the funeral, my feelings took a bit of licking. But then, you girls had stopped palling around, so I figured it was natural. My duties as Mayor keep me pretty busy, especially the last few years, so it's on me as well. I could have stopped by to check on you."

"I always meant to come see you, Mr. Harrison. It's just somehow, I don't know... I felt so *confused*. I saw you at the funeral, and... I know it sounds stupid, but I got scared."

"Unfortunately, as someone who's lived more than three times the count of your age, I can tell you life gets scarier the older you get. Time doesn't help because it only picks up speed as you go. One minute, you're eighteen; the next, you've left seventy behind."

The reminder of Harrison's age surprised Lisa; her father was still in his fifties, and comparing the two men seemed an incongruous juxtaposition. In her head, James Harrison was still the man she'd grown up with, not this... wraith.

"How are you that old?" she asked, turning red when she realized she'd spoken out loud. Mr. Harrison definitely inspired Lisa to drop her guard. "I'm sorry. That was, like, crazy rude."

"Bull. Lisa, I'm old; it's okay. I've had a good life. Well, except for losing all my women. After Ruth got into drugs and left me, I was destroyed. You girls didn't see it; you were too young. I hit what some call rock bottom. I remember one night I actually contemplated whether your father would adopt Annie if I killed myself."

"Oh my god."

"I'm sorry if that's a bit much, but it's what happened. If it hadn't been for you girls..."

Mr. Harrison sipped his tea and held eye contact with Lisa a little longer than felt comfortable. Something changed; she couldn't quite put her finger on what, just that this was not the same man she remembered in more ways than just the physical deterioration.

"How's your dad?"

"He's good," she lied.

"Has his hands full, I'd imagine."

"He still hasn't found the killers."

"He will."

"You think?"

"Gerald is a smart man, Lisa. Don't make the same mistake a lot of the folks in this town do. Don't underestimate him."

"I don't, it's just..."

"Just what, dear?"

"You know that Angela Walters was one of the kids murdered, right?"

"So I read."

"Her father is... a mess."

"I don't doubt it. Lisa, do I detect an ulterior motive for your visit?"

"My boyfriend was one of the kids killed at the fire pit."

"I'm so very sorry, dear."

"I know my dad will find the murderer. I mean, this has to be tied into what happened to Onya O'Sullivan five years ago, right?"

"Well..."

"You represented her father."

"I *offered* to represent him, but it never went to trial because your father had the wrong man."

"What made you think that?"

Mr. Harrison stood and approached her, went down to one knee and enclosed her in his arms. The smell of him, his shirt and hair and breath triggered fragments of long-gone summer days and birthday parties spent in this room, just the three of them: Lisa, Annie, and her father. It was a welcome flood of warmth amid an otherwise icy string of days, and despite her attempt to control her emotions, Lisa once again began to cry.

"It's all right dear. Everything will be better."

"Will it? I mean, sometimes I just... I just want to leave and never look back."

"I suppose that's one way to deal with your feelings. But Lisa, I always pictured you as made from sterner stuff."

This stopped her cold.

"I don't mean to say there's anything wrong with you wanting to leave. You're a young girl in a new century, trapped in a small town. But these doubts about your father..."

"Do you think he's going to run against David Bradley?"

"For Mayor? Lisa, who *have* you been talking to?"

"I thought..."

"You thought I tried to talk him into running."

"Yes. Especially now that Mr. Walters won't... can't."

"I did. Many times. I think he's afraid of finding out how people in this town really see him."

"Why?"

"Because your father is more powerful than he likes to let on, and I think that scares him."

The phone in the kitchen rang.

"Please excuse me for a moment, dear."

Lisa nodded and watched Harrison step through the swinging door that divided the two rooms. She sipped tea and let her eyes wander, taking in sights she'd missed. Her eyes landed on the massive bookcase that still housed some of Annie's favorites: *Interview with the Vampire*, *The Lion, The Witch and the Wardrobe* and all of the original *Bunnicula* books they'd loved as children.

Lisa walked over and ran her fingers along the familiar spines. The feel of the clothbound volumes provided a strong sense memory. Something she didn't recognize caught her eye: an old, tattered volume bound in cracked, black leather. She slid the book from the shelf.

"The town history of Sundown Hills," Mr. Harrison said, reentering the room.

"Oh, you startled me. Didn't mean to -"

"No need to apologize. I love that you love books, Lisa."

"Well, that's where I grew up. I mean, when I wasn't here."

Harrison smiled.

"That's a fascinating one. This town goes back a long way; maybe not as long as the book's condition suggests, but that's probably because it was bound and written by hand, passed down since before even good ol' Samson struck oil."

"Sounds interesting."

"If you like, you can borrow it; might give you a new appreciation for Sundown Hills."

"You must think I'm awful, talking about leaving."

"Not at all."

"I just... I feel so claustrophobic sometimes. Like I can't get out from under what people expect of me because of my dad."

"I can see how you could take that as a burden, but maybe try to think of it differently."

"What do you mean?"

"Lisa, you've been given a great gift. You have a keen, analytical eye. I've always known that. Remember, you were the one who figured out what really happened between Ruth and me."

"Oh god, I'm so sorry."

"Nonsense. At the time, it was... inconvenient. It just meant more terrible shit I had to explain to my daughter *and* the town. But I never hated you for your deductions; quite the contrary. I admired the fact that even as a little girl, you didn't take things at face value or swallow whatever story the adults in your life fed you. You looked for the truth. A girl with that kind of awareness, you could really help your father out right now, don't you think?"

"You think so?"

"I *know* so. You're strong, Lisa, and that strength can help him. The doubters are wrong about Gerald. You'll see."

Suddenly, the excitement she'd felt from Michael Bradley's offer felt treasonous.

"Oh god. Where do I even start?"

"Do you remember when Annie broke her arm? Shortly before you two stopped hanging out?"

"Yeah."

"After that, I had a tough time with her. Against my better judgment, I let her doctor prescribe a pretty heavy-duty pain medicine. And Lisa, Annie developed a dependency."

"What?"

Mr. Harrison nodded regretfully.

"I didn't realize it at first, but she'd started hanging out with that other crowd, chief among them David Bradley's daughter and her drug dealer boyfriend. I was skeptical when Annie asked for a refill on her first prescription, so I didn't allow it. I spoke to the doctors, and they thought I was being overprotective; this was before the whole 'opioid epidemic' that's come to light in the last few years. Doctors used to give that garbage out like candy. I'd seen it, you know, with Ruth, and I didn't want to trigger any inherent addictive tendencies Annie might have picked up from her, so I put the kibosh on the refill. But, well..."

"Misty and Vic got it for her, didn't they?"

"I've never proven that, but I'd be willing to bet. I also have it on pretty good authority the same thing happened to Angela Walters after she broke her leg playing Volleyball last year."

"Oh my god."

"You mentioned Onya. Back when Frank was the primary suspect, the police found a rather large cache of prescription narcotics when they searched the O'Sullivan house. Considerably more than a doctor would prescribe, if you catch my meaning."

"Are you saying Frank O'Sullivan is running drugs into Sundown Hills?"

"Frank O'Sullivan didn't kill anyone, but maybe Onya was attacked *because* he's involved with the drugs. He worked for Peppermill Pharmaceutical from the moment Roland Bradley sold them that piece of land, so he had access to the chemicals and a clientele that would come to him. Also, a complicit boss."

"I just... I saw him today on the way here. He's still there, behind the fence. Lurking."

"Doesn't surprise me in the least. Frank's been obsessed with that land for years, which is why he can't stay away from it even now. I've seen some of the police reports about the night those kids were killed, the night your boyfriend, god rest his soul, was murdered. Those reports found something I believe points to it being the same person who attacked Onya."

"The older man they found?" Even before she'd said this, Lisa knew she was correct.

"Yes. He worked for David Bradley. Some transient hired on at Inner Earth."

"Jesus. I'm not imagining any of this, am I?"

"Like I said, you've a keen eye. Now, on the night of the murders, several of those kids had narcotics in their system. I'm sorry to say that I don't have specific enough information to confirm or deny that your boyfriend was one of them."

"He wasn't. Bill didn't even smoke pot. Have you told any of this to my dad?"

"That's why I'm telling you, Lisa. You're his daughter; information like this might help bring him around to your value in this case."

"Mr. Harrison, can I ask you a question about Annie? About after she died?"

"Of course."

"Do you really think Ruth killed her?"

"No. Not at all."

"Then who?"

"I can't say, but not Ruth. She had many problems, but she would never have harmed Annie."

"And you told my father that? During the investigation?"

"I did, but there's that pressure again, and the stress to accept things at face value."

The grandfather clock against the wall struck eight; Lisa's father would be home within the next thirty minutes.

"Mr. Harrison, I have to go. Like, now."

"I hope I haven't upset you."

"No, you've helped me more than I can ever explain."

They embraced a final time, and Lisa hurried out into the night, chilled at the realization that she would now *have* to cut through Peppermill if she wanted to make it home before her father.

———

The moment she closed Mr. Harrison's door, Lisa dug into her pocket and dry swallowed another of Vic's pills.

As she began the trek home, a steadily mounting fear encroached on her every thought.

"He won't still be there. No way."

She tried to put Frank O'Sullivan out of her head and focus on everything Mr. Harrison had just told her. Doing so, Lisa's first question was how had Mr. Harrison seen the police reports about the Peppermill murders? Did the Mayor have access to toxicology reports and itemized lists of evidence? Maybe in some towns, but if Lisa knew her father, he wouldn't be sharing information like that outside of office ranks. She suspected this meant someone on the force had broken protocol. Or could Gerald have been responsible, possibly because he felt indebted to Jim over Annie?

This led to her next question: did her father share the theory that the murderer was the same person who attacked Onya?

It was a lot to process. The sun now long gone, the three-quarters moon did little to dispel the invisible tapestry of darkness that surrounded her. The "seedy underbelly of the small town" was a cliche because it was the truth, and while it excited Lisa to think Mr. Harrison might be right, that she might be able to help her father expose that darkness for the entire town to see, it also chilled her that she'd been so naive for so long.

"All the more reason to help."

Only problem - where should she start?

In reviewing the facts, Lisa found two main threads: the Misty/Vic drug connection and Onya. Vic felt like the best place to start, as he'd given her his business card; she could call him under the auspices of getting more pills and then find out what he knew.

More pills...

Lisa breathed deeply, enjoying the cold air in her lungs. This was the first moment she'd exhibited the prescience to appreciate her freedom. Despite everything else, she wanted to savor that. Autumn nights had always been her favorite, and she felt thankful for being able to enjoy this one, the first waves of the purple bringing feelings of contentment.

'Contentment maintained chemically is the opposite of contentment!'

No sooner had this occurred to her than the purple pushed it out of her mind.

Just enjoy the moment...

A moment that came to a screeching halt at the edge of the Peppermill property. Lisa looked at the time on her phone, already knowing what it would say and what that meant: At a quarter-past-eight, there was simply no way she could make it home before her father *unless* she cut through the woods.

Lisa took a deep breath, stepped up to the drainage tunnel, grasped the corrugated metal's edge, and pulled herself up into its maw.

"Fuck him. I can do this."

She lifted herself up and into the tunnel's mouth. As soon as she did, someone stepped onto the path before her, hidden by cobwebs and shadows.

Lisa froze, but she'd expected this. Every muscle in her body tensed, then released as she instinctively slipped into fight or flight. Not a good choice; regarding the first of these options, the reality was that, despite pummeling Misty, Lisa entertained no illusions as to her effectiveness as a fighter. For the latter, running in this wet darkness increased the odds that she trip and fall.

Then what? What other choice did she have? Talk to him?

"Mr. O'Sullivan?" Lisa's voice came out shaking, her fear unmistakable.

No answer, but the shape took a step closer. He held a bottle in his left hand.

"Hello?" this time, her tone demanded a response. Inside the pocket of her hoodie, Lisa clutched the keychain-sized can of mace her father had given her for birthday number twelve.

"Answer me!"

"I'm sorry. I didn't mean to scare you," the voice was soft. Weak. Hearing it made Lisa ashamed of her fear. Frank sounded... drunk. "You came by here earlier, yes?"

"That was me, Mr. O'Sullivan."

"Did you see my daughter? At Mather's?"

"I did. Onya's doing good."

Frank took a long sip from the bottle and then did the most unexpected thing - he stretched out his arm and offered Lisa a drink.

"Tell me about Onya. What she does, what she says. Does she still have... episodes?"

"They've gotten better," she answered, waving off the bottle.

"Does she still say it? About me? That I tried to kill her?"

"Yes, but no one believes her."

Frank snorted. Lisa was unsure if that was dismissal or laughter.

"Mr. O'Sullivan... I don't think Mather's is a good place for Onya. Bad things happen there.

At this, O'Sullivan definitely laughed; it was an ugly sound born of cynicism, not humor.

"Bad things happen everywhere, girlie. Especially in Sundown Hills."

Lisa leaned forward, suddenly aware she might have a source of information directly in front of her.

"Why is that? I mean, what is it about this town? Drugs, murder, girls who prostitute themselves..."

O'Sullivan stepped forward abruptly and Lisa nearly fell over while trying to keep her distance.

"My Onya never did nothing like that!"

"No! I mean, I know that Mr. O'Sullivan. I'm not talking about Onya."

"She was too young, even at her age. I told Bradley. It's his soul. His goddamned soul."

Confused at this last bit but unwilling to concede, Lisa rushed to reconfigure her strategy.

"Onya is fine. She has her good days and her bad days. She told me to tell you hi if I saw you. That's why I came back. I had to tell you that."

One final swig and then Frank dropped his hands; they hung limp at his side, the bottle clattering on the metal ridges of the tunnel.

"That sounds just like her, always 'hi' instead of a proper hello."

O'Sullivan sounded wasted, and again, Lisa made a mental note to stay on her toes. She wanted to ask him why Onya would change her accusatory mantra, why she would say Frank wanted to kill Lisa, but talking with him now, she realized the answer was simple: because the mantra was the same as everything else that came out of Onya's mouth: gibberish.

"You don't come here, do you? With the others?"

"I'm not much of a partier."

"Good girl. This place..." Frank leaned in and spoke with a conspiratorial flourish that suggested they were not safe.

"You want to know why this place is the way it is?"

"I do."

"The demon."

"Demon?"

"No one believes until it's too late. Come here, I'll show you."

O'Sullivan turned and began to walk away.

"Wait! Mr. O'Sullivan! I can't-"

"For answers, we have to go further in. We have to go down."

A quick glance at her phone forced an ultimatum: follow Frank O'Sullivan or risk her father's wrath. On the path ahead, Frank tripped and stumbled to the ground, making the decision for her.

'Who am I kidding,' she thought, 'even if he does have anything useful to share, he's hammered. Maybe another night.'

Lisa rushed to help O'Sullivan up, but he waved her away.

"Mr. O'Sullivan, I really have to get home. My dad is going to kill me if-"

"He'll kill you, all right!"

"My father would never hurt me!"

"That's what she said, too. Doesn't matter, run back to your fake safe world."

"I could come ba-"

"GO!"

CHAPTER FIVE

In the wake of Frank O'Sullivan's anger, Lisa hopped back out of the drainage tunnel and ran until she no longer could. Halfway home, she watched headlights pull to the shoulder ahead, and Lisa braced herself as she came up on the all too familiar silhouette of the Police cruiser. The tinted window rolled down, and Lisa closed her eyes in anticipation of a furious outburst.

"Hey, you know your dad's looking for you, right?"

Deputy Matt Hartman! 'Thank god,' Lisa thought. Matt, she could deal with.

"I figured as much."

"Come on, don't be like that. There is still a murderer loose."

The moment the words left his mouth, Matt regretted them.

"Shit. Sorry."

"It's okay. Give me a ride, yeah?"

"Hop in."

Once in the truck, Lisa relaxed a bit. As they drove, an uneasy silence filled the space between them. Two years ago when Matt was still a Senior, they'd shared a brief period of flirtation. Like Lisa, Matt didn't have a lot of friends at school, and when they partnered in Home Ec for the "egg-raising" project, they hit it off. Both possessed slightly more collegiate taste in music than most of their peers, thanks in part to older siblings who introduced them to bands like The Cranberries and Death Cab for Cutie, as opposed to the pop and metal most of the other students at Sundown High seemed obsessed with. During their partnership, there'd been a fleeting, wonderful moment when Lisa thought Matt would kiss her, but it never happened. They earned a "B" with the egg; Matt graduated at the end of the year and then moved on to Community College and Police training. And while they still saw one another occasionally, they hadn't spoken beyond "hi" since.

"How're you doing?"

"That a polite way of asking if I'm still nuts?"

"No... I... ah... okay. If you like. Still nuts?"

They both laughed; it surprised Lisa, how good it felt to laugh about her recent woes.

Well, some of them, anyway.

Her mood lightened. The purple had now fully flooded her system, its calming influence prompting Lisa to unburden herself of the day's events. She told Matt about Harrison, Frank, and her fight with Misty, which he knew all about from station gossip. This didn't bother her; Lisa remembered how easy talking to Matt was, something she could not say for most people.

"Matt, if I asked you to help me do some snooping around, would you?"

"Hmm... I guess? We'd just have to set limits, you know? I won't be breaking into the department's mainframe or anything like that."

Lisa laughed.

"I should be so lucky. Do you even have computers at work?"

"Of course we do - and they are off limits."

Matt pulled the truck into Lisa's driveway.

"Thanks for the lift. I'll tell my dad how awesome you are."

"Ha. Sure."

She was out of the truck and about to close the door when Matt stopped her.

"Hey, ah, we should meet up some night this week so you can give me a better idea what you're thinking."

"Perfect. Thank you."

"No problem. See ya later."

———

Later that night:

Inside her room, Lisa found it impossible to settle down after the shouting match her late arrival provoked with her father. The fight culminated with Lisa retreating to her room, where she slammed the door hard enough to shake the frame while the requisite tears bled her ducts dry.

Reintegrating into her normal life seemed as much work as her first week in Mather's.

She remembered that first week, how she'd yell and scream at anyone who questioned her grief or tried to make her locate something useful it might hold. Strength, growth, whatever. Angry, hurt and sad, Lisa laid awake at night and spent the day little more than a zombie. Observing her behavior, the doctors arrived at a pharmaceutical treatment to help Lisa find peace.

The little purple pills.

Antsy, Lisa stared at Vic's business card.

The pills. Lisa didn't understand why she was so obsessed

with these things; she'd only been taking them for a month and a half, surely not long enough to become addicted. Also, with the opioid epidemic a hot-button news issue, she found it difficult to believe doctors would still prescribe anything that might be habit-forming so quickly. Lisa decided she'd have to do some research - she didn't even know what the drug was called - but for now, when she thought about those long nights in Mather's, the screams from down the hall, the memories of Bill, of *hearing him die over the phone*, Lisa's skin turned clammy and cold.

"Stop it! You're doing this to yourself."

Further unsettled, she turned her attention back to Vic's card. Printed on flimsy paper stock, the font a tired example of the same old Comic Sans people like Vic always thought so novel. The card read:

Vic Lamb
Party Favors 4 All Occasions

241-7611

Thinking about it now, Vic's generosity felt extraordinarily sweet, especially since Lisa's dad was the Sheriff. He'd gone out on a limb for her; was it possible Vic's reputation might be unfair? There was no question he sold drugs, but did that make him a bad person? What about the idea that he might be mixed up with the killer? Staring at his card's stupid font - something only a child would mistake for professional - Lisa couldn't help wondering if she had Vic all wrong.

"Only one way to find out."

Lisa picked up the phone and dialed the number on the card but hung up before the first ring.

The phone in her hand startled her by ringing back.

"Vic? Sorry I called so late..."

"Whoah! Hey, kiddo, who's Vic?"

Ashley! Lisa missed her older sister as a calming, guiding influence on her life and a stalwart go-between in her struggles with Gerald. Ashley realized early on the best thing to do was get out of a town like Sundown Hills, where the people who stayed eventually became their parents. Talking to her always helped put things in perspective.

"Thank god."

"C'mon, gimme the dirt."

"No dirt. Just someone at school who was... nice to me."

"Oh. Shit. Sorry, I hope I didn't..."

"It's okay. Bill's dead; I have to accept that to get better."

"That's the spirit kiddo. Man, I was really worried about you. I wanted to be there when you got home, but I've got this damn paper due, and it's like, fifty percent of the grade in this impossible Abnormal Psych class."

"You don't have to explain, Ash. I know you wanted to be here."

The conversation touched the things sisters discuss, but only in a superficial way. Ashley told Lisa about college, and Lisa listened, feeling her goodwill toward Michael Bradley slowly slip behind a sneaking suspicion about his motives. When Ashley asked about school, Lisa told her about the fight with Misty, the Dean, and Vic. She didn't realize it, but Lisa had a lot to say about Vic.

"Okay, I don't want to pry, and I'm not judging at all, sis, but it sounds like you like this guy."

"Oh god no. I mean, he's-"

"Lisa, you just spent ten minutes describing what he was wearing when you talked to him."

"I did, didn't I?" Lisa reflected with a giggle. "It doesn't matter, he's Misty Bradley's boyfriend."

"Hmm... well, from what you just told me, sounds like he might be tired of having a stuck-up bitch for a girlfriend."

"Maybe," Lisa responded before she remembered she was supposed to be grieving. "I hope so for his sake, but I'm not interested. I mean, isn't it too soon?"

"Not if you have to ask."

Ashley's smile beamed through the phone. Lisa realized she was still holding the business card. Embarrassed, she set it on the dresser.

"Look kiddo, I know things are weird right now, and I'm sorry I'm not there. But I'm only a phone call away."

"I know, Ash. Thank you."

"And listen to yourself, will ya? You sound so different to me. You know how they say what doesn't kill us makes us stronger? Well, rate you're going, you'll be able to bench press a pickup by the time I see you next."

"So when do you think you'll make it down?"

Ashley hesitated before answering.

"Sorry Lisa, gotta go cram. Tell Dad I said, well, don't tell him I said anything."

"Gotcha. Good luck on the paper."

"Thanks, gonna need it."

———

Lisa tried to tell herself she couldn't sleep because she was confused, upset, too this, too that. She found herself staring at Vic's card again, remembering his words, the demeanor with which he'd delivered them. Lisa was no flirt, and she often didn't recognize when she was on the receiving end of an advance until the boy made an overt maneuver. Still, she couldn't help feeling this was *something*. And just like that, her anxieties slipped beneath the waves of teenage lust, and something new came straight to the top. Something erogenous.

Her hand found its way beneath her covers; it was a quick and easy maneuver to quell this kind of thought. When Lisa's buzzer popped two minutes later, Vic's face burned brightly before her. Sated, the thrill of the fantasy drained away, replaced by disgust. Juxtaposing thoughts of Vic with Bill's murder seemed the final straw, a betrayal beyond compare. One more parapet added to Lisa's fortress of guilt, the foundation of which she'd still not addressed. Was Vic merely a distraction from that? Bill's death had brought with it not just the horror of murder but the swell of unbidden relief because, in its wake, Lisa realized she had *never* loved him. Less than a week before he died, she'd instigated the fight that ultimately drove Bill to that party because, as she could admit only to herself, Lisa had been all but finished with the relationship.

What's more, Bill knew this. It's why he called that night: to try and win her back. Did it invalidate a person's grief when they were about to dump the person who died?

Now, here she was thinking of Vic, a drug dealer who slept with Misty Bradley and didn't even profess to like her very much. Lisa wondered what was wrong with her that she behaved this way?

There was no answer. Disgusted and exhausted, she closed her eyes and finally fell asleep.

———

A threshold yawned before her, beyond which the night loomed cold and infinite. A faint, familiar aroma tickled her memory. It brought vague images from the past... distant, just beyond reach. A doorway to some Archetypal well; she became aware for the first time of a place inside her that predated the parameters of what she thought of as 'Lisa.'

She stepped inside and closed the door. To her left, sunlight poured through the picture window in the front room. The light made Lisa feel exposed, so she stepped into the room and closed the large purple drapes. The light died.

"Lisa."

The voice came from the second floor, just at the top of the stairs. The ornate wooden balustrade invited her to climb. As she did, Lisa examined the picture frames that transformed the wall's surface into a record of the past. Three steps up, she stood level with the first, a family portrait. Her father stood at the rear left, Ashley in front of him and Lisa beside her. To Lisa's left was a woman with a blurred face.

She climbed three more steps and stood before the second picture, this one just Gerald and the woman with the blurred face. In both photographs, she could tell by the way the woman's clothes hung on her that it was her mother. The obscuration troubled her deeply.

"Lisa," the voice from above recurred.

"Mom? Is that you?"

"Who else would it be, silly. Ready for your big day?"

"I think so."

"Good. It won't be long now."

"Will Dad be there?"

"Well, yes, but you might be sorry you invited him. Your father isn't going to be able to protect you the way you can protect him."

"What'd you mean protect him?"

"Well, wouldn't you like it if he didn't have to die like I did?"

"But you're here now, Mom."

"No, dear. I'm just here to bring you a message."

"Mom...?"

"It works both ways, darling."

"What? Mom, I don't understand..."

The scene stuttered, deposited Lisa in the corridor that led to their living room. Another stutter, and she sat in a chair by the fireplace. A text appeared on her phone, the number listed as "Unknown."

He killed my mother; now he wants to kill you.

A cold wind reminded Lisa she'd left the front door open. She moved to remedy her mistake.

"Honey? Can you shut the door? You can't be too careful with a killer on the loose."

Lisa was just about to pull the door closed when, from somewhere outside, screams erupted in the night.

PART TWO

CHAPTER SIX

Wednesday, September 2

When she woke, Lisa's head felt choked with fog, no doubt the after-effects of the fight with her father for having disobeyed him. Lisa held back the information that she'd gone to see Jim Harrison, instead citing a need for fresh air after being cooped up in the house all day. Perhaps because of this, the one good thing that came out of the conflict was Gerald finally understanding Lisa's need to come to terms with Bill's murder in her own time.

"You need time to pull yourself together; I see that now. If I push you, well, we've already seen what happened your first day back with the fight. Another episode like that and Dean Laramie is liable to tell me to put you back in nuthouse."

Lisa winced, but also, she recognized that this was likely about as sensitive a response as she was going to get. And, of course, Gerald wasn't wrong; she was a mess and dreaded the idea of being anywhere near her so-called peers.

Part of the suspension had come with the agreement that she would stay in contact with her teachers via the school's online portal. In this way, Lisa could stay current on her schoolwork. Upon waking, she made note of the day's assignments, made coffee, and puttered around most of the morning. Thoughts of Onya haunted her; she knew Philip as the type to retaliate, and Onya was an easy target. She considered calling Mather's and asking to speak to Nurse Landing, but after the incident the other day, Helen no longer felt like an ally.

By early afternoon, Lisa's anxiety snowballed. Luckily, she had a lot of work to catch up on. She put her game face on and dug in. Schoolwork would provide a welcome distraction from her fears.

While Michael Bradley had been correct about Lisa having already earned enough credits to graduate, her poisoned disposition toward his offer inspired a new commitment to her Senior year. Necessary or not, Lisa did not intend to get anything other than "A's." Sociology, Trig and Advanced Chemistry were little more than electives, but they would bolster her GPA and help her get into a good school next year.

'I'm going away no matter what.'

Lisa told herself this repeatedly while she worked. She wrote it on the little chalkboard that hung above her desk.

College Bound!!!

While she worked, another distraction began to circle her thoughts like a persistent fly.

Matt.

Seeing him, riding in his car, old feelings resurfaced. She remembered how... safe she'd felt in his presence.

Like kismet, her phone chimed.

How's it going?

Hitting the books. Behind in all my classes.

It felt weird, the excitement she experienced seeing such a simple message. When she responded, Lisa did so with her lower lip tucked gently beneath her front teeth, a tiny jolt of coquettish energy underlying her message. Smiling, she added:

Could use a break.

The moment Lisa hit send, her phone rang.

"Hey hey. You wanna grab a coffee or some lunch? It's my day off."

"Sure, but maybe a little later, if that's okay?"

"I'll come by around... 4:00 PM?"

Lisa blushed when she realized her father would not be home until after eight.

"Sounds good."

Something occurred to her.

"Hey, can I ask a favor?"

"Anything."

"Can you wear your uniform? Or at least bring it with you."

Meaning he'd have to change into it, meaning he'd have to remove his clothes...

"Ahhh... sure?"

"It's nothing kinky."

"Too bad."

As she set the phone down, Lisa's anticipation swelled as she danced around her room in pirouettes of joy.

"I need to get into Mather's."

To say Matt had been hoping for a completely different reason for the uniform request would be an understatement.

"I'm confused. The other night you said the thought of ever going there again scared you more than anything."

This was true; Lisa had confided that since Mather's, her greatest fear was losing her mind. She had tasted the flavor of mental illness and found it revolting.

"I meant as a patient. Look, I don't *want* to go there. I *need* to. I have to make sure Onya is okay. Things happen there, Matt. Bad things. You know the third floor's supposed to have been shut down for decades, but there are always lights in the windows, and you can hear footsteps on the ceiling from the second-floor rooms. People say they do experiments up there, that they pass people off as dead, then release the wrong body for burial and keep some for experiments."

"Who says that? I don't know that I'd take the gossip of a bunch of-"

"Crazy people?"

Matt apologized instantly.

"Okay, tell me your plan."

They would arrive as though on official police business. When it came to his career, Matt wasn't a risk-taker, but before Lisa even finished, he was in. Her passion for the truth, for protecting the innocent, was one of the most endearing qualities he'd witnessed in anyone from his generation. Matt had to keep reminding himself Lisa was not quite eighteen yet; an important fact as he began to relive the feelings he'd developed during their Home Economics partnership.

Unannounced visitors weren't generally welcome at Mather's, but Lisa hoped that with Matt in uniform, they could bypass policy. Of course, she'd also been banking on Matt driving his police truck, but as it was his day off, he arrived in his 1979 Dodge Charger instead.

"Okay, what the hell. Let's give it a try."

They pulled up to the gate at Mather's Sanitarium at half-past five, not even a week since Lisa's release.

When Matt identified himself over the gate's intercom, he did so with a professional degree of severity. The gambit worked; several moments later, they coasted up the winding blacktop driveway toward the main building. Lisa stared at the third floor: several lit windows served as a reminder that things here might not be what they seemed.

Built in the late 1920s, Mather's Sanitarium looked like something from a nightmare, the bold gothic dormers adorned with wrought iron finials, the windows old and, in some cases, broken. There were even gargoyles on the roof, old and battered, the details of their original carvings obscured by weather and time, ominous nonetheless.

"I can't believe you were here for two months; place looks like it's about to collapse in on itself, like the end of Poltergeist."

"When a community tucks their skeletons into a place such as this, it's so they don't have to think about them anymore," Lisa paraphrasing one of Michael Bradley's press releases about the Children's Hospital she had helped him save. His email was still kicking up dust in her head.

They parked and approached on foot. Nurse Landing met them in the lobby.

"Lisa McCready, I didn't think I'd ever see you here again."

"I'm sorry. I know this isn't exactly protocol, but I asked

my dad if we could perform a wellness check on Onya. I'm worried about her."

Nurse Landing's smile did little to disguise her polite suspicion.

"How very thoughtful of you. Was there something in particular that made you fear for your friend?"

The way Landing said, 'your friend' made Lisa think that, despite her pleasant facade, Helen Landing was anything but happy they had come.

"No. Well, it's just that–" Lisa's mind went blank. She didn't know what she should say to Helen because, for the first time, Lisa realized she considered her the enemy. Did she know about Philip's extracurricular activities with some of the girls?

"It's fine, dear. I appreciate your compassion. Come, I'll take you to her."

As they walked, Lisa's pulse quickened, and the walls began to push in on her.

Matt saw the sweat on Lisa's brow. He wanted to reach up and take her hand. Such familiarity, however, would definitely shatter their ruse. Likewise, he held back when Lisa began to nervously over-explain.

"It's just... I know she's been having trouble lately, and I thought that maybe if I visited her, it might help."

"Onya has indeed been having trouble lately, and I'll tell you that I wondered if it didn't have something to do with you leaving us."

Again, 'you leaving us' felt angry, as though Landing were blaming Lisa.

"She took quite a shine to you while you were here, Lisa. If you don't mind my asking, why do you think that is?"

"Because I listen to her."

They passed through the double doors that separated the recreation room from the isolation ward, turned a corner, and there was Philip. Creepy as ever, he stood outside a patient's room with a mop in one hand and the other on the front of his pants, staring into the small square window set into the door.

"Philip!" Nurse Landing hollered, mortified.

Philip jumped, shot Lisa a look that made her skin crawl.

"That's him, Matt," Lisa said so he could hear. She'd told Matt *all* about Philip on the drive over. "That's the guy I told you about."

Matt took two imposing steps toward the orderly.

"You wanna end up on the sex offenders list, buddy?"

Philip took off so fast he nearly tripped and fell before disappearing around the nearest corner.

"Looks like you might want to... reassess some of your staff, ma'am."

"Don't worry, Deputy. Philip will be dealt with. Swift and brutal."

The remark caught Matt off guard, as did the image of Landing consciously struggling to turn her enraged visage into something that only faintly resembled a smile. They continued briefly down the hall and came to the door marked 'VISITATION AREA.'

"You two wait here and I will return with Onya shortly. Just so you know, visitation in the isolation ward normally ends at 4:00 PM sharp. However, since you have the Deputy here with you, please take as long as you need to help Onya feel better. I am truly sorry I ever doubted you."

They thanked her and stepped inside the small room. The walls were drab, off-white with flaked paint and periodic holes, but no windows. It looked like someone had lost their temper and punched through the drywall.

When the door closed behind them, Lisa's heart began to pound in her chest. She'd done all right so far, but once the door closed, all her fears about winding up here again came flooding back. She wasn't crazy.

Just. Breathe.

Matt turned away from her, taking in the room, and Lisa used the distraction to quickly pull one of Vic's pills from the tiny pocket on the front of her jeans and dry swallow it with a cough.

"You okay?"

"Lump in my throat."

Matt put an arm around her shoulder.

"Don't worry, You've got this."

"I hope so..." she said, relaxing into his embrace.

———

"Lisa!"

The two girls embraced, Onya overjoyed and going so far as to give Lisa a huge kiss on the lips. An awkward moment for sure, and one that took Lisa a few minutes to shake off. To help recover, she began to ask Onya questions.

"How are you doing? Are they treating you okay?"

"I guess. I'm... sleeping a lot; sometimes I think I'm... sometimes I think I'm just going to go to sleep one day and never wake up."

"I know the feeling. It's the meds. Without them, though, you might not be able to sleep."

"Is that what happened to you when you went home?"

Before Lisa could answer, a loud, concussive sound from outside the room startled them. In its wake, Onya promptly reverted to a trembling wreck.

"It's okay, honey. You're okay. It was nothing."

"No! You don't know! You don't know about the walls! He does! He knows you're here! You shouldn't have come! He killed my mother; now he's going to kill you!"

Before she could even shoot him a look, Lisa felt Matt's hands on her shoulder. The gesture proved far from calming; Lisa could feel he was shaking, too. Lisa knew Matt had heard the stories about crazy Onya O'Sullivan, but he'd never actually experienced her firsthand.

"Onya, it's okay. I promise you."

"NO! He knows! He knows!"

"Who is 'he?' Is he a real person? Or is he like Arturo?"

"Who's Arturo?" Matt whispered in Lisa's ear.

"Her stuffed turtle."

"Gotcha."

"You shouldn't have come here! Shouldn't have come!"

Lisa began to panic. She knew if she didn't calm Onya in the next few seconds, her cries would bring the staff and their visit would be over.

"Onya, I saw your father the other day. He wanted me to tell you hello and that he loves you more than anything in the -"

"He's lying! He's lying! He's lying!"

Onya began to shriek, each iteration of the phrase louder and more disturbed than the previous. Lisa looked to Matt but quickly realized he was well outside his experience.

The door to the room opened with a BANG! and Nurse Landing entered flanked by two orderlies. Lisa recognized one as Andre, who had handcuffed her on her final day. The other was new to her.

"Please leave and let us handle this," Nurse Landing commanded, directing the orderlies to restrain Onya.

Lisa bolstered for a fight but caved when Matt took her by the arm and led her from the room.

"She's in charge, Lisa. We're visitors, and if you want to be able to come back, we gotta do what she says."

Onya's words devolved into an indecipherable scream, a siren that ricocheted off the stark, white walls. Lisa felt as though she might vomit. Then the door shut, and a moment later, Onya's voice evaporated. Lisa was left standing with Matt in the hall, quaking so hard her teeth rattled.

"So, should we talk about what just happened? I mean, first, it's a good thing we came. You totally saved some girl from that pervert, Lise."

They were in the car on the way back to Lisa's.

"I've never had concrete proof of anything; more a gut feeling. But my gut's pretty good," saying this, Lisa's thoughts turned directly to her father and his endless lessons and lectures on instinct, awareness, and "O & E" - Orient and Execute, Gerald McCready's own personal version of the OODA loop.

"I'm not surprised, being raised by your dad."

"He took me to the firing range, taught me how to get out of cuffs, rope, all kinds of stuff. He was always like that, but it really ramped up after what happened to Ashley."

"I remember. Jeez, she was what, a senior at the time? Bad luck seems to run in your fam- I'm sorry; I'm such a jackass."

"No. No, you're not. I mean, you'd be insane not to make that observation. I've felt like a black cloud has followed me my entire life. Never knowing my mom, Ashley's attack, Annie, now Bill and Mather's."

"I'd never been in that place, you know? I mean, we weren't in there very long, but it got to me. It's creepy as hell, and I totally saw the lights in the third-floor window when we rolled up. I'll have to ask around at the station, do some digging."

"Being locked inside that place, screams echo through the halls at night. It's unreal. When you said it looked like a nightmare, you hit the nail on the head. I still wake up hearing those screams; feels like I'll be hearing them for the rest of my life."

This was something Lisa hadn't actually admitted to herself, but it was true, this idea that the screams might be a curse she could never outlive.

Madness - Only the purple can fight the madness.

The voice was right. After two months of Mather's, sometimes Lisa felt like something inside her had broken, leaving only the tattered, insane wreckage of the person she'd always identified as. Without thinking, her hand slid into the tiny pocket on her jeans and removed a pill, then stopped when she realized she'd just taken one.

"Look, I know you're still hurting. Two months in any facility isn't going to change the fact that Bill's dead. I just wanted to say I'm sorry because, well, I've never said it before."

It irritated Lisa that people still thought she was upset about Bill because, more and more, she realized her grief for Bill had passed. This, in turn, made her feel callous and wasn't easy to admit. Deep down, however, an anchor had lifted. She looked at Matt and thought about the nights she'd spent with Bill, the way their rudimentary teenage sex had slowly, over their time together, become something better. Something she'd wanted to explore with others...

"You okay?"

"What? Yeah, uh... thanks. Really, you're so nice to me. It means a lot."

She leaned in and they kissed, fully immersed in each other. Her thoughts spiraling into the first feelings of this new romance, something new occurred to Lisa. She disengaged before things could get heated.

"Matt, what do you know about Annie Harrison's death?"

"Not much, really; that was before my time on the force."

"Do you think you could find anything out? Like, from the database or whatever?"

"You think her death might be tied into this, too?"

"I don't know, I just... people are talking about my dad. Saying he covered for her killer."

"I've never heard anyone say that."

"Yeah, well, think about it. You wouldn't hear stuff like that because you're a cop. I'm his daughter the target, remember?"

"Point. Sorry. I thought it was Annie's mom who-"

"Stepmom, but that explanation never made any sense. When I asked Mr. Harrison about it, he said the same thing, that Ruth would never have hurt Annie."

"Annie's father said that?"

"Yeah, and Misty said something the day I... the day we fought. She said Annie was killed by transient workers and my dad covered it up."

Lisa was ad-libbing, walking a tightrope with her emotions, but she needed a source inside the Sheriff's Department that wasn't her father. What's more, she knew she could get Matt to be that source. It was manipulative, but she didn't care.

"That's crazy. Your dad's a ball-buster, but he's a good man. A good sheriff. He cares about this community."

"I know he cares about Sundown Hills, and I know he cares about me, but that doesn't necessarily mean that he can't make mistakes. The whole thing has me sick, and I wanted to know if you could find something that would help *me* help *him*. Or at least make me feel like I'm not losing my mind."

For a moment, Matt didn't say a word. He stared at Lisa as though trying to decide whether or not her concern was legitimate. After a moment, his eyes lightened and a smile lifted his face.

"Sure. I'll... well, I'll look into it, anyway."

They pulled up in front of Lisa's house and Matt put the truck in park. Was he disappointed in her? Maybe, but manipulative or not, Lisa knew she could count on him.

"Okay, thanks for everything today. I mean, really."

Lisa loosed her safety belt and leaned into Matt, their mouths meeting in a kiss that danced on the edge of becoming something more.

CHAPTER SEVEN

Thursday, September 3

In the middle of the night, Lisa woke to screams. Panicked, sweating through her clothes, she jumped from bed, tears already in her eyes before she realized the screams were in her head, ghosts courtesy of Mather's Sanitarium.

Shaken, she laid back and focused on calming herself. To do this, Lisa used a mantra Miss Galdykas had taught her:

Just breathe

Just breathe

Repeating this, she focused on her body, relaxing it one section at a time. Her bladder called for release, but Lisa knew if she interrupted the process now, she would have to start over again. She zeroed in even tighter on breathing, and before long, peace settled over her.

She had just entered a twilight state when the sound of the front door brought her smashing back to reality.

Lisa slipped out of bed and tentatively stepped into the hallway. Across the hall, her father's door stood open, his bed still made. At the top of the stairs, she caught a quick glimpse of movement followed by the familiar creak of the kitchen door.

Someone's in the house...

Lisa ducked back into her room and grabbed her mace. Images of Frank O'Sullivan, of a masked intruder, of Vic Lamb assailed her. In the first, Frank cried and became violent. In the second, a bloody meathook hung at the intruder's side, a smile visible through the black mask's open mouth. With Vic, a chill of a different kind nipped her, and she had to push the image from her mind to stay present. No matter who was in the house, she wasn't taking any chances.

Quietly, she crept down the stairs, turned left and approached the kitchen door, behind which she could hear the low murmur of a man's voice. Lisa pushed the door open and stepped over the threshold only to find a masked figure in nondescript black clothing before her. Before she'd barely registered the intruder, he charged her with a forearm in the midsection and all of Lisa's air exploded from her lungs in one giant burst.

Lisa fell to the floor, missing the chance to catch her breath before the first boot caught the side of her head. Lazy beacons bubbled before her eyes, silver and black spots that ate her consciousness, threatening to replace it with void.

Don't black out...

No sooner did she think this than the next boot caught her in the small of the back; her bladder exploded, urine soaking her, washing over the floor.

"Sick, bitch!" The attacker reconnoitered to avoid the expanding puddle, and Lisa caught the next kick in the upper right thigh. This hurt worse than the first two, but with the pain came a thousand-kilohertz shock that jolted her into a primal state of awareness.

When the next boot came, Lisa moved her head just in

time, slipped both hands behind its return arc and pushed her attacker's leg straight out in front of him. His planted foot hopped once for a save, hit the puddle and disappeared from beneath him, sending the bastard straight onto his ass with a jarring THUD!

Vision blurred, leg muscles cramped and barely operational, Lisa began to pull herself across the tile by her arms. As a kid playing Marines, they called this the alligator walk. Fingertips, forearms and shoulders working in tandem, her homemade lubricant sped her along the floor toward the kitchen's island. She could hear her attacker groan and knew she had seconds at best. Re-focused, she pulled herself up into a cobra pose. As she'd hoped, once back on his feet, the attacker moved around the island to come at her head-on, trying to avoid the puddle. She waited until she saw his eyes appear over the edge of the marble countertop, then flung the door of the first cabinet open hard enough that when it hit his shin, he howled in pain.

The inside of that cabinet was home to several cooking implements. Lisa grabbed the first one she saw, a meat-tenderizing mallet, and brought it down hard across the back of his other calf.

For the second time, Lisa brought her attacker down to her level.

This was the first chance she'd gotten to actually look at this person. Definitely a man based on the voice, dressed in a long-sleeved black thermal, black cargo pants and a ski mask. With his lanky build, Lisa smiled at the realization that simply by pissing herself, she'd gained the advantage in this skirmish.

With her right thigh still little more than a bundle of clumped, raw nerves, Lisa pulled herself three more big moves across the floor and brought the hammer down again. This time, Mr. Mask moved in time to avoid the blow.

"What the fuck, you crazy bitch?"

"You're asking me what the fuck?"

Lisa practically threw herself on top of him. He turned and started to gain his feet, but she caught his calves, and just the contact made the tender little sticks fall out from under him again.

"Jesus Christ!"

"Don't go breaking into girls' houses and attacking them, you fucking piece of shit!"

She was shrieking as she climbed up over his ass, back and shoulders, gaining a grip on the fabric bunched at the back of his skull and driving his face into the piss-soaked tile.

"How's my piss taste, fucker? Tell me! Tell me!"

When relating this later, Lisa would not remember what she said or the sequence of the maneuvers that won her the day. In the heat of battle, though, she proved more than capable of the hostility needed to win. There was more of her father inside her than Lisa McCready realized.

As she pounded the attacker's face into the floor, everything turned red. Her breath whistled through her nostrils, and the pores on her scalp flared open, a burst of heat driving her into a sudden bout of exhaustion. A moment later, two things happened in tandem: Lisa fell close to unconscious on top of Mr. Mask and the kitchen door flew open. Gerald rushed inside just as the world began to fade to black.

"Lisa!"

"He killed my mother... now he wants to kill me..."

There was more violent motion and screaming, but it amounted to little more than waves breaking against a distant shore as Lisa drifted into the waters of unconsciousness.

———

Lisa opened her eyes and panic immediately gripped her. The clinical white walls and smell of disinfectant brought Mather's screaming back, and for a moment, she thought her release had been a dream. Then she saw her father, hat in hand, sitting at her bedside and the image of the intruder returned to her with a stabbing blast of pain and fear and embarrassment.

Her mouth tasted of copper, like when she used to suck pennies as a kid. Lisa's eyes felt hot and dry, and a low-grade throb of pain radiated through her entire body, especially her right thigh.

For the first time in her life, Lisa saw tears fall from her father's eyes. She opened her mouth to speak, but the back of her throat felt coated in sand, and her tongue refused to function.

"Dad?" she croaked.

"Sweetie, I'm sorry. I'm so sorry..."

"She's probably thirsty. Give her this."

Matt stepped into view and handed Gerald McCready a small plastic cup with a bendy straw that, with a bit of maneuvering, Lisa caught between her lips.

It was the most refreshing water she'd ever tasted.

"Easy, girl. Easy," Gerald let her have a bit more, then set the cup on the table at her bedside. Most of the sand now washed away, Lisa tried again to speak.

"Who... who was it?"

Her father looked as though he'd not anticipated the question. He turned to Matt, then turned back to Lisa; another first - he looked embarrassed.

"Let's not talk about that right now, honey. The doctors say you're fine, just a mild concussion and-"

"Who was he?" she asked again with a fierce enough edge that both men reacted.

"We don't know, baby. We think he's a transient - maybe a laborer. We're waiting for dental records."

"What..." Lisa's voice caught in her throat, and Matt jumped up and handed the cup directly to her this time. She finished the contents in three big gulps.

"What did he say when you questioned him?"

Her father and Matt traded a look, then dialed back on her.

"I couldn't question him, sweetie. You... he... died."

Lisa sat up and immediately regretted it.

"Died? Was it me? Did I kill him?"

Neither man answered, so Lisa lay back against the pillow, closed her eyes, and willed herself back to sleep.

CHAPTER EIGHT

Friday, September 4

When Doctor Tulane released Lisa from the hospital the next morning, Matt drove her home.

"How did you get stuck picking me up?"

"I didn't get stuck, Lisa. I asked to pick you up."

"Oh, sure. So my dad's not, like, avoiding me because I killed a guy?"

"Lisa, what you did was self-defense. I mean, Christ, that guy broke into your house and attacked you. I think what you did wasn't just warranted, it was, well, kind of awesome."

"Yeah? I don't really remember most of it, but I remember being scared and then, in like a flash, I wasn't. Or, at least, I wasn't as scared as I was angry. I mean, what kind of fucking psycho breaks into the Sheriff's house and attacks his teenage daughter?"

"See?"

"Yeah, but Matt, my dad never even came back to see me after he told me the guy died. What does that say?"

"It says he can't face you until he finds out who that guy was and why he did what he did."

"You don't think it was random?"

"Are you kidding? After the fire pit? No way."

"Wait a minute. What are you saying?"

Matt pulled the cruiser to the side of the road, put it in park and turned in his seat to face Lisa directly.

"Look. I don't want to make you paranoid or totally fuck you up, but ya ask me? Someone has you and your dad in their crosshairs."

"Fuck."

"Yeah. Your father would kill me for saying that, but way I see it, you're better off knowing. Offense beats defense every time."

"How do I run offense on an unknown person who wants me dead?"

"Maybe not unknown. My money's on David Bradley."

"Seriously?"

"There's precedent: Angela Walters."

"Oh my god. Is he the suspect for the fire pit?"

"I can't comment on -"

"I mean you, Matt. Who are *you* looking at?"

"Way I see it, David Bradley has reasons to hate both Angela's father *and* yours. I mean, think about it for a moment. You're David Bradley. Your younger brother not only abandons the family business, he tries to bankrupt it by blasting you to anyone who will listen for all he's worth, every chance he gets."

"What the hell does that have to do with me? Or Angela?"

"I can't speak to ongoing investigations our department might have, but I can tell you that, in my opinion, James Harrison is right. David Bradley is absolutely running drugs into Sundown Hills. He's got a captive audience with both his workforce *and* the men on Craig Walters's construction crew.

Only now, Walters is a shell of his former self because his daughter's been murdered, and Project Pegasus is a chicken with no head. Kinda convenient, right?"

"Okay, so David's trying to ruin his brother's support network. Why me? What's he have against my dad?"

"Are you kidding? If you're running drugs into town, who's your biggest opponent?"

"Why now?"

"Well, like I said, I can't discuss ongoing investigations, but..."

The lightbulb nearly blinded her. Matt couldn't discuss ongoing investigations, meaning *an investigation was in progress.* This meant Lisa was definitely a target IF it was David Bradley.

"Now I'm scared. David Bradley has money, influence and power."

"Something else that points to David. I think his brother suspects him, too. I think that's why he offered you a job in Seattle. To protect you."

This had not occurred to her, and Michael Bradley instantly became a brighter star in Lisa's sky. That far away, she would surely be safe, same as Ashely.

"Okay, Matt. What the hell do I do?"

"We need to figure that out."

They finished the drive to Lisa's, went inside and sat at the kitchen table where, not twenty-four hours prior, she had beaten a man to death.

———

Two years ago, Matt Hartman told his best friend Skeeter Sherman that he was in love with Sheriff McCready's daughter. Skeeter, whose dad Leonard had worked for McCready for going on ten years, told Matt that if he knew what was good for him, he'd squash those feelings like a bug.

"Trust me. When it comes to his girls, the Sheriff doesn't play around."

The idea wasn't that he shouldn't date Lisa because she was the Sheriff's daughter, but that if Matt wanted to be a cop in Sundown Hills, conflict of interest didn't even begin to describe *that* situation.

Since early childhood, Matt knew in no uncertain terms he wanted to be a police officer. His father had been one in Upstate New York, where Matt's family lived until just after his tenth birthday. Matt turned ten in June, his father was shot in the back twenty-eight days later. The bullet did not kill him, but it paralyzed his right side. Six months later, Officer Darryl Hartman committed suicide. In the note he left for his wife (which Matt was not supposed to see), Darryl spoke of how he was a broken person. A 'disfigured, discarded, disaster of a man."

Disfigured.

In the tsunami of grief and fear that his mother suffered as a result, she moved herself, Matt and his older brother back to the town she grew up in: Sundown Hills. Matt's brother Kevin left for school in New York six months later, and Matt and his mother tried to put the past behind them and make a new life for themselves. For the most part, it worked. Matt's mom found solace as a functional alcoholic, while Matt decided to follow in his father's footsteps.

During his final semester of high school, Matt's Guidance Counselor put him on the work-release program; Matt left after fifth period to intern for the Sheriff's Department. He mainly did rudimentary work: filing reports, data entry, etc. The Sheriff's secretary, Bridget, had requested a leave of absence to care for a dying sister in Florida; during her absence, Matt pitched in and tackled as much as he could for a few hours every afternoon. Sheriff McCready took a liking to him, and one night over takeout, he got to talking about his daughters, how he struggled with living in the same town as the two assholes that had assaulted Ashley, and how her departure for college meant he couldn't protect her anymore.

"I'm not takin' any chances with Lisa. Any guy even comes near her, I'll lock his ass up so tight, he'll never see the sun again."

Matt took this comment to heart, and despite his feelings for Lisa, he forced himself to remain platonic. At the end of the semester, he graduated and began his training.

The thing was, Matt might have moved on, but his feelings for Lisa couldn't be negated. Whenever he'd see her at the station, or if he had to stop by the Sheriff's house while she was home, any interaction brought those feelings right back to the surface.

When Matt parked the cruiser at the foot of Lisa's driveway and shut off the engine, he spoke to her with an earnest compassion that proved enough to get the old juices flowing. Matt could see by the look in Lisa's eyes that she still liked him, too. Over the next fifteen minutes, the more they talked about Lisa's predicament, the more they slipped into sync. When she suggested they go inside to talk more, both knew an ulterior motive was already at play. So, when five minutes after sitting down, Lisa put her hand on Matt's knee, the action was charged with two years' worth of sexual tension. As with all increasingly volatile potential energies, one spark was all it took to make the keg explode.

———

When Ashley McCready first left for college, the four hundred-plus miles between Sundown Hills and Indiana University did not seem adequate distance from her father.

Overbearing was the word Ashely would use when she talked to her therapist about him. Overbearing and sometimes suspicious.

Six months before graduating high school, Ashley was attacked by two drunk jocks beneath the bleachers at a school football game. While the attack was interrupted and Ashley suffered no serious physical injuries from the incident, the assault decimated her psychologically. She spent the next three months in her room. While initially sympathetic, Gerald eventually began to push a self-defense agenda that Ashley had zero interest in.

"Learning this stuff is like asking for it to happen again."

"Ashley, honey, that's just not true. You're not asking for it just because you carry mace or know how to throw a punch."

"Oh really? But I was asking for it by the way I dress?"

This had been a point of contention between Ashley and her father since Freshman year. Gerald never directly blamed his oldest daughter's penchant for fishnets and halter tops for the assault, but his regular admonishments for her sense of fashion laid the subtext bare. Lisa knew Gerald's *concern* for Ashley was legit even if misinformed; however, she also knew that, in his mind, the conservative platform he brought to his office took an arrow every time someone saw his daughter running around town 'tarted up,' to use one of his less-sensitive phrases.

So, while Gerald never mentioned Ashley's clothes after the incident, he didn't have to; Ashley already knew how he felt. More than anything, this fueled the anger she carried for him - and, by extension - the town he worked for. Anger that still seethed to this day.

The two boys who attacked her were expelled from school and given adult sentences of six months probation. Big whoop. Slightly more satisfying was that, as starting varsity athletes, both had previously been shoe-ins for scholarships at prominent Universities. After the dust settled on the incident, both were rejected from every school sans community college.

Despite all this, or perhaps because of it, those three months in her room became something of a chrysalis for Ashely, and she emerged as a suddenly willful, positive person. She finished Senior year as a runner-up to Valedictorian and was accepted to several colleges. Her plan to move as far away as possible was subsequently undercut by her fears of leaving her younger sister alone.

"I'm a six-hour drive away. Seven with a lunch stop," Ashley told Lisa while secretly hoping she wouldn't have to return at all. In the stark interiority of Ashley's newly refurbished mind, she didn't give a toss if she saw Sundown Hills or her father ever again.

When Ashley saw Gerald's name on an incoming call just after dark, her first impulse was to ignore it. Eventually however, something told her to pick up.

"Dad. What's up?"

"Ashley honey... I wanted to tell you..."

Ashley's impatience with her father always went from zero to sixty in less than a fraction of what it did for anyone else.

"Dad, I'm cramming. If you called to stutter..."

"Your sister was attacked."

The air around her caught fire, and Ashley suddenly found she couldn't breathe.

"What?"

"I don't want to go into detail over the phone, but someone broke into the house last night and attacked her."

"And you're just telling me now? Jesus Christ, Dad! Is she okay? Who was it? Did you shoot the son of a bitch?"

A sigh, then Gerald continued:

"He's dead, all right. But honey, I want you to be careful,

okay? Is there a... is there a boy you're seeing that you could maybe stay with for a while?"

"What?" Gerald's question both frightened and infuriated Ashley. Never one to acknowledge his daughters as sexual beings, she knew for him to broach such a subject - let alone suggest she stay with someone - meant Gerald's concern was genuine. Yet, Ashley couldn't help but lash out in return. After everything between them, anger had become her automated response to the man who helped give her life.

"That doesn't make any sense, and you know it. You're just looking for a reason to try and start up your same old argument again."

"Ashley, look. I know you can't forgive me for - "

Ashley clicked off a second before she burst into tears. Outside, the man watching her through the window smiled. Emotional moments like this were the best time to strike. He knew this from experience.

————

After only fifteen minutes of discussing strategies to keep Lisa safe, they spent two hours in Lisa's room.

Lisa could not remember the last time she'd felt so happy.

She lay on her back, Matt curled next to her, his head nestled on her breasts as the sun crept behind the horizon. They dozed, woke up and went for another round. After, Matt began to grow antsy.

"Wow. If you'd told me I'd be here last month, I wouldn't have believed you."

"Tell me about it."

"We really need to talk about how to handle the situation, because I'm not going to feel comfortable until we figure out a fool-proof way to keep you safe."

"I feel pretty safe with my dad's favorite deputy inside me."

The moment she said this, Lisa regretted it.

"What time is it? He should be home soon, right?"

"You work with him, Matt. Don't you know his schedule?"

Matt leaped from the bed and found his phone.

"Half past eight."

Now, it was Lisa who sat up, alarmed.

"He's usually home by eight-thirty. Nine latest."

"Shit!"

Matt retrieved his pants from the floor and hopped into them, one leg at a time. Lisa ran for the bathroom; as she did, her phone pinged.

"Check if that's him!" she shouted as she closed the door. Matt grabbed the phone from the nightstand and instinctively breathed a sigh of relief when he saw it *wasn't* Lisa's father. Relief bellyflopped when he saw the message's preview. A dark photo of a girl through her window, framed by branches. It read:

talked to ashley lately cunt???

Lisa returned to the room fully dressed.

"Not him?"

Matt handed her the phone.

"Lisa..."

———

Ashley's apartment was just off campus. The ground floor of a three-flat, it wasn't the nicest place she'd looked at, but it was the best bang for her buck, no doubt. Plus, she considered the fifteen-minute walk to campus each day a huge win, as she had developed quite the taste for craft beer. The walk would help her fight off the added calories accompanying this newfound love.

Since the call from her father, Ashley had put down two IPAs with a fairly steep ABV. Her tastes lay more in line with a good Kolsch or Sour, but as the saying went, any port in a storm.

Fried from a combination of cramming and the news about her sister, the beers didn't seem quite enough. She stepped outside to finish the joint Sam had left in the ashtray last night. Sam definitely wasn't a long-term investment, but he was nice to her and had great weed, so for the time being, Ashley was content.

The air outside was crisp, and the smoke felt good in her lungs. She scrolled through her Instagram while taking her time with the smoke.

RUSTLE

A sound to her left caused her to look up. Instinctively, her right hand slipped the phone back into her rear left pocket even as her left retrieved the keychain-sized can of mace from her front hoodie pocket.

The building sat alone near an overpass, with the parking lot stretching out to the cross streets of Everett and Vans. Behind, a steep hill led up to the Interstate. Ashley remained perfectly still for several long, frozen moments, the only sound traffic on the highway.

"Hello?"

No answer. Of course not. Ashely knew her neighbors were all out bar hopping because she'd turned down an invite to join them so she could prep for this damn psyche test.

RUSTLE

Ashley nearly jumped when she heard the sound a second

time. There were only a few leaves on the ground and no trees in the parking lot. What was she hearing?

"C'mon girl, you know Sam's weed can make you paranoid," she said out loud with a hint of braggadocio, as though this might be enough to ward off any trespassers. She flicked the remainder of the joint away from her and turned to head inside. Mara, Ashley's therapist, had warned her that smoking weed might exacerbate some of her negative feelings. "PTSD never really goes away," she could hear Mara say in her thick, Minnesota accent.

Once back inside, Ashley plopped on the couch and realized she was *way* too high to study.

"Great job, Ace."

She thought about it for a moment, then called Village Pizza. Small Pepperoni, extra cheese. Food would cut her high in half, maybe make the world manageable again.

While she waited, Ashley took a quick shower and clicked on the television. A self-professed 'Murder Junkie,' she had been waiting all week to watch a new documentary on Richard Ramirez.

The bell rang, and struggling into sweats and an old Cure t-shirt, she went to the door with a five-dollar tip in her hand.

"You're even faster than they promise in their ads, so you get a big tip. In fact, if you're cute, you might get something more than a tip-"

Ashely opened the door and the knife went straight into her throat, severing her vocal cords and trachea in one shot. Air rushed in around the blade's edges as the killer worked it back and forth. When she dropped, one black-gloved hand caught Ashley's body at the small of the back, even as the other swept the door closed behind them.

When the pizza man came not five minutes later, it was to be the third prank order he'd dealt with that day. His exasperation probably explains how he missed the arterial spray that decorated the door and front porch of the apartment.

———

Lisa tried calling Ashley, but her phone went straight to voice mail. She tried two more times in rapid succession, then called her father.

"Dad! I just got a really freaky text. It's like someone outside Ash's apartment, stalking her!"

Gerald told her to hold tight, hung up, and immediately called Rick Thompson, captain of the University police. The day that Ashley announced her enrollment, he'd driven up and introduced himself to Thompson, took him out for a few beers and asked him to keep an eye on his oldest daughter.

Lisa didn't know any of this.

"What are we gonna do? Matt, someone is going to kill her!"

A moment later, her phone dinged. When she opened the message, she fell to her knees, the tears like blades in her eyes. Lisa cried so hard she began to vomit, and for a moment, Matt thought she was on the verge of convulsions. When he looked at the phone, he saw the picture of Ashley with one knife in her throat and two more, one in each eye. Scrawled in black marker across the hardwood floor where she lay was the word "Bich." The accompanying text read:

guess ash ain't as tuff as U. 2 bad 4 her

CHAPTER NINE

Lisa,

I've wanted to write since Ashely's death, but I thought it best to give you your space. Words cannot express how truly sorry I am for the loss of your sister. I did not have the pleasure of knowing Ashely as well as I do you; however, what little I know about her suggests she shared your indomitable spirit, love of life, and the perspicacity I have seen when working with you. I will not overextend my grief; let it just be said that I feel very deeply for you at this time.

The Seattle situation will be there when you are ready. We have maneuvered things into a stalemate I am willing to live with for now. I hope that, when you feel up to it, you will contact me. I would still so love to have you on my team.

Until then, please do not hesitate to reach out if I can assist you or your family in any way.

Best,

Michael R. Bradley

Friday, October 30th

The days that followed were the darkest Lisa had known. Between Ashley's funeral and her father's grief piled atop her own, Lisa was fairly certain she would have wound up back in Mather's if it wasn't for Matt. Their bond deepened quickly, and the night after Ashley's funeral, Lisa told Gerald her intention to begin a relationship with his deputy. To her surprise, he gave his unconditional blessing.

"Matt's not just a good guy; he's a good cop. You know I don't like to talk about this stuff with you girls... with you... but I'm happy for you."

Gerald excused himself, and Lisa knew it was to cry. She also knew that the strategist in him had a lot to do with his acceptance of her relationship with Matt.

"He's a good cop."

Meaning, if Gerald couldn't watch over his daughter 24/7, he was happy to have someone else he trusted who could help.

But Matt couldn't be with her 24/7 either, and in her loneliest moments, Lisa's depression became the immutable law that governed her life. She hadn't been back to school, nor did she intend to return any time soon. Gerald's grief caused him to act erratically, and when he nearly shot someone on accident at the firing range, he agreed to take time off. As a result, Matt stepped up and began to work longer hours, effectively leaving Lisa alone with her father for long stretches. They started family therapy with a colleague Mrs. Galdykas recommended, but Lisa and Gerald only exacerbated each other's sorrow. Their time together became one long, heavy ordeal. She began to withdraw, and Gerald took to fishing for long hours during the day and spending his evenings at the Deep Six Bar, a dusty shot-and-a-beer joint at nearby man-made Lake Bradley.

After a few days of this near-total isolation, Lisa dug Vic Lamb's card out of her dresser.

She'd managed to stretch what she had, primarily by spending time with Matt. Without that anchor as a regular option, her mind fixated on

Purple

She punched in Vic's digits, then hung up and played around with the apps on her phone, mindlessly opening and closing social media platforms, seeking distraction in these methods of communication she barely used, deleting emails she'd never read. None of it was important; that's what being so close to death taught you. "Modern Life is Rubbish" - the title of one of Ashley's favorite albums - resonated so strongly with Lisa now. People yammering for something to say, desperately searching for a place to make their stand against the world around them, the veritable machine that threatened to consume them. All nothing but distractions, distractions from the fact that sooner or later, everyone is going to die, Ashley sooner than so many others.

Lisa put the phone down and began her deep breathing.

Just Breathe

Just Breathe

She wondered suddenly if Onya was better off in Mather's than out, faced with the same battery of decisions, problems, tragedies, and triumphs. This last was the hardest to come by, of course. She hadn't lied to Matt about the dark cloud; the fact that there were so few real triumphs was proof of its existence.

Enraptured by her darkness, Lisa picked up Vic's card again, this time dialing the number completely.

For the favors, she told herself. For the favors.

———

The night was colder than expected, and Lisa immediately regretted not wearing a coat. Add to that cutting her palm scaling the trellis from her window to the ground, and her walk to Christmas Park was anything but pleasant. Almost midnight now, and her breath served as Lisa's only companion, visible against the moonless night. It took fifteen minutes that felt more like an hour, but finally, she saw the pointed gazebo roof in the distance. A few more moments and, if Vic was on time, Lisa would be back in the arms of

Purple

For the final stretch, she cut through Adele Johnson's backyard and jumped the small fence that divided the autumnal remains of her prize-winning garden from the Southern end of the park. From this view, walking up through the softball field, Lisa saw Vic's old Datsun pick-up truck pull into one of the spots near the gazebo. A tiny thrill set into her stomach and she began to walk faster, her anxieties melting away.

"Hey, there she is," Vic said, rolling down the window and revealing Misty Bradley sitting shotgun, "Jeez girl, where's your jacket? It's freezing."

"I'm stupid."

"I'll say," Misty said, and Vic shot her a 'We talked about this' look.

"Here, climb in."

Lisa circled to the passenger side, stopping at the sight of a bullet hole in the rear of the truck's body.

"Long story," Vic said as he rolled his window back up.

When she opened the passenger door, Lisa saw the utter misery on Misty's face. She clearly did not want to be here, sharing space with the girl who blackened her eyes almost two months ago. Those eyes were pinpoints now, and as Lisa slid in and forced Misty into the 'bitch' spot in the center, she caught a whiff of the social queen's breath; it reeked with the sour stink Mather's had taught her went hand-in-hand with heavy methamphetamine use.

"Glad you called," Vic said, handing Lisa a small pill bottle.

"Thank you," she said, handing Vic a previously agreed-upon sum. He held up a hand to ward off payment.

"The least I can do."

"Give me a fucking break!" Misty cut in. "You charge your own girlfriend for drugs, but with this bitch it's on the house?"

"I hope you're not still mad about the fight, Misty. I'm... well, I'm not really sorry for what I did because of what you said about my dad."

"Whatever. You kicked my ass, congrats. Next time, you won't be so lucky. Maybe you'll be the one who ends up dead."

"Misty!"

Vic grabbed Misty by the arm, and she turned and smacked him hard in the face.

"Fuck you, Vic. Take me home if you're gonna be such a fucking pussy. Maybe you can come back and fuck this stupid bitch instead of me tonight."

"Why are you always such a bitch?" Lisa asked, slipping one of the pills into her mouth and feeling somewhat skeezy for doing so in front of Misty.

"Cunt!" The truck's cab became a whirling sea of fists, and Lisa took a hefty shot to the chin before climbing back out onto stable ground. Suddenly the cold air didn't feel so bad.

"Misty! Jesus fucking Christ!" Vic hollered, climbing from the truck and slamming the door behind him. Muffled by the window, Misty laughed hysterically.

Lisa offered the money again.

"Look, don't worry about the money, okay? I've got to get this nightmare home."

"We are not going back to my house!" Misty shrieked from inside the truck.

"Of course not, baby."

"Vic, just take it, okay?"

"Look, Lisa? Just... get home safe, yeah?"

"I'm not going home," Lisa said, leaning into the manic energy that had been twisting her insides over the last couple of days, building to this moment.

"You got a party to hit or something?"

"Nope," she said as she climbed the three steps into the gazebo and sat down.

Vic did a double-take. Behind him, Misty began to scream.

"Let's go, mother fucker! I'm fucking cold!"

"You're going to sit out here, in the cold, without a coat?"

Lisa sighed, and Vic hopped over the three steps and landed in front of her. It was the kind of move a little kid pulls, and in that moment, Lisa thought she understood Vic a little better. Just a big kid who does whatever he can to avoid growing up.

"You okay?"

"Someone murdered my sister. I'm anything but okay."

Vic considered this for a second, then sat down beside her.

"I never got a chance to tell you how much that sucks. I mean, not that you don't know, but... ah..."

"It's okay. I get it."

"Do you know who did it?"

"No. But I think... I think I have to go talk to Frank O'Sullivan."

"Frank? Why?"

"Well, back around the time I was released from Mather's, I ran into him. I think... I think he was trying to tell me something. To warn me this was going to happen."

"Frank O'Sullivan?"

"You know him?"

"Where you been girl? Everyone knows Frank. He's like the troll that lives under the bridge, 'cept in Frank's case, it's behind the fence. Guy's a whack job. I'm surprised he could even string a coherent sentence together for ya."

"You sell him drugs?"

"Yeah. I mean, I sell a lot of people drugs. That doesn't mean I'm the reason he takes them. I'd imagine that has to do with whatever fucked up shit made him attack his own daughter."

"He was cleared of that."

"Yeah, well, like my dad says, where there's smoke, there's fire. Look... if you really think he might know something, it wouldn't be right for me to let you go alone. I mean, fucking guy might attack you or something."

"I can take care of myself."

"Yeah, I believe you. Still, we're not talking about beating the fuck outta some stoned cheerleader in the girl's room. Lisa, you're playing with murderers."

She let that sink in, found she did not have a rebuttal.

The fact that she had killed an attacker in her own home less than a month ago was somehow not yet public knowledge.

"C'mon - I'll drive you. He's probably not home, though. He's always out at Peppermill. Fucking guy's obsessed, ya know?"

"Why help me?"

"Look, you got me all wrong, Lisa. I might be a drug dealer, but I'm not the kind of guy that leaves a girl alone to wander the night when there's a killer on the loose."

The sincerity with which Vic said this brought down Lisa's defenses.

"I think whoever killed my sister might be the same person that killed Angela Walters and attacked Onya. I think Frank knows something, and I'm going to ask him."

"Well, Frank knows me, so maybe I can, you know, help you get him to talk."

"You want to help me, even though it will also help my dad?"

"So?"

"I thought drug dealers and Sheriff's were natural enemies?"

"Maybe we are, but that doesn't make you and me enemies."

Lisa smiled.

"Come on back to the truck."

Misty was not pleased with this development.

CHAPTER TEN

They returned to the truck to find Misty had pulled the keys from the ignition. To move things along, Lisa explained where she was going and why. She left out any mention of her suspicions concerning Misty's father.

"I forbid you to go with her, Vic!"

"You 'forbid' me?"

"Yeah, I forbid you. I mean, what the fuck? I'm your fucking girlfriend, for fuck's sake!"

"Look, I just want to make sure nothing happens to her. We all know it's not safe right now. Here, shut up and play with this."

Vic tossed Misty a joint.

"Great. Light?"

Vic held his lighter out in the palm of his hand, closed his fingers over it when Misty tried to take it.

"Be nice."

"Fine. Whatever."

Misty slid over, and Lisa climbed back into the Datsun.

As soon as Vic popped the truck into gear, he turned on the radio. The eerie sounds of Led Zeppelin's *No Quarter* leaked into the cab from two rear speakers that had certainly seen better days.

"Love this song," Vic said, turning the volume up.

It took roughly ten minutes for them to reach Frank O'Sullivan's house. When they did, they saw no lights and, what's more, a massive hole in the large bay window beside the front door.

"What the hell happened here?"

"No idea," Vic said, gliding the truck to a stop at the curb. "Wait here, let me go up and look around."

The moment he stepped from the truck, Misty lowered the volume on the radio.

"I hate Les Zeppelin. I hate all his stupid 80s rock."

"Ah, that's Led Zeppelin, and they're from the 70s."

"Whatever."

The silence that followed proved painfully uncomfortable. Something about Misty Bradley not leveling a flurry of angry profanity at her made Lisa uneasy.

"So, is it because Angela wanted to fuck Bill?"

"What?"

"You know, like, why you hate me so much?"

"I... No. It's because you're the fucking Sheriff's daughter and the Sheriff has it in for my dad."

"Okay. Well, just so you know, I don't work for my dad. I mean, I love him, but I don't have anything against-"

"Fucking save it. We're. Not. Friends. And if you try to fuck my boyfriend, you'll regret it."

Vic knocked on the passenger window and Lisa jumped.

"Whoah. Sorry."

Misty laughed.

"It's okay."

"Looks like no one's been here in a while. Can I take you back home?"

Lisa hesitated for a moment. Then: "Can you drop me somewhere else instead?"

———

"You're getting out *here*?"

Vic's Datsun idled on the side of the road next to Peppermill's fence.

"Yeah. You said yourself, if Frank's not at home, he's here."

"I did say that, didn't I? Shit."

Vic pulled back out onto the road.

"What're you doing?" Lisa and Misty asked in unison. Vic laughed.

"If I wasn't gonna let you walk to Frank's house by yourself, I'm sure as shit not gonna let you go wandering around Peppermill alone at night."

Vic passed the section of fence with the drainage tunnel, pulling off after the small access road that ran about a quarter mile into the woods. Here, a chain-link fence blocked further progress.

"Where are we going?"

"Better way in. Trust me."

"What the fuck, Vic?"

"Look, babe, you don't have to come," he said, killing the engine and pocketing the keys.

"Then leave it on!"

"Haha, yeah, right. So I can walk home? C'mon, babe. I ain't stupid."

"I'll freeze out here."

"You'll stay a lot warmer if–"

"If I help you break into my Uncle's property?"

"Like you haven't come here to party hundreds of times."

"Whatever."

Misty stared daggers at Lisa, and although it felt good to

have Vic take her side, it occurred to her that Misty might be a better friend than foe. Lisa wasn't sure she wanted Michael Bradley's niece following her through the fence, but she also realized there was no way she could disappear with Misty's boyfriend and not solidify her stance as the girl's mortal enemy.

They hopped over the fence and walked about another eighth of a mile before coming to a small building. A corrugated metal door rattled against the deadbolt that did a half-assed job securing it against the elements.

"There's water and electrical meters inside. This is how the city used to monitor the facility before the scandal."

"Isn't this where all those old stories about satan worshippers and demons and shit started?"

"Babe, you guys are so much alike, it's crazy to me that you're not friends."

"Oh, please. Look Vic, you might want to fuck her, but leave me out of it. No three-way with this one, dude."

"Whatever. Don't listen to her, Lisa. She's just jealous I'm helping you."

Vic stooped near the door and removed a small ring box from beneath a rock. Inside, a corroded metal key sat on faded purple velvet.

Purple

"VIP entrance."

They went in, and Lisa instantly stepped into a cobweb. Misty laughed as Lisa struggled to free herself from the gossamer tendrils that engulfed her hair and face.

"This way," Vic said, stepping around a bank of defunct industrial meters and opening a second door. Beyond, a path led into the trees.

"Wow," Lisa breathed softly. Vic was definitely a useful guy to have around.

They followed a small trail. Further up, the mouth to

another drainage tunnel yawned. Lisa could hear water trickling over its edge.

"Careful, this ground is weak from run-off; you step wrong and you'll go down. A friend of mine broke his ankle here when we were kids."

"You came here as kids?"

"Yeah man, we used to come here, get high and shoot things with my dad's rifle. It was the shit."

Lisa and Misty sighed in unison, and surprised, their eyes met in camaraderie for a moment.

"What?"

Despite the previous air of hostility between them, both girls giggled at Vic, their shared dismissal of his boyish stupidity.

"Whatever. You want in? This is the best way."

Vic made a point to walk close to Misty as he led them into the tunnel about three feet above the path. Lisa went first, grasping the metal edge and pulling herself up, no problem. Misty followed, and Lisa felt a jealous twinge as Vic placed his hands on her bottom to help boost her up.

Stop it! They're together, and you're with Matt, for god's sake.

"See," Vic said, pulling himself in last. "That wasn't so bad, right?"

The tunnel's natural reverb elongated his words, made them sound eerie, almost robotic. Vic took the lead, Misty behind him, Lisa bringing up the rear with her phone's flashlight. She noticed the tattoo on Vic's right calf, some heavy metal monster she'd seen on posters and t-shirts.

After only a few steps, Lisa stepped in a puddle of icy cold water, the chill instantly penetrating her thin canvas sneakers.

"Ah! Jeez, that's disgusting."

"Yep. Gross." Misty said with a subtle laugh.

Lisa increased the lumens on her phone to avoid a repeat. Up ahead, the tunnel forked and Vic veered to the right.

"Hey, where's this go?"

"Who cares? This is the way to the pit."

Lisa hesitated at the fork, taking two steps into the other tunnel. Further up, she could see the corrugated metal disappear, replaced by wet, sodden walls of black earth. The sound of run-off trickling onto the metal from above disappeared the deeper into this new tributary she went, the light literally swallowed by a darkness that felt tangibly oppressive. Lisa raised a hand before her face; she could no longer see anything. A thin, jagged sound startled her, and Lisa's breath caught in her throat. Silence, then, there it was again:

Screams?

"Hey!"

She jumped, frightened out of her mind as Vic put his hand on her shoulder.

"Come on, you're gonna get lost."

"What is this place?"

"Well, if you believe the old stories, it leads to an underground room where Nancy Walters and her Satanist buddies sacrificed the folks they abducted."

Vic laughed, but Lisa knew he only did so to cover his own fear.

'What have I gotten myself into?' Lisa thought as Vic took her by the hand and led her back into the main tunnel.

————

When they emerged into the woods, Lisa's bearings were gone. Ashley once told her how, back when she was in grade school, some of the kids with older siblings would repeat stories about Peppermill and the infamous scandal that revolved around crystal meth and black magick.

"Did you really mean that? About an underground room

for sacrifices?" Lisa asked, unable to keep the fear from her voice.

"Oh, come on. Don't believe his bullshit."

The slight tremor in Misty's voice said she didn't feel nearly as certain as she wanted Lisa to believe.

"My uncle Lane used to work here back in the day. He swore up and down that shit was true."

"Whatever. So where do we find your Hobo?"

"If he's here, he'll find us," Lisa said, aware of the tremor in her own voice.

The night grew painfully still as they walked through the thick, damp trees. Lisa's head began to waiver and she realized Vic must have given her a higher dosage than what she'd received at Mather's. She'd have to be careful with that.

Because apparently, you're going full-time pill popper...

"Let's just get through this, okay?" Lisa said out loud, not meaning to.

"Huh?"

"Nothing."

Several minutes later, they entered the clearing, the fire pit cold and dead before them.

"Should we light a fire or something? Ya know, to attract his attention."

"Sure."

The girls sat on the fallen logs and stared at their phones while Vic took to conjuring fire. Once the flames began to whisper their intent, he sat next to Misty and sparked a joint.

"Think that's a good idea?"

"You got your pills, yeah? Why you wanna shame me for my coping mechanism?"

He passed the joint to Misty, who took a massive drag, coughing violently when the smoke came rolling out of her. She passed it to Lisa, but she waved it off.

"Whatever," Misty said and took another massive drag, exhaling cleanly this time.

Lisa tried to text Matt as a grounding exercise. The woods had other plans: no reception, phone or internet. She thought of Bill's broken communication the night he died.

Everyone settled into their respective buzzes; they watched the flames lick the shadowy trees surrounding the circle.

"So your Uncle worked at Peppermill?"

"Lane. Yeah. He said some fucked up shit happened. Couple kids disappeared into thin air out here one night."

"That's messed up."

"Lane said the rumors got it all wrong; the Peppermill Execs didn't summon a demon to Sundown Hills, but that whatever Black Magick they fucked around with actually moved this entire piece of land. Way Uncle Lane explained it, once you reach this side of the fence, you're actually *in Hell*."

A shiver passed through Lisa. She fought the urge to wipe sweat from her brow, as though acknowledging the temperature would prove Vic's crazy story. Nonetheless, it took a moment before her brain re-engaged with logic.

"Oh, come on. Aren't you an Atheist or something?"

"So was Lane. Well, before he became a Satanist."

Misty laughed at this.

"Um, hello? I've met your Uncle Lane. He's, like, fifty and braindead."

"That's because when he realized the shit he'd done, he tried to blow his brains out. Missed anything vital, basically turned himself into a fourth grader again."

"Not buying it, sorry."

Lisa said the words, but her anxiety insisted they were lies.

"What's maybe even more fucked up is that Lane told me he knew which one of the Peppermill employees was responsible for *making those kids disappear*. Said the guy's name was Frank."

"Vic! That is *not* funny."

"Take it easy, babe. It can't be the same Frank. He'd be, like, too old."

"I thought Satanists get, like, eternal life or whatever."

"Lane sure as Hell didn't. Har."

The inherent strangeness of the world around them brought with it a sudden silence. The three teenagers sat in the dark, straining to hear the woods in all directions, sonar searching for something to ping. Lisa closed her eyes, but the light from the fire followed her into her head, the flames inspiring an inner vision. Her thoughts swam. Something felt different about the pills. The purple wasn't just stronger but seemed independent of Lisa's mind. *Suggestive*, like it was leading her thoughts to bad places. She opened her eyes and saw the flames rising so high they looked as tall as the trees. An alarm began to sound somewhere far off in the back of her head, but when she tried to say something about it, Lisa couldn't speak. Nor could she move. It felt like she was asleep and awake at the same time, like the sleep paralysis documentary Annie had shown her a couple of years ago.

That's when Misty started to scream.

Lisa was so preoccupied with her paralysis that, at first, she thought the new sound was the town's tornado sirens. Then she saw Vic on his feet, trying to calm Misty. She tried to turn her head to see why Misty was freaking out, but she couldn't move.

Reality flickered, and the world grew dim and slow. Misty's screams, the crackle of the fire, the wind - everything drained away until Lisa was trapped in a pitch-dark vault.

Slowly, from somewhere nearby, the sound of footsteps entered her awareness.

Clik-Clop

Clik-Clop

Lisa knew the steady, heel-toe rhythm of the boots all too well. It was a sound she'd heard every day for two months.

"Lisa Lisa. Time for that bedtime story, baby."

Eyes still glued to the ground, Lisa watched as spit-shined boots stopped just inside the circumference of her vision.

"Once upon a time, you and your friends went to Hell. You've all been bad little girls and boys, and when the Devil came to welcome you in, he decided you would have to work off your sins. So he gave you to me, Lisa Lisa. He gave you to me so I could do whatever I wanted. And no one cared or believed you because everyone knew you'd gone just as crazy as that other little bitch, Onya."

She was shaking so hard Lisa felt like she would explode. She tried to scream, but when she opened her mouth, she could taste Philip's bleach-stained fingers inside, moving over and beyond her teeth and tongue, growing, feeling their way toward the back of her throat and then down toward her stomach.

"When you get to Hell for real, Lisa Lisa, I'm gonna own you."

The terror grew to overwhelming proportions until something exploded inside her, breaking Lisa's paralysis. She pushed Philip away and raised her head to stare him in the eyes. Only it wasn't Philip she saw before her, but Angela Walters?

Angela rolled over in a backward somersault and came up flawlessly on her long, tan legs. She stood and brought both arms up to point at Lisa.

"You're a lying, sanctimonious bitch, so you're perfect for it. Get ready, Lisa McCready, because in no time at all, your only friend is going to be the demon that eats your soul!"

Angela dropped onto all fours, her arms locked beneath her knees as she scurried forward again.

The image nearly broke Lisa's brain. Human beings were not supposed to move like this. Lisa turned away, but from every side, she heard scratching that peppered the air with the smell of loose dirt. It sounded like people were clawing their way out of shallow graves all around her. The fire roared, the flames so high and bright they blotted out all the stars in the sky and threatened to burn a hole in the night. A hole something might use to climb into their world...

"Keep her away from me!"

"I didn't do anything to you, bitch!" Misty retorted.

"Keep her away from me!"

"Who? Who, Lisa?"

"Angela! She wants to kill m-"

When the smack came, it burst the scene before her, bringing Lisa up and out of herself. Suddenly unstuck, her arms pinwheeled in such an exaggerated fashion that she sent herself backward into the dirt.

"Ow!"

"Jesus! Sorry Lisa, but you were... you were screaming and thrashing around - I thought you were going to throw yourself into the fire."

"Wait, what? Misty was screaming!"

"Yeah, right. Don't try and pull me into your crazy psycho-bitch routine."

Lisa lay in the dirt, startled that the fire had died. Misty looked bored, her lack of concern as evident as Vic's empathy. In her head, Lisa fought to dismiss the episode.

"I... I thought..."

"Hey, it's okay. You must have fallen asleep or something."

"Vic, those pills you gave me, are they the same as the ones you had the day outside Laramie's office?"

"I think so."

"Where do you get them?"

"I can't reveal my sources."

Lisa jumped to her feet and grabbed Vic by the throat.

"I'm not fucking around. I won't tell my dad, but I need to know."

"A guy who works at the sanitarium."

Lightbulb.

"Philip?"

"How the hell did you know that?"

CHAPTER ELEVEN

Marty Rollins brought his burnt orange T-Bird to rest in front of his cousin Craig's house. The interior light clicked on as Walters attempted to climb from the car. His left foot caught on the safety belt and Craig slammed face-first into the dirt just as Sheriff McCready's police cruiser sped around the corner, high beams blinding them.

The cruiser came to a rest at the end of Craig's driveway and the passenger window rolled down to reveal a scowling McCready. He'd been prowling for confrontation since Ashley's murder.

"You all right there, Craig?"

Marty stared back with the vitriol he'd come to reserve for the Sheriff.

"He's fine. Just took him out for some quality family time, get it? Trying to keep him on the straight and narrow."

McCready regarded Marty with open disdain. The two men hadn't gotten along even before Angela's murder. Marty lived farther out in a trailer park just off the highway on the edge of town. Marty and Craig were about as different as two people in the same family could be. As a kid who graduated a few years before his cousin, there were rumors Marty was involved in weird shit. He'd worked for Peppermill in the early 90s during the disappearances. To this day, the Sheriff harbored a suspicion that Marty knew something.

"How about you, Martin? If I pull you out of that car for a breathalyzer, you gonna pass?"

"I believe so. You're welcome to test me, though. Civic duty and all. Just mind we're on my cousin's land, so if you ain't got a warrant, some might call that trespassing. Still legal to shoot trespassers in this state, Sheriff? Asking for a friend."

McCready held the other man's gaze for a moment, then drove off.

"Fuckin' asshole."

"Yeah, well, you just mind your business around that man, all right? After his daughter being murdered and all, hard to say what a man like that might do if pushed."

"Yeah, think I have a pretty good idea about *that*."

"Get in and lay down, will ya? If I gotta come back tonight to bail you outta jail, I'm gonna put my boot up your got-damned ass. Got it?"

Craig slammed the door and shielded his face as Marty popped the car into second and showered the lawn with gravel. The T-Bird skidded through the rocks and hit the black-top highway at fifty-plus miles an hour.

Craig stopped to urinate in the overgrown lawn next to his driveway before stumbling up the stamped concrete steps and through the front door, which he failed to notice was unlocked. Still grumbling, he made his way through the large, empty house, past the bookshelves filled with first editions he'd never read. The living room looked like something from an interior design magazine. Above him, a crystal chandelier sparkled in moonlight that filtered through multiple stained glass skylights. At the other end of the room, Walters passed through another door and into the kitchen, where a bottle of twelve-year Glenfiddich waited for him in the cupboard above the sink.

"Fucking McCready. He's going to get his one'a these days."

Craig plopped into the chair at the head of the kitchen table and set the whiskey and a crystal tumbler before him. The table's dark cherry finish reflected light from the room's recessed bulbs in a way that added extra shadows to his countenance, making him look considerably older than he actually was.

At fifty-two, these days Craig looked closer to sixty. Although possessed of a sharp business acumen, Walters hadn't always been the success he'd become later in life. His early years had been quite different - closer to his cousin's: fast cars, loose women and a never-ending party funded by the fortune his family amassed via Peppermill's success. When Craig's Mother, Nancy, was charged with supplying local crystal meth manufacturers with methylamine, that fortune dried up pretty fast. This, more than anything else, proved quite the wake-up call.

Craig got sober and earned a Real Estate license. He met Angela's mother, Jamie, when her father hired him to his agency. Starting at the bottom, Craig worked his way up until he had enough money and contacts to start his own business. After that, Real Estate was all he cared about. When Angela died, Jamie left him and brought everything he'd worked for down in flames. Craig poured half a glass of the whiskey and tossed it back in a single gulp.

A noise from outside the kitchen drew his attention. There, in the door to the back porch, stood a lone figure dressed in dark camouflage, a black ski mask over their face.

"Hey dumbass! Trick r' treat's tomorrow night!"

No response.

"Ain't got no candy, so fuck off!" Craig took another belt, this time directly from the bottle. As he did, the figure surged forward and drove its palm into the underside of the glass, sending it so far down Craig's throat that he began to choke.

His air cut off, Craig thrashed in the chair, blood pouring from his nose and mouth, every sense in full panic as the bottle strained against the back of his throat, gagging him. With all his attention focused on the crisis at hand, he didn't see the intruder raise the ball peen hammer until it connected with his face, shattering both his right cheek and the bottle lodged within. The obstruction dislodged, Craig's body instinctively took a large gulp for air, swallowing dozens of glass shards that shredded his throat on their way to his stomach.

Face-down on the cold linoleum floor, Walters scrabbled for purchase like a wounded animal. Blood poured from dozens of wounds perforating his face and throat. The figure kicked him once in the chest, flipped him on his back and straddled him. It was from this position Craig stared into his attacker's eyes, holding the gaze until he felt the claw end of the hammer slip into his throat. Using their leverage, Craig's attacker pulled his skull off his spine in one quick motion and kicked it across the room. It bounced once against a ten-thousand-dollar curio cabinet and came to rest on the blood-spattered linoleum.

———

After they let Lisa out just down the street from her house, Vic dropped party favors off at a colleague's apartment. Lately, he'd taken to having others sell to everyone but his closest associates. The Sheriff's grief had made him a nightmare for criminals, and Vic avoided nightmares at all costs.

Well, most nightmares.

"Got anything for *me*, baby?" Misty asked as Vic pulled back onto Highway 24.

"Yeah, right."

"C'mon Vicky Vic, give Misty a little bit? Pah-leeze. She'll make it worth your while."

"All right, just stop talking in the third person."

He tossed her a small, intricately folded piece of paper.

"There is no third person, dummy. We already dropped her off."

Vic rolled his eyes as the Datsun turned onto the broken blacktop driveway. He pulled off into the dead grass beside the ramshackle two-car garage which, like the faded, baby-blue Craftsman, had long ago fallen into a state of disrepair.

Burke Lamb had inherited the house from his father. As part of Burke's escalating ambitions, he'd recently told Vic to expect to move into Artisan's Ridge by "First Quarter next year." Vic didn't know when his dad had begun talking like that, but as long as they were moving up in the world, he was fine with it.

"Just don't expect me to wear a suit or nothing."

"Wouldn't dream'a it, kid. You take care'a your business, it helps me take care'a mine."

Stepping from his car into a box of rusted-out car parts, Vic couldn't wait for the change to come. Misty on the other hand, didn't seem to even realize the car had stopped moving.

"Let's go babe."

Vic came around and opened the truck's passenger side, trying unsuccessfully to instill a sense of urgency in this girl who had overstayed her welcome in his life. Misty was great at first; her bleach-blonde hair, tiny waist and wonderfully pointy breasts made her hard to ignore. Those attributes came at a price, though, because Misty Bradley was so emotionally disfigured that she often felt impossible to tolerate for more than a few hours at a time. This was especially true when she was high, which lately seemed to be always.

"Where we going, Baby?" she cooed, trying to raise the bindle of white powder to her nose. Vic snatched it from her.

"To my room where I can put you to sleep; no way I'm taking you home like this. Your old man would have one of his goons kill me."

They entered the house and miraculously made it to Vic's room without incident. Misty bounced down onto the bed and immediately began removing her clothes.

"You gonna fuck me stupid?"

"Be hard to do."

"Huh?" Misty snarled, finally realizing she no longer held the drugs in her possession.

"Give 'em back!"

"Look, you need to sleep, okay?"

"You know what I need first, Vicky wick?"

Vic had a bit of a buzz himself, and seeing Lisa lying on his bed naked...

Misty! As soon as he saw *Misty* lying there naked. Jesus! Where had that come from?

Smiling, Misty took Vic by his hands and pulled him down to the bed, where she started the fun by burying her head in his lap. Vic's eyes rolled back in his head, and the last image he saw before he closed them was Lisa McCready's face superimposed over his girlfriend's.

CHAPTER TWELVE

Saturday, October 31st

Lisa woke around 10:30, a rarity for her. She lay in bed until almost 11:00, thinking about the night before. The events at the fire pit felt distant, more like a dream than reality. Maybe Vic was right and she'd fallen asleep, or maybe she'd gotten a contact high from their weed. It didn't really matter. Lisa's main concern was Vic's revelation that Philip supplied his pills; her mind drew all kinds of horrifying scenarios with that.

"Take your pills Lisa Lisa, or you'll end up just like your poor little friend Onya..."

Lisa dug the bottle from her nightstand and threw it across the room. It was a half-hearted gesture with no real conviction, but in a symbolic sort of way, it gave her the strength to get up and face the world.

After a long, hot shower, she dressed and headed downstairs. Halfway there, Lisa saw the door to the kitchen propped open; she could hear her father on the phone.

"Yeah? Well, no goddamn thank you. Nope. I don't believe that. You've done nothing but lie to me. Yeah? You go ahead and do that, see what happens!"

She heard the phone slam against the table, followed by sobbing. Lisa returned to her room as quietly as she could, located the pills and took one without a second thought. Shaking out two more and putting them into her pocket, she lay back down on the bed and cried quietly, waiting for that sweet oblivion that, for some reason, never came.

Somehow, the disappointment settled her. Curious, Lisa returned to the stairs, descending them loud enough to announce her presence.

"Dad? You home?" she called, still barely holding it together. As she entered the kitchen, she turned a massive sob into a fake yawn.

"Yeah," his voice cracked, but Gerald McCready pulled off his own facade so believably; Lisa realized that had she not accidentally eavesdropped, she would never have known anything was wrong.

Lisa pushed all her questions from her head lest she give herself away. Composure regained, Gerald McCready sat with his hands on a large, leather-bound book she didn't recognize. His phone was nowhere in sight.

"What's that?" she asked, intimating the book. Gerald's mask slipped for a moment, as though reminded he held something he did not want his daughter to see. He recovered gracefully, and Lisa once again recognized the man who raised her.

"The station's ledger. Expenses and the like. Trust me, you'd rather read a trigonometry textbook."

"I like trigonometry."

Gerald smiled, "Of course you do."

He stood and gathered Lisa into his embrace. It felt wonderful.

"When did you wake up?"

"Just now," she lied, "slept like crap; there any coffee?"

"Sure honey, come on. I'll make you breakfast."

Gerald set a steaming mug of coffee in front of his daughter, picked up the book and left the room.

"Too much for me. Be right back."

Lisa heard him on the stairs, immediately followed by a series of brief hammerings. She was about to get up when the toilet flushed. A moment later, Gerald returned and dropped a thick pad of butter in the skillet. The sound of it frying reminded Lisa of better days.

"Can I ask you a question?"

"Sure, honey."

"Do you know much about those old Peppermill legends?"

Gerald pierced his daughter with a serious glare.

"You're not hanging around there, are you?"

"Of course not! I just... I've always been curious. I read something online last night and wondered what the Sheriff thought about all that devil worshipper malarky."

"I know that Nancy Walters was using that facility to supply drug manufacturers with the ingredients for crystal meth."

"That's Craig Walters's mom, right?"

"Yeah. When the sting happened, Nancy made bail pretty quick, which raised a lot of eyebrows. Some said she bought her way out. Others said she signed a deal with the Devil. Which version you wager I believe?"

Gerald cracked the first egg into the deep brown butter that now coated the pan. The smell proved intoxicating.

"I don't know," Lisa said, sipping coffee. A new, bitter blend that made her lips pucker. Lisa reached across the table for the sugar and spooned in two big clumps, stirring as she spoke. "Just curious. What about all those kids who went missing there back in the 90s?"

"Druggies and criminals."

Her father looked up from the pan, his arched eyebrows an unmistakable signal that Lisa had entered forbidden territory.

"This is all ancient history, honey."

"Is it? Seems awful familiar..."

"Look, I'm doing my best, okay?"

A harder edge crept into his voice. Lisa watched him switch the skillet with the eggs to the back burner and move one with three sausage links onto the flame.

"I know you are. It's just... well, I want to help."

"Help? Lisa, you know what kind of maniacs I'm looking for here? Christ's sake, all three guys at the fire pit that night are varsity athletes."

"*Were* varsity athletes."

"I know you want answers, Lisa, but I don't have any yet."

"That's why I want to help. Look, I think I can-"

"Enough."

"Dad! I know you're worried about what happened to Ashely happening to me, but I have to do *something*. I'm scared *all the time*! When I close my eyes, I think about the guy who attacked me or whoever murdered my sister, wondering if I'm still a target."

'*Or that part of our town is actually connected to Hell,*' she refrained from adding out loud.

"Goddamnit, Lisa! Look, I'm sorry - I'm not mad at you, but why are we still talking about this? After all the goddamn money I paid those people at Mather's, I thought you'd be -"

"Normal again?"

"Yeah," this, Gerald said indignantly.

Lisa wondered what he'd say if she told him someone on Nurse Landing's staff was selling pills to the local drug dealer, then realized she'd probably receive the same response she did when she told him about Philip's extracurricular activities with the female patients.

"I'm never going to be normal again. Never! How the fuck could I be? First Annie, then Bill, now me and Ashley!"

"Watch your mouth!."

His phone rang from the other room and Gerald bolted for it, eager for a distraction.

"Yeah. Yeah. Jesus H... I'll be right there. Roust Len outta bed and send him out to find the dealer."

He hung up and turned to Lisa.

"I have to go."

'Dealer?' She thought.

"Did Vic do something?"

She regretted the familiarity her question communicated.

"Lisa... you better not be hanging around that scumbag."

"I'm... not. I just need to know-"

"The words 'need to know' shouldn't be in your vocabulary unless you're talking about school. Now, I have to go."

"No! Every time I try to talk to you about this, you run off."

"I am the goddamned Sheriff, aren't I?"

"Yeah? Well, you know what, Sheriff? I'm sick of you acting like you're disappointed because I'm no longer the girl I was three years ago. I don't want to do debate, or yearbook, or whatever. Seems to me that in a town where a sizable portion of the high school population has been attacked or murdered, the only "need to know" is how to stay alive."

Gerald slammed the breakfast plate down in front of her, turned and put on his coat and hat.

"You do whatever it is you plan to do today, so long as it doesn't involve leaving this house. You may have let popular opinion convince you I'm not doing my job. Fine. I've still got a killer on the loose and until I find them, I do not want you outside these walls. Are we clear?"

"Crystal."

———

Lisa dumped the burned breakfast in the trash and made another pot of coffee. She was too close to realize it, but her anger was born as much from her experience at Peppermill the previous evening as from the argument with her father. Was she losing her mind? Even the pills seemed to have turned against her. The one last night hit her so hard; why did she feel nothing now?

"Fuck it," she said, dry swallowing another that instantly caught in her throat. The sensation sickened her, and she ran to the toilet, retching. The pill came up intact, surrounded by dark, coffee-stained bile.

Lisa's head swam; when she opened her eyes, the little purple oval lay at the bottom of the basin. As she watched, it sprouted dozens of tiny legs that moved it in a sweeping frenzy, then disappeared an instant later through the trap at the bottom of the bowl.

Lisa gagged with revulsion, more bile and coffee exploding from her in a veritable fountain that emptied her so completely she collapsed to the floor, her head resting against the tile, the cool porcelain a welcome balm. Lisa's sobs soothed her, smoothing out the frustrated fracture from the classical reality she knew and loved, but now realized was barred to her. A world where Ashely was alive and Sundown Hills was an annoyance, not a threat.

I'm not like Onya. I'm not insane. I'm not insane. Just breathe. Just... breathe... Just...... breathe.........

Flashes of her vision at the fire pit returned to her, and she remembered Philip's voice, clear as though he were standing beside her now.

"When you get to Hell for real, Lisa Lisa, I'm gonna own you."

"Not if you do what I ask," a second voice said inside her, down where the purple once again began to thrum in her blood.

Curled up on the bathroom floor, Lisa lost consciousness.

———

The sound of someone on the front steps woke Lisa. How long had she been out? Cautiously, she pushed up onto her feet and crept out of the bedroom, the waning afternoon light her only guide. Not wanting to reveal herself, Lisa tiptoed down the stairs and placed her eye on the front door's peephole.

No one.

She opened the door and caught a particularly eerie chill. A beat-up cardboard box lay on the welcome mat. "Sheriff's Daughter" was written on top in a childlike scrawl.

She wanted to run upstairs, crawl back in bed and pull the covers over her head, but something inside her insisted she investigate. After hesitating for a tiny eternity, Lisa grabbed the box, locked the door and returned to her room. Inside, a stuffed turtle just like Onya's looked up at her with large cartoon eyes that seemed to offer the answer to all her secrets.

Was this real or an elaborate hallucination? Unable to decide, Lisa snapped a photo with her phone; the turtle was real. At least as real as a Jpeg.

She called Matt, but his phone went straight to voicemail. Lisa hung up and texted him a picture of the turtle, along with the message:

Did you send me something?

She waited for the message to show he'd read it. A moment later, Matt responded:

No. WTF?

Lisa ran back outside in her socks and took the porch's stairs in a single bound. She landed in the grass and ran to the sidewalk, checking both directions. Nothing. No sign of whoever had left the turtle, no strange cars parked nearby.

What if Onya's in trouble?

She dialed Mathers and asked to speak to Nurse Landing, who wasn't available.

"This is Nurse Racine. Maybe I can help you, dear."

Lisa didn't recognize the name or the voice but figured it was worth a shot.

"I'm calling to talk to Onya O'Sullivan. I'm a friend and just wanted to say hi, tell her I was thinking about her."

"I'm sorry, but it's well past visitor hours. Could you call back tomorr-"

"Please! It's... it's the anniversary of her Mother's Death. I got stuck at work and couldn't call until now. I'll only be a moment."

"Well, okay. What is your name, dear?"

"Lisa McCready."

"Okay, Lisa. Hold on while I go see if Onya is awake."

Gentle music piped in over the line while she waited; it reminded her of the muzak they played in the rec room, essentially an aural sedative. At that moment, it just added to Lisa's anxiety.

"Miss McCready? I have Onya here for you."

"Thank you."

"He..hello?"

"Onya? It's Lisa."

"Lisa?" Onya's voice perked up.

"How are you doing? Everything okay?"

"I had pancakes for dinner! Isn't that funny? And Nurse said I get to go on the elevator before bed tonight."

Lisa smiled. She wondered what it would be like to have such simple pleasures ensure the sanctity of your day. She was about to ask after Arturo when something occurred to her.

"Onya, did you say you're going on the elevator?"

"Yeah! Isn't it exciting?"

The elevator meant they were taking her upstairs.

"Onya, I don't think you should go on the elevator. I think you should-"

"All the other girls who go in the elevator get to go home! Nurse said I'll go home, too."

Blinding panic seized Lisa.

"Onya, don't go in the elevator, do you hear me? Don't go-"

"Don't yell at me!"

"I'm sorry. I'm... Onya, do you still have your turtle? You know... Art?"

"Arturo? Yes. He's here. Wanna talk to him?"

"Ummm...."

"I can go get him and come back."

"No Onya, that's okay. I just wanted to call and see how-"

"Arturo used to have a brother."

"You mean, like, another turtle?"

"Alberto. Arturo and Alberto. I think the nice man has him now, though."

"What? Onya-"

There was a brief interruption on the other end of the line, after which a new voice came on, one Lisa recognized immediately.

"Hello? Hello, who is this?"

Startled, Lisa hung up. Adrenaline surged through her

body; she felt like she'd dodged a bullet but couldn't say exactly why.

She texted Matt again, returned to the kitchen and poured a cup of old coffee. One minute in the microwave and Lisa used the first sip to swallow another pill. If they were taking Onya upstairs, that might be it for her. Lisa knew she had to stop this, but without Matt, what hope did she have?

Depressed, she stared out the window. The sky was cold and barren. As Lisa watched snow flurries swirl across the yard, one question stabbed her with a frustrating urgency she could not accommodate:

"Who the hell is the nice man?"

CHAPTER THIRTEEN

"That's what I'm telling you, Mr. Bradley-"

"Doug, please. It's Michael."

"Right, right. Sorry, Michael. Well, like I said, the boys called me in when they found it. I wasn't necessarily surprised, but then I've told you the story about what I found back in the day when I was part of the -"

"State inspection crew. Yes, Doug. You told me. Look, it's okay. I believe you. Now, *show* me."

Doug Creed had only known Michael Bradley for a month, but if asked, he'd tell anyone and everyone that Michael was the best damn thing that ever happened to Sundown Hills. "Helluva boss, too," Doug intoned on numerous occasions.

Formerly an employee of the state, Doug held the title of Chief Building Inspector for years before Michael poached him. That's a hell of a pension to dismiss, but Doug was tired of his boss, and Michael paid better. Sure, Doug's wife had questioned the longevity of the position, "Assuming Prop 72 passes, once he's up and running, what then?"

Doug didn't sweat the small stuff. Michael hired him to

assess the structures comprising the former Peppermill compound. He put Doug in charge of contracting everything needed to bring his former family land up to code and into the new Millennium.

No small task.

A layman might theorize that turning a former pharmaceutical manufacturing plant into a high-tech grow facility would be closer to a 1:1, but that was *not* the case. Especially with how long most of the property had lain dormant. Doug knew the work would be difficult but also believed it would be worthwhile. He understood firsthand that when Peppermill came to Sundown Hills in the 90s, they'd brought evil with them. Now, because of Michael Bradley, the town might finally have a chance to be free of that evil once again.

Doug was just a young man in 1992 when Inner Earth Oil laid off nearly one thousand local employees. The effect this had on Sundown Hills was noticeable even to him then. Doug remembered how, that same year, then-Mayor Yogi Horton began to court large industrial manufacturers with tax incentives designed to make moving their operations to Sundown Hills lucrative. Mayor Horton succeeded in bringing in several companies, the largest of which was Peppermill Pharmaceutical.

Owner and CEO of the company, Nancy Walters, had inherited everything from her late husband, Arnold. Three years after arriving in Sundown, Nancy was arraigned on conspiracy charges when a federal drug task force connected Peppermill to the manufacture of the street drug Crystal Meth. The Federal Government ordered Peppermill to cease operations while Nancy prepared for a trial she had no hope of winning.

Only she *did* win that trial.

Two years after her arrest, Nancy Walters walked out of the courthouse a free woman, all charges dropped. This was

the Zapruder moment for young Doug, and it had stayed
with him ever since. With the airtight case the government
built against her, how did Mrs. Walters manage to avoid
sentencing?

Throughout the months leading up to that verdict, the
disappearances began. Every couple of months, a few teenagers
would go missing. Two government workers overseeing the
plant's shutdown went missing. Rumors began to take root: all
the disappearances occurred on or around Peppermill's land.
One former employee gave an interview with local news where
he talked about seeing an "abattoir" in one of the buildings, a
sort of ritualized 'murder space.' Residents began to see Nancy
Walters's freedom as the reward for an infernal pact.

By the time the rumors became Urban Legend, Nancy
had disappeared and left the Peppermill land to her son
Craig, a local real estate agent with grand designs and no capi-
tal. Craig sat on the land out of spite for David Bradley.
When Michael Bradley returned to Sundown Hills, he
bought the land from Craig and the two started a company.
Shortly after, Michael became Craig's angel investor for "Artisan's Ridge." The rest, as they say, was history.

As a teenager, Doug obsessed over the Peppermill story.
He acquired a set of the compound's blueprints from City
Hall, and while his friends partied at the fire pit, Doug used
his own trespassing to conduct a series of explorations.
Breaking into each building in turn, all of Doug's suspicions
were validated when he discovered a room not on the
schematics.

A sub-basement below a secondary building used for
reagent storage, the room measured approximately 10' x 12'
and was lined with a slick, black material unlike anything
Doug had ever seen or felt. It was greasy but left no trace on
the skin. Inside, someone had drawn a large Pentagram on

the floor in what looked like red wax, and the charred and rotting corpses of at least one hundred cats hung from the ceiling. Terrified, he ran from the place, certain he'd been marked for death.

Doug lived on to graduate a year later. He began an internship with the city building inspector, and at twenty-one, Doug maneuvered himself onto a Peppermill inspection detail. Part of the condition for the charges being dropped against the company required regular oversight of the land as long as it was owned by Nancy or anyone in her family. The bad press might have killed Peppermill's legitimate business, but the city was taking no chances on any more criminal enterprises.

Doug planned to officially put that room on the record during that inspection. Only he never found it again. The room had disappeared.

Now, years later, Doug walked Michael Bradley through a door and down two sets of stairs that went further into the Earth than any of the property's records showed. At the bottom of the second set, the two men stopped on a metal platform suspended over a cavern that, judging by the reverberations of their footsteps, must be massive.

The walls hewn into the Earth, a single electric lantern revealed the only path just to their left.

"This way, Mr. Brad- Michael."

Michael nodded, following deep into the Earth until they came to the room Doug had described to anyone who would listen for nearly three decades. The room everyone thought he'd imagined.

"My god. She did do it here. I mean, I'd heard the rumors like everyone else, but I didn't think... Well, it doesn't matter what I thought now, does it Douglas?"

"Just Doug, Michael. Wait, so you knew about this?"

"Everyone knows about this, Doug. Well, everyone who's anyone."

Doug nodded, happy to be included in the sentiment, completely oblivious to the fact that Michael Bradley's definition of "everyone who's anyone" most certainly did not include him.

When they arrived at the door, Michael caught Doug's hand a moment before he turned the knob.

"May I?"

"Of course."

With his left hand, Michael Bradley grasped the rusted old knob and slowly pulled the door open, releasing a neon green light from within.

"What is that?"

"This is... everything, Doug. Everything."

———

When Misty opened her eyes, she couldn't tell what she was looking at. She'd slept with her contacts in, and the resulting residual crust washed the world in opaque distortion. At first glance, she deciphered the object in question as one of those landscape paintings you find at thrift stores, the kind that were always set into gaudy, gold frames. A series of brown pine trees ran over the arc of a hill; below it, a sloping beige waterfall led to an arched pool filled with strange striations that suggested artificial development - boating skiffs or filtration equipment. She stared harder, but her confusion only multiplied until, finally, Misty heard a voice.

"Hey sleepy head. How you feel?"

Misty sat up and, with her right thumb and forefinger, peeled the dried sheaths from her pupils. Vic stood before her, his brown, sloppy hair spiked like he'd just removed a hat, nose and mouth somehow blurred together as the phantom waterway she'd glimpsed, his entire person framed by the gold border of the vanity attached to his dresser.

"I thought you were a painting."

Vic laughed, "Never heard that before. Last night was amazing, babe," he leaned in and kissed her on the head. Misty placed her shaky hands on either side of his face. Vic's sharp, jutting cheekbones - a model's cheekbones, really - incited her to guide his lips to hers. They kissed passionately, and although Misty fell into the moment, the maneuver was also a ruse, as she could not remember the previous evening *at all*. She moved a hand between her legs and discovered she was still wearing panties. The moment escalated, and Misty began to worry as she felt the intensity of Vic's kiss; his lips moved down the curve of her jawline, skipped to her neck, working down to her breasts. Built like a porn star since fifteen, it was no wonder Misty was the most popular girl in school *and* the most sexually active. She'd moved beyond guys her own age Junior year, preferring instead a certain level of experience. Vic was a second-year senior, and although she'd taken a step backward from her last boyfriend, who was thirty when she was seventeen, her relationship with him was almost at an end. As Lisa suspected, Misty 'worked' at the club on the edge of town and, in doing the rounds there, had met someone who lavished her with money, gifts, and attention.

"Where'd you go?"

"I couldn't sleep, so I went out and sat in front of the TV. Passed out watching re-runs of The Jeffersons."

"What's The Jeffersons?"

"Really? Never mind."

The banality of the conversation eroded Misty's anxieties. She kissed Vic again, this time bringing it hot and heavy herself. The next twenty minutes melted most of her hangover away in a haze of rare intimacy and pleasure.

When they finally crawled from Vic's bed, Misty threw on a pair of his sweats and an old band tee. She followed him downstairs to the kitchen, where Mr. Lamb greeted them at the breakfast table with a look of abject horror. Misty had spent the night there plenty of times, none of them a secret, so she wasn't sure what his problem was until she followed his gaze to the tv at the end of the table. The words "Breaking News" blazed across the screen in the amateur font local station KFTT favored for its news programs.

"Jesus Christ, that poor bastard."

"Who?" Misty asked, suddenly terrified.

"Oh shit! Isn't that Craig Walter's place?" Vic asked.

Behind them, someone knocked on the door.

———

When Sheriff McCready arrived at the crime scene, deputies Matt Hartman and Jeff Wilson were having trouble keeping local news reporter Ted Owens from crossing the police line. This brightened the Sheriff's morning; he felt like taking his anger out on somebody; Ted Owens would do just fine.

"You giving my guys a hard time, Ted? Because I believe you and I have talked about this before."

"Look Sheriff, there are a lot of people upset with how you're handling the rising tide of murder that's come to Sundown Hills, and-"

Before Ted could continue, the Sheriff stepped directly into his face, nose to nose.

"You get one warning and one only. Get off my crime scene or I'll cuff you, then kick your ass for resisting arrest."

Ted took an immediate three steps back, paused, then another half dozen well away from the police tape surrounding the Walters' front yard.

"That's fine, Sheriff. You just keep digging that grave

deeper. Pretty soon, it'll be so deep, when they drop you in, no one'll hear you hit bottom."

The Sheriff's left hand went to his holster and Ted turned and ran. Satisfied, McCready returned to the dark business before him.

"That the only trouble so far?"

"Yeah. Fran's inside now, doing her thing."

"That's fine," Sheriff said, lifting the tape to step beneath. With Matt and Jeff in tow, he walked toward the house.

"Thought you were on leave, Sheriff?" Deputy Wilson asked, and Matt hit him with an elbow to the ribs.

McCready ignored Wilson, stepped into the house and made a bee-line for the body. County coroner Fran McDelmond was hard at work taking pictures of everything in the room, first and foremost, the mutilated body in the center of the kitchen.

"Morning, Frannie."

"Sheriff. I know Craig wasn't your favorite person..."

"Maybe so, wouldn't wish whatever the hell this is on anyone. Jesus H., where the hell is his head, Frannie?"

"Over there," Fran pointed toward the far wall.

"You gonna be the one to tell the ex-wife?"

McCready started to answer, then caught a full-throat sob before it exploded from his face. He quickly waved Fran off and hurried outside, shutting himself in his cruiser. A moment later, gravel flew as McCready hit the gas and fish-tailed out onto the road.

"What the hell was *that*?"

"Still recovering from having to bury his oldest daughter," Matt said. "Shit like this ain't gonna make it any easier."

"Jesus Christ. Could it be any worse?"

"Smart money says yeah, it can."

———

Gerald McCready drove two miles to the old abandoned access road that led to what was left of the Bradley family's Oil land. He pulled to the side, obscured from passing eyes by a copse of Birch trees. Turning off the engine, Gerald cried so hard that, for a moment, he thought his heart would stop.

———

Twenty minutes later, the Sheriff returned to the crime scene with a tray of coffees and a box of donuts.

"Sorry about that. Didn't have time for breakfast, felt a bit woozy."

Fran and Matt eyed their boss sympathetically. Fran set her camera down, removed her gloves and accepted a Boston Creme from the pink box. McCready motioned for them to follow him out back.

"Intruder came in this way," Matt pointed to marks on the door's frame and jamb that supported this theory, then wiped maple glaze from the corner of his mouth.

The Sheriff paused at Craig Walters' severed head and winced; Gerald was not a squeamish man, but even he had limits.

The Walters' backyard was a large, rolling blanket of once-well-kept Kentucky Bluegrass left wild since Angela's death.

"Heard he fired the landscaper the day the wife took off. Got in the guy's face and ended up getting his ass kicked."

"Doesn't surprise me. Craig really wanted someone to hurt him; looks like he finally got his wish."

"Things are heating up. I hope I'm not the only one thinking this is all connected?"

"It's connected, all right. Bradley."

"Which one?"

"David. His brother has him backed into a corner, and

he's fighting to get out and remake the town in his family's image again."

"Isn't this just about the Peppermill land? I mean, why would you be on that list, Sheriff? Why your girls?"

Matt winced when Fran asked this, but the Sheriff clearly agreed with the Coroner's read.

"David has a narcotics operation and he lost a large part of his workforce when the town voted to shut down his fracking operation. If he's voted in as Mayor, he can change the rules in his favor. Toss out 72 and his brother in one fell swoop."

"I think you mean 'when' he's elected. This crime scene means David's now running unopposed."

Matt said this with Lisa in mind. He wasn't sure she wanted her father to throw his hat in the race in the eleventh hour, but they both knew it might be the only surefire way to stop what was happening. McCready didn't take the bait.

"Here's a question for you guys: anyone even seen Michael Bradley in town lately? The email he sent Lisa mentions an office in Seattle. Think he's laying low in the Pacific Northwest?"

"What email?" McCready asked, and Matt instantly realized his mistake.

"Ah, yeah. I think. Um..."

"Deputy..."

Matt felt the Sheriff's gaze like a hot coal on his forehead. He decided he would have to be more careful navigating the new boundaries of his relationship with Lisa.

"She interned with him few years back. He offered her a job."

"Selling pot?"

"Sheriff..."

"She gonna-"

"Nope," Gerald interrupted Fran. Matt hoped he hadn't created yet another nightmare for his girlfriend.

Fran nodded, finished her donut and turned back toward the house.

"Back to work. I'll have a report on your desk by tonight."

"That's fine. Thank you, Frannie."

"One thing: so Michael Bradley has an office in Seattle. Pot's already legal there, right? You think he might already be bringing drugs into town?"

"If so, he's his brother's biggest competitor."

"Exactly. Might be you should look at Michael, too."

"She should have my job," Matt said with something less than a smile.

"She's good at everything, a real 'think outside the box' kinda mind on that one. What the hell is this about Michael Bradley emailing my daughter?"

"Look, maybe I misunderstood what Lisa told me -"

"Don't bullshit me, son. I know I'm a hard ass, but I like you and I like that you're seeing Lisa. Just watch what you talk about in front of the rest of the force. Especially if I don't know about it."

"I didn't know-"

"Finish up here," McCready cut him off, his patience taxed. "Make sure that prick Ted Owens keeps his distance. If he gets a shot of this, it'll be all over the internet in an hour."

"Do I take it then, Sheriff, that you're more worried about bad publicity than the murders?"

Gerald and Matt turned to see David Bradley looking over the top of the fence.

"Crime scene, David. Not gonna tell you twice. Git."

"You're lucky I didn't bring a press junket, Gerald. Seriously, when is this gonna stop?"

"Why don't you tell me?"

"Ha. That's a good trick. Maybe I should run for Sheriff

instead, see if the town has more faith in my ability to stop this horror show."

"I bet you'd be able to stop it in a day, huh? Maybe sooner? No sweat for you, right David? You just call off your hired killers, they stop murderin' people."

David Bradley's countenance darkened. Matt would later tell the other Deputies he put his hand on his gun because he would have sworn David was about to jump the fence and charge the Sheriff.

"You go on say that to anyone who matters, I'll sue your ass *and* your department for slander."

"Yeah, then we'd really be able to catch the killer," Matt didn't mean to say it out loud, but he did and immediately drew David's ire.

"Watch your ass, kid. You're awfully young to have me as an enemy."

"That a threat?" the Sheriff asked, removing the handcuffs from his belt. "Cuz I can take you in for that."

"Sure. Do that. I'll make sure it's on the news that you took time out of trying to catch a killer to arrest me for telling you to do your damn job."

A pause followed, loaded for bear. When it popped, nothing happened and David Bradley took his leave.

"Killers."

David stopped and turned back around.

"Come again?"

"Plural, David. Killers."

Bradley's self-righteous momentum seemed to run out of him for a moment, then he puffed his chest back up and retorted, "Whatever. Just catch 'em."

"You really want me to, or do you just want everyone to think that?"

David was already out of earshot.

Sheriff and Deputy returned inside the house to find Officer Amanda Holloway had arrived.

"Got Vic Lamb in my car."

The Sheriff stepped past the others and followed Amanda out to where Vic sat in the back of her squad car. McCready opened the door and fixed his stare on his suspect for several long, unblinking moments.

"You do this, Vic?"

"You fucking crazy? I'm no killer, Sheriff."

Vic leaned forward to emphasize his point, and McCready took the opportunity to slam the door. Vic screamed when the glass collided with his forehead.

"Jesus!"

McCready opened the door again, pulled Vic out and passed him off to Deputy Len Sherman, who had little trouble dragging him into the house and pitching him to the floor directly before the body.

"You do this?"

"No, all right? What the actual fuck?"

"Len here saw you drive by out front last night, 'bout the time it happened."

"I was at home. You can ask Misty."

"I'll do that."

"Ask me what?"

As if on cue, Misty entered the house. She'd followed Vic.

"Hold on there, girl. This is an active crime scene-"

Misty saw the body on the floor and gagged, began to back away.

"Vic, what did you do? What did you do?"

Matt caught a firm grip on her shoulders and steered her outside.

"Who the hell's watching the perimeter? Jesus H. Christ, next thing we'll have Owens and a camera crew in here! Get that girl outta here!"

"Misty, I didn't do this! I swear!"

"She followed you here, Romeo, not because she cares we arrested you. Didn't know your girlfriend had a sugar daddy, huh?"

Vic's brow furrowed; the implication set his brain on fire with rage.

"You don't know what you're talking about! Fucking pig!"

Vic wrested his right arm from Len's grip and socked the Sheriff square in the jaw. Gerald took the punch like a man who had taken many, turned back with a smile as he watched Vic try and scramble out of Len's renewed grip; Len was a hulk of a man, smart as a whip and retired state wrestling champ. Vic wasn't going anywhere.

"Thank you, Mr. Lamb. I didn't have anything to actually hold you on until now. Good work. Officer Sherman, would you do the honors of booking this jackass, please and thank you."

"My pleasure, Sheriff. C'mon kid, we got a nice cell with your name on it."

————

The phone call to Onya left a bad taste in Lisa's mouth. If that *was* Alberto on her doorstep, then who left it and why? Lisa's first inclination was to take the turtle's appearance as a warning. Despite her reluctance to put Matt in another awkward situation, she texted him to please check on Onya when he had a chance. He didn't reply.

Sitting on her bed, Lisa turned over as many angles as possible while fumbling absentmindedly with the stuffed turtle. That was when she first noticed the odd, rectangular bulge in its belly. It felt like something hard and plastic and entirely out of place. A discovery loomed before her, and she went into her bottom dresser drawer and removed the small knife her father had given her for her tenth birthday; it made quick work of the soft fabric, revealing a wad of fluffy white stuffing. Bundled inside that was a folded ziplock bag containing a USB flash drive.

"Holy shit. Holy goddamn shit!"

Just holding the drive in her hand was an overpowering revelation. Until now, the conspiracy her mind sought to assemble was only theoretical. Now, here was the ultimate validation; Lisa had tapped into a mystery, something bigger than her, something that made her feel... important.

She fired up her laptop and inserted the drive. Once the LEXAR icon appeared, she double-tapped it, and her Preview app launched. A moment later, a large PDF document opened. Clocking in at over two hundred pages, Lisa saw copious amounts of notes and diagrams: it looked like pages from an old medieval Grimoire, like the Book of the Dead in the Bruce Campbell movies.

Detailed drawings made by a talented hand covered the pages: images of buildings, oil derricks, tractors - a crude attempt at a map of Sundown Hills. Further on, there were minutes from meetings - dates sometimes absent, sometimes present - denoting the late 1800s and early twentieth century. She turned to a random page and read:

December twenty-one, eighteen hundred sixty-six:

...and the stranger telleth of a mixture, pure yet ineffective in the servitude of She with the Black Eyes, She with the Black Heart. She who makes the blood pumpeth and watcheth from the light of darkness...

"What in the world?"

A few pages later came sketches of men in featureless masks standing around some kind of raised dais, one in the center holding a woman by the hair, a curved blade at her throat. Blood poured from a jagged wound into a black pool before them. The name "Mammon" was scrawled hundreds of times around the images, the handwriting erratic.

Lisa flipped forward several pages and read anew:

July twenty-seventh, eighteen hundred sixty-seven:

The blood is steady, the town healed. I care not for the cost when this being we have conjured continues to make our family stronger than all others. What is the cost of one life in the pursuit of such power? In what will become the tradition of my ancestors, my Daisy will die so that our family's reign is sealed. Charles will watch, that he may understand what is required when the power passes to him.

Lisa flipped a dozen more pages. The handwriting became drastically different.

January sixth, nineteen hundred twenty-six:

He does not understand. He says he does,

but in his eyes, I see a lack of resolve. It is that damned Hershal girl who has poisoned my son's head with her Christianity, her weakness and lies. I have already taken steps to make sure they can never be together. A union such as that would be travesty for our lineage. My father would kill...

Lisa flips ahead again, only a few pages this time:

March twenty second, nineteen hundred twenty-six:

With Betty removed, Roland has accepted his destiny. Still, when I look at him, I wonder if this change will last. I will instruct Wright to institute a contingency plan, in case Roland reneges again after my death.

Lisa's cell phone buzzed in her back pocket, and she nearly jumped out of her seat.

"Hello?"

Sobbing from the other end of the line.

"Hello? Who is this?"

"Lisa. I'm sorry. It's... it's Misty. I didn't know who to call. Can I see you?"

"Uh, yeah. I mean, I'm at home, but..."

The other end of the line went dead, and a bad feeling seized Lisa. A moment later, the phone buzzed again. This time, the message was from Matt.

Can't talk. At crime scene. Craig Walters murdered last night. Vic suspect.

CHAPTER FOURTEEN

At the rear of its main dining area, The Red Lion sported not one but two large banquet halls. Behind the second, a smaller space dubbed "The Brass Room" served as a makeshift hall where David Bradley sometimes held business gatherings. It was here he had called a meeting with his closest associates.

Donald Governor was one of the prominent nouveau rich that had taken up residence in town since the *Artisan's Ridge* development began. He was the Bradley campaign's biggest financial supporter. Ingrid Freitag was a recent addition to David's inner circle. On the books as an "advisor," she was six foot five inches tall and all muscle, more of an Olympic athlete than a logistician. The man next to her was David's lawyer, Ben Inoue. Rounding out the group, Inner Earth's two most senior board members, Miriam Harrison - James Harrison's cousin - and William Rottenbury, representatives of the other two original families that settled Sundown Hills beside Samson Bradley. Both were in dampened spirits this evening despite the free-flowing alcohol, as it had become increasingly apparent that Michael Bradley's Proposition 72 was on its way to realization, certainly an indication that the citizens of Sundown Hills were beginning to think outside the box the Bradley family empire had kept them in since the town's inception.

"The latest poles put the community almost sixty-five percent in favor of legalizing Marijuana."

"Just because my brother gets to grow and sell legal pot doesn't mean the community is against oil."

"I'll tell you what they're against, David. You. I knew from the moment we handed you the keys to the kingdom that we were fucked. Defending fracking in 2015 is pretty much akin to publicly standing in favor of child abuse. You should have stuck to our anti-pot campaign."

"Listen to me! With my brother ramping up his "this is what big oil has done to our town" routine, we have to *kill* his credibility. BLAMMO! Dead! There's no time to waste trying to talk people out of what they already know they want. Instead, we have to poison the man spreading the message. Hell, once Proposition 72 passes, anyone can sell weed with the right approval."

The room was small but open, eschewing tables in favor of a beautifully hand-crafted Cherry-Maple bar. Seven stools lined the front, all built with gorgeous, polished brass. Likewise, the room's lighting fixtures, bottom runner, and beer taps were also brass.

Miriam sipped from a glass of white wine and looked past the others, fixing her eyes directly on David.

"No one is questioning your methods, David. We're simply reacting to unexpected developments. It might help if we had some idea of how you plan to pull us out of the fire?"

"My methods are exactly that, Miriam: my methods. Trust me when I say you *do not* want to know. Also, you've forgotten; now that Craig's daughter is dead, I'm running unopposed. Once I'm Mayor, I can do whatever I damn well please. That's how it's always been."

"We've already shown tradition is dying in this town; you really expect us to believe that's your secret weapon?"

The brash cacophony of Bradley's crystal snifter shattering against the wall stopped Rottenbury cold. A small man, William scared easily and did not know how to handle physical displays of aggression. He breathed a visible sigh of relief when David stormed from the room, his absence creating a vacuum.

Freitag shot Inoue a look, and the two stepped out to the patio and lit cigars.

"Our boss has quite the temper," her thick German accent molded the words into quick, guttural bullets.

"This is the first you're seeing it? Might I ask you, Mrs. Freitag, how long you have been in Sundown Hills?"

"Miss. Just under six months. I am a long-time family friend of the Bradleys. David contacted me just after my father died last month, offered me a distraction by bringing me in to help him."

"I'm sorry for your loss."

"Time is a monster, a ravager of our bodies and spirits. Coming here, David has given me a new purpose. I enjoy it very much."

"Funny then that this is the first time we're meeting."

"A lot of what I have been working on is off the books, so to speak. I expect David to integrate me into the day-to-day operations after we bring this... unpleasantness with his brother to a close."

"Excellent." Inoue nodded, checking his watch.

"May I ask you something, Mr. Inoue?"

"Of course."

"You work for the firm, yes?"

"Geist-Wilhelm? Yes."

"Do you find it disturbing that David sits on the throne

instead of his older brother? It seems to me Michael has a more robust... business acumen?"

"If that is your polite way of saying David is a low-rent thug pretending to be a businessman, then I agree with you one hundred percent. That said, I'm sure you must know Michael's only interest in the family business lay in destroying it."

"One can never be sure."

"There is a... contingency. It has been applied before."

Ingrid smiled.

"Sounds... mysterious."

"Not really."

"A powerful family is a volatile one. There is always a dissenting voice or, at the very least, bad blood."

"Funny, that expression. There are those who would say all Bradley blood is bad blood."

Ingrid laughed at this, took a large drag from her cigar.

"There is a pattern to the birth of all male Bradley children," Inoue continued. "It's actually rather uncanny to look at a family history where all but two successive heirs were born on the same day of the year."

"Roland and Michael."

Previously distracted, Inoue refocused on Freitag. This woman was not what she seemed.

"You know more than you let on."

"I told you, I am long-time family friend. In fact, my family and David's go back much further than the two of us. Tell me, do you think it was a coincidence that Roland's first-born son has followed in his footsteps? I've heard some reports he has been seen leaving the church on Sunday."

"Reports?" Inoue felt a chill run the length of his spine. He inhaled deeply and eyed the door, not fifteen feet from where they stood.

"Tell me about yourself, Mr. Inoue."

Anything but friendly, the request sounded more like an instruction. Inoue imagined a tiny red dot on his forehead.

"Not much to tell. When I took over for the family's previous representative, I learned that Roland's father, Charles - that would be David and Michael's Grandfather - believed his son's aberrant birth date to be a deviation that would affect the family fortune. With Roland, Charles had no choice, as the only other child he sired was a girl, and the company's bylaws are very specific on the matter of female leadership."

"Not allowed."

Inoue nodded. "That might not be politically correct in today's world, but Sundown Hills has always followed its own path."

"A path that Brother Michael has managed to fork if the conversation from earlier is any indication."

"Roland did indeed prove to be a disappointment, so Grandpa Charles took steps to ensure any future heirs who break the cycle would be... ineligible to head the family business."

"I happen to know that is not exactly true. What's more, I believe you know this is not true. You and your *other* employer."

"Come again?"

"Please, Mr. Inoue. We have seen your phone records. Not the phone you carry in your pocket, the other."

"Look, I don't know what you think you know-"

"I know nothing. Please, continue to talk to me about the Bradley Account."

Ben stared at the woman across from him. Her hair was pinned back so tight it stretched the skin on her face backward with it. Her nose and chin were small, almost non-existent, but her brow was large and somewhat out of place on her otherwise graceful face. Ingrid Freitag's mouth rested in tight, sphincter-like repose. When she smiled, her lips cut far enough across the lower portion of her face that the corners of her mouth touched her ears. Ears that were large, almost elven.

Inoue felt compelled to follow her instructions to the letter.

"Roland balked at his responsibilities and was deposed as CEO. He'd kept Inner Earth profitable for much of his life, but things began to fall apart closer to the end. What's more, a scandal that damaged his reputation in the community came to light."

"The half-breed."

"Yes. Roland's daughter Linda left home at seventeen. Disappeared. Years later, her son showed up in town with a family of his own. Michael and David consider Linda's son a 'half-blood.' They think he wants part of the fortune."

"Who knows about him?"

"Family. That's all. Well, no. That's not quite right. Harrison and Rottenbury must know - they've sat on the board long enough."

"How could something like that stay a secret in such a small town? Seems to me everyone knows everyone else's business, and David is not very good at keeping his... darker side hidden."

"You'd be surprised."

"Would I?"

Inoue's phone buzzed. Without looking at it, he took a final puff from his cigar, dropped it and stamped the cherry out with his thousand-dollar Italian loafer before leaning in with a conspiratorial flourish.

"Duty calls."

Ingrid smoked for a few moments longer, watching the lawyer cut quickly across the room and out into the Lion's main bar. A moment later, she stubbed her cigar out in an ashtray on the table closest to the door, turned and took the stairs at the back of the patio down to the parking lot.

————

By the time Sheriff McCready arrived back at the station, Vic was already in a cell, the coroner had taken possession of Craig Walters's body, and David Bradley had been, temporarily at least, put in his place. All McCready wanted was a half hour to sit and drink his coffee in silent reflection, a temporary reprieve from a day that had started poorly and done nothing but devolve since.

The opportunity for that reprieve would not present itself.

"Sheriff, you haven't returned any of my calls in longer than I can remember. If I didn't know better, I'd think you were avoiding me."

James Harrison. He looked considerably worse than the last time McCready had seen him in person, which, admittedly, was some time ago.

Harrison stepped into the office and pulled the door closed behind him. A half a tick later, an abrasive knock startled the man before he could sit down. Bridget, the Sheriff's secretary, popped her head in.

"I made a fresh pot of coffee, Sheriff. Figured you might need it after this morning."

"You're a lifesaver, Brig."

"Don't you forget it," she said and closed the door again, but not before giving Harrison a scolding look.

"Ever think I might just be busy burying my daughter and trying to stop a killer?"

"Never one for social niceties, were you Gerald? Or tact, for that matter. I'm sorry about Ashley. Truly. Believe me - *I can relate.*"

"Yeah, well, unless you're here to tell me who killed her, I don't have time for you right now."

"Sadly, no. Is there anything I can do?"

"Know anyone that drives a dark black Lexus?"

"Half the folks who live in Artisan's Ridge? Why?"

"University police say there's a video from the School book store right next to Ashley's..." Upon saying her name, Gerald's composure cracked. It took a moment, but he regained and continued. "A black sedan, possibly a Lexus, passed by not two minutes after the murder. We know the timeline because she'd... Ashley had ordered a pizza. She must have answered the door expecting the delivery guy."

"My god."

Silence hung between the two men, twisting in their guts. They had been friends once, long ago. Gerald had come to Sundown Hills to be Sheriff based on Jim's recommendation.

Those days seemed a lifetime ago.

"What can I help you with, Jim?"

"You have me all wrong, Gerald. I'm here to help you."

"Is that so?"

"It is. Look, we both know if David runs unopposed, there can be only one outcome."

"Jim, we've had this conversation before."

'We have, but never with these stakes on the table."

"The election is Wednesday."

"Gerald, I respect your decision. However, I am here to tell you it's the wrong one. When I approached you about this previously, I may have come across as hyperbolic. Still, I backed off once Walters began gaining ground, right?"

"So?"

"So? Gerald, if David Bradley is to be removed and his family's oil dynasty laid low, you are the only viable alternative."

McCready stood, crossed the room and exited through

the door. A moment later, he returned with a steaming cup of coffee and returned to his desk.

His feet hurt, his head hurt, and most of all, his heart hurt.

"So let's say I enter the race at the eleventh hour. Kinda late to convince the constituency I'd do better at being Mayor than I have been at being Sheriff."

"The murders?"

McCready nodded.

"You'd have the outgoing Mayor's endorsement. And I could write a speech for you. One and done. You call Ted Owens, give him the scoop, he'll have you on the tube tonight."

"You'd have me come up pro 72."

"You bet. It's here, regardless of what you or I want."

"Town definitely seems to want it."

"Gerald, do you know the kind of money other states are making off legalized marijuana?"

"It's drugs, Jim."

"It's the future, Sheriff."

"Not in Sundown Hills, it's not. Let them smoke themselves into a coma on the West Coast."

"Illinois. Minnesota. It's not just the hippies anymore."

"Still illegal on the Federal level, regardless how many states say otherwise."

Harrison was clearly having a difficult time disguising his frustration. He hesitated a moment, then tried a different tack.

"Gerald, I know you want David gone and Inner Earth with him."

"Doesn't mean I want to legalize drugs."

"Okay, what do you propose we substitute for Oil? Where are people going to work? What will keep our town on the map, successful and moving forward?"

"I don't know, Jim. Guess that's the problem."

"72 is going to pass, Gerald, and if you've convinced yourself otherwise, you're not listening to the town. People are ready for something new. Honestly, did you forget that I brought you in? That I was the one who reached out in the first place, brought you to Sundown Hills when others would have rather you stayed where you were? Or better yet, been 'dealt with' the way they'd always planned to with Linda?"

"My mother's name should never cross your lips. None of you."

"She was supposed to -"

"I know what she was supposed to do, Jim. The fact that didn't happen is the first clue the town wants out of the endless loop it's been stuck in since 1866."

"You see? There's no need to treat me like an enemy when I can be an enormous asset to you."

A burst of static from the Sheriff's walkie interrupted them.

"Sheriff - come in, Sheriff McCready, over."

McCready pulled the walkie off his belt and brought it to his mouth without breaking eye contact.

"McCready here, over."

"Sheriff, got something here I need you to see, pronto. Over."

"On my way. Over."

McCready wasted no time heading for the door.

"Maybe another time, Jim. Thanks for stopping by."

As he passed Harrison, the older man caught McCready's right wrist.

"Gerald. I believe in you. I believe you can lead this town out of the bad times, the same as Samson Bradley did way back when."

"Bad times. Yeah, that's exactly what we're up against, isn't it, Jim?"

As he said this, a tear slipped from McCready's right eye. His hand came up so quickly to catch it that Gerald broke Jim's hold on him in something resembling a defensive maneuver.

"I hope you're not growing hostile with me, Gerald. That wouldn't go over too well when the time comes."

"Hostile? Jim, you don't know the meaning of the word. Now go home, will you? You look like death warmed over."

———

Deputy Jeff Wilson sat reading the newest issue of his favorite hunting magazine, periodically slipping into dozing reveries that revolved around the day he would shake off the rustic confines of the Sundown Hills Sheriff's Department for the considerably more exotic State Police force. Only with the department for six months, Jeff was born and raised in Sundown, and at twenty-two years old this past March, he'd had his fill. There were things about the place that he loved, but considerably more he did not.

Jeff wouldn't dare talk about it at the station, but he'd definitely be voting "YES" on Proposition 72. Not because Jeff smoked marijuana but because he was one of those starstruck citizens who saw Michael Bradley as the town's own Elon Musk. Sure, starting with pot maybe wasn't how he would have done things, but it was an easy money maker, and legalization felt progressive in both a social and economic sense, so much so that if it passed, Jeff thought Prop 72 might actually pull the town out of the 1950s and into the present. Jeff had read interviews where Michael outlined a business plan for the town that, following a successful pass on 72, included solar energy, an electric car dealership and a "robust rebate program" for anyone who bought one. Some people thought this was all talk, some thought Michael's main goal was destroying his family empire, but Jeff believed everything the man did was in the name of progress.

That's what Jeff wanted: progress.

Too many people in town stuck to the old ways, suspicious of technology, fearing change. That mindset was dangerous. Jeff saw the allure of status quo - everyone did, especially the older you got. He saw a path for himself in local law enforcement, but without Michael Bradley, anything he did would amount to little more than maintaining the stagnation. No, if Jeff stayed, it would only be if Michael got his way.

Two months ago, Jeff had begun volunteering for Bradley as a security guard on the old Peppermill land. Since then, Michael had hired him on as a salaried advisor for the Sundown Hills he saw on the horizon. Once 72 passed, Michael would use his new-found political leverage to ramp up his anti-oil campaign.

Jeff liked the sound of that; he saw 72 as a bellwether for the town: if it didn't pass, things would remain the same here forever.

In that event, Wilson's plan was to transfer to the State Police, maybe eventually try and move on to the FBI. As a kid, Jeff had been a big X-Files fan, and although he didn't expect to be chasing shapeshifting aliens, it was his dream to drive around in one of those lean, unmarked Federal cars dressed in black, scaring the bejeezus out of anyone he didn't like. He was in the middle of imagining the scene again, a recurring fantasy where he rooted out Chinese super spies from inside the White House, the President shaking his hand in grateful fascination with this agent who had come up in the ranks of the organization so quickly when the Sheriff's fist slammed on his desk and startled him so bad Jeff almost fell out of his seat.

"Keep your goddamn eyes open, Deputy. This isn't kindergarten."

In the face of the Sheriff's anger, Jeff quickly reacclimatized to the waking world.

"Sorry, Sheriff."

McCready stared holes in Wilson, his anger slowly subsiding.

"I was just... just... nothing. Sorry. What can I help you with, Sheriff?"

"What's with you and that damned cologne, Deputy? You smell like an Elks Club meeting in 1958."

Jeff had worn "Ship Wrecked" cologne since his Junior year in high school. It'd been his father's favorite when he was alive.

"Huh? My Colo-"

"Never mind. I need you to drive Mr. Harrison home."

"Isn't that his Range Rover in the lot?"

The Sheriff eyed his Deputy suspiciously for a moment.

"Everything okay, Sheriff?"

"You know Jim Harrison?"

"Well, yeah. Doesn't everybody? He's the Mayor."

————

"He say anything to you when he came in?"

"Just hello; couple minutes of small talk."

"Uh-huh."

Jeff began to squirm under the Sheriff's lingering gaze.

"I could, ah, *follow* him home?"

"That's fine, Deputy. Follow him and make sure home is where he's going. When he gets there, make sure he goes in and the lights go on. Got it?"

"Yessir. You want me to stay there, keep watch on him?"

"Jeff, that's the first good idea I've heard come out of your mouth since you got here."

"No problem, Sheriff."

The Sheriff went through the door and out into the evening sky so quickly Jeff didn't even hear the bell on the office door jingle.

————

On his way out the door, Gerald clocked Jim's truck in the handicapped spot up front, a legal placard for the disabled hanging from his rearview mirror.

"Even the mighty fall..." McCready uttered, unaware he had done so. The Sheriff's mind was elsewhere; he climbed into his cruiser, pulled out of the station's driveway and circled back, putting the truck into third to climb over the curb and creep around back of the station's small, attached garage. This is where the Sheriff kept the department's excess vehicles - a whopping two of them - and a make-shift evidence locker. Despite Craig Walter's ceaseless expansion of the modern amenities in Sundown Hills, the Sheriff's Station was still a small, impossibly limited structure, and Gerald had long ago been forced to think outside the box when it came to accommodating basic departmental needs. The police cruiser glided silently over the moist grass and came to a rest inside the small grove of Pleached Hornbeams just to the rear of the structure. The sun was nothing but a whisper on the horizon, and what's more, storm clouds hurried the impending darkness. Content to be unseen, Sheriff McCready killed the engine and sat watching until Jim Harrison ambled to his truck and left the way he would if he was heading home. A moment later, Jeff's cruiser came out from around the opposite side of the station and started out after Harrison.

"Good boy." Gerald McCready said, tears in his eyes. In the dark, he removed a picture of Ashley from his wallet. He stared at this for a long, somber moment, then produced the other picture he carried with him. In this one, Lisa's smile ate the entire scene. Barely on the cusp of young adulthood, there was a light of innocence Gerald worried he had not seen in his daughter's eyes for several years now, certainly not since the deaths began.

"Goddamnit Jim. Why do you have to force my hand?"

Staring at the picture, the Sheriff began to sob, and after only a moment, the throes of his tears brought on a violent coughing fit. When it was over, the steering wheel before him was spattered with blood.

CHAPTER FIFTEEN

Scrolling through page after page of ceremonial diagrams, a sickening horror crept over Lisa. Reflecting on her discussion about the Bradley family with Mr. Harrison and juxtaposing that with what he told her about Frank O'Sullivan and Onya, sharp tendrils of unease wrapped around her guts.

"All the other girls who go in the elevator get to go home! Nurse said I'll go home, too."

Should she try and convince Matt to find records on the girls who 'went home'? Surely there must be some way to confirm if they actually made it out of Mather's alive.

Alive: a fleeting lucid moment with the word made Lisa burst into tears. Ashely...

When she calmed, Lisa thought back, tried to jot down bullet points of her conversation with Harrison.

"Those reports found something I believe points to it being the same person who attacked the O'Sullivan girl."

Did the outgoing Mayor know something he couldn't fully cop to? Was that why the second half of her visit felt so weird? Had Jim been trying to tell her something without having to explain how he knew?

"He killed my mother; now he wants to kill me!"

The original form of Onya O'Sullivan's accusations no longer felt so wild.

That Onya's mother died during childbirth was a documented fact, but thinking about the accusation now, what if Onya had witnessed someone else's murder and internalized it? Because someone was killing people in Sundown Hills. A lot of people.

Desperate for answers, Lisa scanned back to the file's table of contents. Written in jargon, the entries told her nothing. Phrases like "Isolation of Loathing" and "Contented Single Offerings" translated into nothing she could use to gain a strategic understanding of how any of this applied to what was happening in town.

Then she noticed the image inlaid over the contents. She'd just seen the same image - what she now saw was a half-moon with a face - on the spine of the book her father had been reading earlier.

She had to find that book.

Lisa remembered Gerald had played it cool when she came upon him with the book. He'd closed the cover casually and excused himself only after a few moments of conversation. After that, she'd heard him climb the stairs, where there were three bedrooms and one bath.

She stepped out onto the landing and walked the short distance to her father's room. The door was closed but not locked.

"Might not be an invitation, but it's not exactly a "Keep Out" sign, either."

To Lisa's surprise, the book was sitting in the center of his desk. She opened it and found the contents identical to the PDF, the only exception a pocket in the inside front cover where several newer sheets were neatly folded and tucked. She slid these out, careful to keep them ordered exactly as they were.

The loose pages consisted of more of the same gibberish, save the top sheet, which had a series of names on it, all paired together in uneven brackets. Near the bottom, Craig Walters and Burke Lamb's names were partitioned together. Turning the page, Lisa felt a chill when she saw two more names written in different color ink and once again paired off in brackets: David Bradley and Gerald McCready.

A knock from downstairs startled her; Lisa set the book exactly where she'd found it and cautiously took the stairs back to the ground floor, approaching the front door so she could see through the small, square window near its top. A disheveled Misty Bradley stood on the porch sobbing, looking over her shoulder repeatedly.

How is it that you've become a go-to for these people? How did your grandiose suspicions lead to this?

The moment Lisa opened the door, she was taken aback. Face to face, she could see the flaked mascara in Misty's eyes; she could also smell the sex on her, like she'd partied all night and forgot to shower upon waking.

"I didn't know where else to go. Vic... the police say he killed Craig."

"Craig?"

"I... I never told him. About us. About me and Craig. Now... do you think Vic's the killer? Oh god, have I been with him while he..."

The word "killer" wound down like a death rattle as Misty erupted into fresh sobs. Lisa realized she might now hold this girl's life in her hands; Misty was at the end of her rope.

Suddenly, Jillian's comment in the girl's bathroom on her first day back at school made sense.

"That wasn't my fault! I didn't realize she was his daughter. At least I wasn't the one who actually set up the deal that night."

"Come inside and slow down."

Lisa ushered Misty in and shut the door, casting a quick eye up and down the street to make sure her new friend hadn't been followed as she obviously feared. It was a strange feeling, this domestic paranoia. Lisa didn't like it at all.

Get used to it.

The voice cooed from inside the labyrinth of Lisa's increasingly complicated inner landscape. It was right, of course, but everything kept spinning further and further out of her control until that dry, purple itch swept up from the tiny hole in her heart where all her dead friends lay rotting; was it time for a pill again already?

Is it ever not time?

The voice asked.

———

Deputy Wilson watched as Jim Harrison piloted his mid-sized SUV into the Gas n' Grab parking lot. Wilson waited for Harrison to enter the tiny convenience store, then pulled into a spot on the other side of the lot from him and waited. When Harrison exited the store, he had a six-pack of beer in one hand and his phone to his ear with the other.

"Trust me. He'll run. Look, just get them there. I'll handle the rest."

Harrison hung up and opened his car door, then spotted Wilson's cruiser. A smile tugged the corners of his mouth and he shut the door again and approached his would-be interloper. Wilson rolled his window down as the older man stopped several feet back.

"Afternoon Mayor."

"Deputy. I take it the Sheriff asked you to follow me?"

"Haha. Yeah. Something like that. Think he just wants to make sure you get home safe."

"Sure he does. Look, pardon my lack of tact, but how much do you make working for the Sheriff's Department?"

Wilson's reaction to the question was an almost comical double take.

"Well now, sir, I'm not really sure that information is -"

"Can it, Deputy. I need someone in the Sheriff's Department I can rely on. Interested?"

"Um, Mayor Harrison..."

"The position pays exceptionally well."

"Can we talk somewhere a little more private?"

Harrison held up the six-pack.

"Follow me to my house, I'll buy you a beer."

Once inside, Lisa planted Misty on her bed, careful to shut the laptop before she might get a glimpse of the screen. Lisa hurried back downstairs to the kitchen and popped a pill from her pocket before grabbing two bottles of water. When she returned, she found Misty pacing the room, her anticipation apparently nearing a crescendo.

"Hey, c'mon. Drink this and tell me what happened."

Misty tried to sit but would stand back up every few seconds while she related the fractured narrative. Lisa picked up the basic outline of her and Vic's night after dropping Lisa off, straight through to when the police knocked on the door.

"I don't know what they think happened. It was terrible."

"You followed them?"

"Yeah."

Misty's face twisted with another sob and it was at that moment Lisa realized she was not crying over Vic's arrest - she was crying for Craig Walter's death.

"Misty, were you, um, involved with Mr. Walters?"

"You wouldn't understand."

Now it was Lisa who stood and paced. This town!

"What the fuck is wrong with you people? Even the adults act like a bunch of fucking children!"

"Don't say that! It's not what you think."

"How is it not what I think when you just told me it's exactly what I think?"

"Look, I know what everyone thinks of me, about what I do. Even Vic knows; he hasn't had sex with me without a condom for months; most of the time he doesn't even want to, calls me the BJ queen to try and make me feel better about the fact that my own boyfriend doesn't want to put his dick in me."

"Misty! Listen to yourself! Can you fucking blame him? I mean, Jesus, you're right that everyone knows what you do because you broadcast it. That day we fought in the girl's bathroom? You came in with the Misty Bradley Fan Club and I listened to you basically hold a whore audition!"

"J and Jenna don't get it. They've been to Slo Motion before, but they think it's about climbing some kind of social ladder, like they're mingling with people above them, fucking men for money. That's not it."

"Then what? Were you in love with Angela Walters' dad?"

"Don't say it like that. I wasn't in love with him, but I loved him. He cared. He really cared. I mean, the sex was part of it - there's just no competition when it comes to an older man versus someone our age. But with Craig, it was more about being taken care of."

The memory of Misty's proclamation that day in Dean Laramie's office returned to Lisa:

"My dad isn't going to come for me; he doesn't give a shit about me."

Lisa cringed; it really was all about daddy shit with some girls. Lisa shut the door on that particular train of thought before she could turn it back on herself.

"Okay, so you think Vic killed Craig out of jealousy? You said he was with you all night."

"I think so, but I was fucked up. He could have slipped out. I heard your dad say one of the other cops saw his car drive by Craig's place around the time it happened."

Lisa thought for a moment.

"Could someone else have taken his car?"

"I suppose his dad, why?"

Something clicked; Vic's dad. Burke Lamb in the book right next to Craig Walters.

"I don't know, but I'm definitely starting to see a common thread here."

"What thread?"

Lisa flipped the laptop back open.

"The sins of our fathers. Does this mean anything to you?"

Misty stared at the images Lisa scrolled through on the screen.

"No."

"Okay, one sec."

Lisa ducked back out to her dad's room and snagged the book. When she returned, Misty remained glued to the laptop, scrolling through page after page, evidently fascinated.

"Weird shit, right?"

"What is this?"

"Not sure. Here, look at this."

Lisa opened the book, removed the loose page that had names of people she knew.

"Whoah. Is this...?" Misty's question evaporated as she stared at the names, stopping cold when she reached both their fathers' names. In that moment, a great, horrible darkness settled over them, bringing with it fear, but also, an incredible, smoldering anger.

"Misty, do you have *any* idea what this is?"

"No, but you said your mom died during childbirth too, right?"

"Yeah."

"Doesn't that seem, like, you know... weird?"

"Wanna know what's weirder? Onya O'Sullivan's mom died giving birth to her, too."

"The psycho?"

"She's not a psycho!"

"Jeez, sorr-ree."

"Onya went through some really bad shit, and she's way fucked up because of it."

"Fine, but what does any of this mean?"

"I don't know. That's why I asked you. You're a Bradley, and this entire town was built by your family. I thought you might know something I don't."

Misty returned to Lisa's bed, plopped down on her back and pressed her fingers into her eyes. Lisa recoiled a bit, imagining the extra wash cycle she'd probably need to extinguish the Misty Sex smell.

"There's... a lot of weird stuff I remember as a kid. Stuff that doesn't make any sense."

"Like what?"

"... It's hard to even talk about. Masks, for one. I always kinda assumed it was a Halloween party or something, but I saw stuff just now on your computer that reminded me of those masks. Like, a bunch of people in masks."

"Hence the Halloween party interpretation."

"Did you know I have an older brother?"

"Wait, what?"

"Yeah. He doesn't live here. My dad shipped him off to some fancy prep school when he was super young. Right now he's finishing college at Oxford."

"I... I'd never heard that before."

"It's weird because no one in town knows about it. Like, seriously. No one. Even weirder? We were both born on August sixth."

"My dad was born on August sixth!"

"So was my dad. So was my great-grandpa *and* his dad."

———

Lisa did the calculation in her head; everyone in town knew the last hundred and fifty years of the Bradley lineage because it was also the town's lineage, "Samson Bradley?"

"Yeah. Before that, I don't know. I don't think there's, like, any records or whatever."

"Okay, this birthday thing isn't just weird, I'm pretty sure it's *impossible*. Did you ever ask your dad about this?"

"It's a big deal in our family. Only Grandpa Roland and my Uncle Mike were not born on August sixth, and I'm the only girl with that birthday. It always seemed kinda freaky, ya know? When I was younger, I used to go to a psychic."

"Really? What did they say?"

"She saw me a few times. She said this was like, super special. She did all this research and didn't even charge me. Started making charts for my entire family. Then she just up and moved, didn't even say goodbye."

A chill ran through Lisa.

"My dad told me that Grandpa Roland had mental issues, that he almost bankrupted the family. He started to cry and apologized for never telling me any of this. But..."

"But what?"

"I don't know. I felt like he was faking it, ya know? The crying. Like, because he didn't want to talk about it."

Lisa flipped back through the book, stopped at the brackets with Misty and Annie.

"Annie doesn't fit. Her Mom didn't die giving birth to her, she died from drugs, right?"

"Actually, no."

"No?"

"Her real mom did die during childbirth."

"Okay, that's even more impossible than the birthday thing."

"Not if all those women died from unnatural causes."

"You mean like..."

"Murder."

"Why?"

"I don't know, but I think I know where to get some answers."

———

As soon as they stepped outside Lisa's house, Misty's phone buzzed.

"It's my dad. He's probably calling because he heard the news."

"Oh my god, don't tell me your dad knew about you and Mr. Walters."

"Of course not. My dad would've had Craig killed if he'd known."

Lisa had to bite her tongue to refrain from asking the obvious. 'Are you sure? Because, ya know, someone just killed him.' She could see they'd both made the same connection.

"It's just... I haven't been home in a couple of days. Normally, he probably wouldn't even notice, but with Craig's death..."

"Must be nice. I can't go two hours after school without my dad sending one of his deputies to look for me."

"That's because your dad cares. Don't hold that against him, Lisa. Seriously, it might be overkill, but it's better than having a dad who only remembers to check if you're alive when there's been a murder."

Lisa didn't know what to say to that, so she didn't say anything. Misty answered her phone.

"Hi, Daddy. No. Yeah, I stayed at a friend's last night. Yes. Yes. No, I'm with, well, I'm with the girls. Yes. No. Yes."

Lisa moseyed farther afield to give Misty privacy and pulled her own phone out to text Matt.

Any news?

Her phone rang instantly.

"Hey, how's it going?"

"Just great. I... it's been a day."

"Especially for Mr. Walters, right?"

"Lisa babe, you have no idea. I think even your dad had trouble with this one."

"*You* okay?"

"I will be. Still a bit shaken."

"Is Vic in custody?"

"Yeah."

"Did he do it?"

"Not for me to say."

"Unofficially, what's your gut say?"

"... Maybe. I don't know; it's hard to look at something like this and picture anyone being capable, let alone a nineteen-year-old."

"Matt, can I ask another favor?"

Matt's pause suggested he was becoming weary of Lisa's favors.

"I think it depends on what it is."

"Can you go back to Mather's?"

"Lisa, we can't keep kicking the hornet's nest. Your dad is tight with Helen Landing; he's going to find out."

"It's important. I think Onya might be in danger. I talked to her and she said she was going to the elevator. And then I found this book, this... I don't know what it is, but I found it in my dad's room and there are names of people we know bracketed together. Onya's is in there and-"

"Babe, where are you getting this stuff?"

"It's... just a hunch, but wouldn't you rather be safe than sorry?"

A pause, then:

"Look, I'll try, okay?"

"This means a lot, Matt. Thank you."

Behind her, Misty moved close enough that her voice carried over the phone.

"Yes. No. Look, I'll be home in a few hours. Fine. Okay."

Lisa walked further down the sidewalk, closer to the white picket fence that partitioned her front yard from the sidewalk and street. She knew it was too late, though, knew Matt had heard Misty.

"Who is that?"

"Misty."

"Misty Bradley? Really? Rematch?"

"No. She was... upset about what happened, said she needed someone to talk to."

"Uh, correct me if I'm wrong, but last time you two talked to one another, you ended up throwing punches, right?"

"Well, that was two times ago."

"When did you see her since?"

"...The other night."

"What night?"

"Oh, ah, earlier in the week..."

"Lisa, *what* night?"

"Last night."

"Last night? As in, the night Craig Walters was killed?"

"Yes?"

"Was she with Vic?"

"Yeah. I... we... went to Peppermill to look for-"

"Are you kidding me right now, Lisa?!"

"Don't yell at me!"

"What the hell's going on that you're hanging around with Vic Lamb and Misty Bradley?"

"I'm trying to help, okay? We went looking for Frank O'Sullivan."

"Oh for Christ's sake..."

"Fine. Fuck you if you're mad."

"I'm sorry, baby. Look, I'm not mad. I just want to make sure you weren't anywhere near the murder scene. If there's even a single fingerprint..."

"Are you serious? You think I was there when... when..."

"No, but Misty Bradley wasn't in Craig's house for more than a second before we had her removed, and *her* prints are all over the place. Any way you cut it, that doesn't look great for her. Or Vic."

"Well," Lisa glanced over her shoulder to where Misty was now off the phone and waiting. "I wasn't there. Can I tell you about it later? Maybe tonight, after you're off?"

"Count on it."

"I'm gonna go. Text me."

"Lisa..."

"Yeah?"

"Whatever you're doing, be careful, okay? I'm kinda starting to feel like I-"

"See you tonight."

Lisa hung up.

"Who was that?"

"Matt. From my dad's office."

"Did he say anything about Vic?"

"Yeah. He said he doesn't think Vic did it," Lisa couldn't

help but lie to try and mitigate some of Misty's misery. She changed the subject quick, though.

"What'd your dad want?"

"See where I was after he heard about Craig."

"Sounds like he cares more than you think."

"No, he doesn't."

Lisa squashed the impulse to argue her point because, honestly, David Bradley probably didn't care where his daughter was unless it somehow suited him.

"So where we going?"

"I have a theory I want to test. Can we take your car?"

Parked in Lisa's driveway was the brand new, white Tesla Model S Misty always drove to school. As Seniors, they were allowed to drive, adding even more humiliation to the fact that Lisa was still being dropped off by her father. Misty's Tesla was only one of two in Johnson County, her uncle Michael being the other proud owner.

Misty hit the fob and the alarm beeped off.

"I've never been in an electric car before."

"Really? Oh shit, you'll love this. Watch."

Lisa never even felt the car start; one moment the seatbelt began to automatically stretch across her chest, the next they were going sixty miles an hour.

" Slow down!"

Misty eased off the gas, let the speed come down automatically to the posted 35 MPH.

"The car do everything for you?"

"Everything except cry."

Lisa didn't touch that one with a ten-foot pole.

———

Matt was on his way back from a much-needed lunch break when Bridget came in over the radio.

"Matt, you back on? Over."

"Hiya Bridget. Just caught me on my way back. What's up?"

"You with the Sheriff?"

"No ma'am."

"Know where he is?"

"Ah... I thought he'd still be at the station, dealing with paperwork or reporters or the paperwork from punching the reporters."

"Don't even joke about that, mister. No, we haven't seen him since, well, since Jim Harrison barged into his office about an hour ago."

It wasn't like Sheriff McCready to leave without telling someone to hold down the fort, especially in times of crisis.

"Gonna ask an obvious one, Bridget. You try calling him?"

"Uh-huh. Here *and* on his phone. No dice."

This felt weird.

"What'd the Mayor want?"

"Don't know, but they weren't exactly behaving in what I'd call a friendly manner. No sir. Jim seemed to have a big 'ol axe to grind with the Sheriff."

"All right, let's start with the obvious - where's Jeff? He came on right after we brought in old Vic rattle head himself."

"That's the thing, Matt. Jeff's not answering his radio *either*."

Just as Bridget said this, Matt passed the Gas n' Grab on Haymarket and spotted Deputy Jeff Wilson's cruiser. Standing at the window was Jim Harrison. The two men seemed considerably more familiar than Matt would have guessed, and something about that got his hackles up.

"Well I'll be. Bridget, you're never gonna believe this, but-"

Matt stopped himself. Wilson might not be responding, but that didn't mean his radio was off.

Harrison motioned for Wilson to follow him, then started back to where his truck was parked closer to the storefront.

"Matt? You cut out? What am I not going to believe?"

"Ah... gas is up another quarter! Damn, Bridget, I tell you, those electric cars are starting to seem like a worthwhile investment."

"Oh lord, not you too! I sure am tired of everyone acting like-"

Bridget's customary spiel about Michael Bradley, electric cars and legal drugs faded into the background as Matt drove three stops up to the empty lot that used to be Al's Pizza and parked behind overgrowth that concealed his car without sacrificing his view of the two men. When Jeff followed Harrison out of the lot, instinct told Matt something wasn't right.

"Matt! Where'd you go, boy?"

"Sorry, Bridget. Ah, long day," it had to be a coincidence. Had to be. Besides, Matt was tired and worried about Lisa. "I'm sure the Sheriff will turn up. I'll be back in five minutes or so."

"Okay. See you soon. Out."

"Yeah," Matt said to himself as he watched Jeff follow Jim Harrison in the direction of his house. "See you soon."

CHAPTER SIXTEEN

David Bradley stormed into the Red Lion like a man possessed.

"Where is he? Where's my goddamned brother!"

Corey Mitchel, the nighttime bartender, looked up from making an Old Fashioned and forced a smile for the man who signed his paychecks. Corey would tell anyone who asked that this would be a great job if it wasn't for the owner.

"He's in your private room, Mr. Bradley. Came in about five minutes ago."

David slammed his fist on the bar.

"You let him into my private room?"

"No sir. Mr. Inoue did."

"Ben's here, too? What the hell?"

"David?" Ben Inoue's thick, marbled voice rolled in from the corridor that led to the Brass Room. "We've been waiting for you."

David Bradley registered his attorney's voice but continued staring at Corey.

"What's your name, kid?"

"Corey Mitchel."

"All right, Corey. Stop what you're doing and make me a Sapphire Martini, neat."

"Absolutely."

Corey left the Old Fashioned half complete and turned to snatch one of the fancy martini glasses that hung on the overhead rack behind him.

"None'a that shit. Use a rocks glass. And Core-dog…"

"Yes sir?"

"When you pour the gin, I want you to look at the bottle of Vermouth, and that's as much of that fucking shit as I want to come anywhere near my goddamn drink. Capiche?"

"Right-o, sir."

Drink procured, David took a large sip and a measure of calm rolled through him from shoulders to toes. He rocked back on the heels of his thousand-dollar Gucci running shoes for a moment before turning to face Inoue.

"Since when do *you* summon *me*?"

"David, make no mistake: I presume no hold or control over you. Your Great-Grandfather hired Geist-Wilhelm and they hired me. I work for you as an Attorney, Advisor, and, I'd like to think, Confidante. It is under the auspices of that latter role that I *asked* you here in an attempt to end this petty feud that currently has you at a forty-three percent approval rating with the public."

"I'm running unopposed, Ben."

"You haven't seen a television today, have you?"

"No."

Inoue nodded to himself, understanding achieved.

"And of course, no one would risk your wrath by telling you…"

"My patience is waning, Ben. What the fuck are you talking about?"

"He's trying to find a way to tell you that I added my name to the ballot this morning, brother."

Michael Bradley stepped from the Brass Room into the hall behind Ben. Seeing the smile on his brother's face, David thought he might burst into flame. He could feel the heat in his brain descend through his body in seconds. Michael had done the unthinkable, and it would either ruin him or finalize his victory over David in the public eye.

"Fifty-six percent, David. Still think Prop 72 won't pass?"

"You son of a bitch."

"We shared her, remember?"

"David, please. Regardless of how it seems, your brother didn't come here to gloat."

"Oh no? What then?"

"We have to talk about the one person who could topple us both."

"The half-blood."

"Got it in one."

"Look, the temperature of the town is boiling. That's one thing about fear, David. It works to your advantage until it shuts down people's rational minds and evokes their amygdala. Once the primordial survival response kicks in, they're a lot more difficult to control."

"And you think if Gerry arrests someone for these murders, he'll be able to take the town away from both of us?"

"He's already got somebody in custody, David."

"He does?" David laughed.

"Yeah."

"Your brother is correct, David. That is why he reached out to me."

David drained the last of his drink and slowly, purposely, set the crystal tumbler on the bar top. His fingers lingered for a moment on the lip of the glass before planting his hand on

Ben's shoulder. It was a companionable gesture with only the faintest undertone of malevolence.

"Rest easy, Ben. I know you're looking out for me."

"Thank you, David. Now, if you'll both excuse me for a moment, nature calls."

———

Ben Inoue walked from the Brass Room into the corridor that led to the private restroom. He entered, closed himself in a stall and exhaled a massive breath of relief. Next, he removed his phone from the inner breast pocket of his jacket, scrolled to his recent calls and pushed the number that appeared third from the top.

"Yes?" The voice on the other end of the line began.

"They're both here."

"Thank you, Ben."

"Don't call me again, Jim."

———

When Inoue returned to the back room, David had racked up half a dozen lines of cocaine on the bar top. He blew the first one back, offered the straw to his brother.

"No thanks."

David didn't bother to offer any to his Attorney.

"There you go again. Look, if we're going to work together, you're gonna have to drop the fucking attitude, Mikey. Otherwise, I just can't help you."

"Help me?"

"Gentlemen. You need to help *one another*. Only once Gerald's suspect is discredited, or he's dead, can you resume your own competition."

"No sense swinging for the fences if the other team's already won, Dave."

"I'll take care of it."

"David. I hope this doesn't mean-"

"Just shut up, all right? You're a goody two-shoes, big bro. Fine. But there's a reason you came to me. Let me be *me*, capiche?"

Inoue shook his head in consternation.

"Isn't this becoming a bit... convoluted?"

"Doesn't feel that way to me, Ben. Cold feet?"

Not for the first time in the past few weeks, Inoue felt a malevolence directed toward him by his employer. Accustomed to keeping the man-baby millionaire firmly in his side eye, the Attorney thought he could almost see gears turning inside David's head. As though intuiting Ben's fear, David cracked a smile before snorting two more lines. When he came back up for air, he was already on his phone.

"Hello? Yeah, I have something... sensitive for you. Yeah. Okay, I'll text the name and location. It may be a bit tricky," David took a small notepad from his jacket pocket as he spoke. He motioned for a pen, and Inoue stepped forward and handed him a gold-plated Montblanc.

"Yeah. Uh-huh. Okay."

David returned his phone to his front right pocket, rolled the paper into a tight cylinder and set it on the bar next to the coke before heading for the exit.

"Read that, Mikey."

As Michael picked up the note, David turned and snapped a picture with his phone. In it, Michael stood over the drugs, holding the rolled-up paper.

"Are you fucking kidding me?"

"Nope. Ben, I'm going to need your team to prep a statement. I want to come out hard against both the Sheriff and my coke-head brother. Should hit like a one-two punch tomorrow morning."

"I came here out of solidarity!"

"Yeah, but you said it yourself, Mikey - once McCready is out of the way, it's you and me. Never too early to gain the upper hand."

CHAPTER SEVENTEEN

Alone in the cell at the back of the Sundown Hills Sheriff's Station, Vic amused himself by running through the lyrics to every song on the first seven Iron Maiden albums. Those were his favorites. He got caught up remembering the chorus on "Only the Good Die Young," the final song on *Seventh Son of a Seventh Son* and switched to the first four Metallica albums.

When he could see the sun had set, worry set in. He'd never got to make his phone call, and Burke never showed up demanding to see him. No one even came to check on him. When Len Sherman put him in the cell, he'd given Vic two bottles of water and a power bar, all three of which he'd polished off within his first hour of incarceration. These provisions hadn't seemed unusual at the time, but now he wondered. They were coming back for him, weren't they?

"Hey! Heahayaay! Anybody out there? Heeeeellllloooo?"

No response. As the light outside faded, the cell lights did not come on.

So much for energy-saving technology, he thought.

"I have to peee-eeee-ahhhh! Hellll-lloooo-ah? Olly Olly Oxen Free?"

At that moment, a lone figure stepped through the security door at the far end of the room. Limned by the soft white light of the cheap florescent bulbs, Vic's brief glimpse into the outer station suggested it was empty.

"Can you let me out of here now? I think you're taking this shit a bit far."

The figure did not move.

"Okay, well, can I at least get something to drink? I'm fucking thirsty as hell in here, chief. And I still gotta piss."

The figure stepped from the shadows: Matt Hartman. Being a small town, Vic knew a little about him, but he didn't think they'd ever actually spoken.

"I'm going to need you to tell me exactly what you and Lisa were up to at Peppermill last night, Vic. I'm also going to need you to tell me if she was with you when you killed Craig Walters."

"How many times I gotta say this, bro? I didn't kill Craig fucking Walters, okay? As for Lisa, she told me she was going to Peppermill and I didn't want her to go alone, so Misty and I went with her. You're welcome."

"What happened?"

"Nothing happened. "

"I don't believe you."

After she hung up with David Bradley, Ingrid took the elevator from her office on the third floor of Inner Earth's Corporate building to the garage. She usually preferred the black Lexus LX, but she'd already established an identity with the tan Subaru in the part of town she was heading to, so she asked Gus the valet for the keys to that instead.

Ingrid maintained a polite thirty-five miles an hour as she drove through town with the autopilot set two miles below the speed limit, stopping at each stop sign she hit. David's admonishment that the job 'might be tricky' blossomed into hyperbole when she read the job specifics in his follow-up text. Ingrid felt a bit like killing him, as well.

"Live to serve."

Ingrid Freitag was, if nothing else, an enigma. The story she'd utilized since arriving in the United States was not entirely fiction, but it wasn't entirely the truth, either. First and foremost, Ingrid's last name was Wilhelm, not Freitag.

The Sheriff's Station came into view, a well-lit beacon on the otherwise darkening street. Only one cruiser sat in the lot.

"Maybe I'll get lucky."

Ingrid passed her destination and turned right at the next intersection. The Sundown Hills Sheriff's Station was located on an otherwise residential block, and part of Ingrid's job had involved weeks of mapping the area, figuring out which houses were empty, where the dog walkers and joggers lived and what their preferred routes were. In a big city, psychologists long ago outlined how, even on an unconscious level, people's routes orbited destinations like police and fire. In small towns like Sundown Hills, that was not the case.

At least it wasn't the case before the murders.

Ingrid's observations bore this out: she'd started the project weeks before the fire pit murders; at that time, the three dog walkers and two joggers in the immediate vicinity might arbitrarily incorporate the Sheriff's Station in their routes, but it wasn't a given. After the Peppermill Murders, however, all her subjects gravitated toward the building that suggested safety. To fix this, Ingrid made sure to make Craig Walter's murder as brutal as possible, thus ensuring no one would be leaving their houses after sundown for the foreseeable future.

Social engineering through murder, just one of her specialties.

Ingrid parked in front of an empty house halfway up the block just East of the Station. She'd visited this one several times before, always dressed professionally, knocking on the neighbors' doors to introduce herself as Julia Richards, a local agent with Craig Walters' Real Estate Company. It was these small flourishes that gave Ingrid the greatest joy.

"You'll see me pokin' around, gussying up the place. Mr. Walters thinks this would be a great home to rehab and sell to one of the families in Olde Creek."

These were the words this community wanted to hear - a rube realtor spreading a rube's idea of prosperity, values and behaviors that reinforced their rube world. Ingrid did not bother to ponder how David Bradley managed to summon her from the sophisticated comforts of the city to this backwater town; it did not matter. Being here was written into her destiny long before she was born.

Dressed in this same business casual guise, Ingrid circled to the back of the house and let herself in through a door she'd previously jimmied. Once inside, Ingrid changed into all-black tactical gear and donned a black ski mask. Next, she moved through the backyard fast and low to the ground, slipping between the worn beams of a fence at the Western edge of the property and into the trees that bordered the two-lane blacktop of Harlow Avenue, across which the rear of the Sheriff's Station beckoned. No windows here, but there was a door to the small, attached garage where the department kept some vehicles and a make-shift evidence locker. She'd scoped this entrance on a previous late-night visit, had timed getting in and out of the Station proper by picking the lock, traversing the garage and entering through a door that led to the Station's small jail. It was this route she took now, mindful she might stumble upon an officer bringing her target dinner, questioning him, whittling with him; she'd given up any attempt at understanding these people months ago.

The garage was minus one of the two vehicles she logged on her previous visit, a black 4Runner with large, off-roading BF Goodrich tires, which meant she had a better view of the caged room that held evidence. It looked like someone had put a fence around a kindergarten cloakroom.

"State of the art."

She banished her contempt as she came up to the door. Disdain could lower her guard and allow her to underestimate an opponent. Ingrid retrieved the triangle pick from a small tool set and carefully popped the lock. The sound proved little more than a ping, but she waited to make sure no one heard it anyway. Satisfied, Ingrid turned the knob and pushed the door open in slow motion. Light spilled across the doorway as she slipped inside.

———

They rounded the turn onto Redbreast Drive at a calm twenty miles an hour, Misty's hands never touching the steering wheel.

"That's just fucked up."

"You get used to it. My Uncle Mike says everyone in town will own an electric car by the time he's finished."

"Next stop, Robot Overlords."

They shared a laugh as the car stopped in the gravel before Frank O'Sullivan's house. The hole in the picture window had grown; nothing remained but jagged glass teeth jutting from the otherwise empty frame.

"This is bad."

Lisa tried to open the car door to exit, but it didn't budge.

"Let me out."

"Oh my god. Are you crazy? You are *not* going in there."

"Come on, look at this place. There's, like, *no one* here. I just want to look around for a few minutes."

Misty hesitated but eventually popped the locks.

"You don't have to come with."

"No shit. I'm not going in there with you, but I'll stand watch or whatever. And you're gonna owe me big time for this shit right here, Lisa McCready."

They walked through the grass, overgrown almost to their hips.

"If I lived next to this asshat, I'd have a fit. This is, like, so freakin' gross."

"Yeah, well, not everyone can afford to have a stable of groundskeepers."

They approached the massive aperture where the window had been; peering inside, Lisa spotted large swathes of dark green mold climbing the walls. As she prepared to step over the craggy edges and into the O'Sullivan house, she noticed dark red stains on some of the window's broken teeth.

"Is that blood?"

Lisa didn't answer. Instead, she took a deep breath and stepped over the lower lip, careful not to catch her flesh or clothing on the glass.

"I'm waiting right here."

Once inside, the smell of decay grew so strong that Lisa felt lightheaded. Not wanting to touch anything, she dropped to her haunches, closed her eyes and repeated Miss Galdykas's mantra:

Breath. Just breathe.

As she did, Lisa realized it wasn't the stink of the garbage or putrescence that made her lightheaded.

"Gas."

With this revelation, she removed the police-issue flashlight her father gifted her for birthday number ten from her bag. Ashley had received one, too.

Don't think about Ashley right now. Think about finding the answers that will lead to Ashely's killer.

Lisa clicked the flashlight on and instantly felt like a target. Standing, she moved the stout beam along the walls.

"Doesn't look like anyone's lived here in months," she called to Misty behind her.

"So Hobo Man really does live in the woods?"

"Guess so."

"Getting kinda cold."

Lisa walked through what was left of the O'Sullivans' modest living room toward the open-plan kitchen. A stack of bricks had been gathered in one corner, an ashtray over-flowing on its upper-most point. Beyond that, the refrigerator was plugged in and running; Lisa opened it and saw a carton of two percent milk and about a dozen cans of cheap beer. The air inside the machine was cold, and the use-by date on the milk was two days prior, meaning someone had been here recently. Finally, she bent by the stove and confirmed that, as she'd thought, the pilot light was out, and all four burners were cranked. She dialed each one back.

"This place may actually be creepier than the fire pit," Misty called into the house.

"I wouldn't go that far," Lisa said under her breath. A very human sound came from the hallway next to the kitchen. It led to the bedrooms at the rear of the house. As she started down the hall, she kept the light angled downward so as not to advertise her presence. Lisa's senses told her she was alone, but her gut said something else entirely.

The hallway proved to be in considerably worse shape than the living room. Obviously the elements had made great strides in reclaiming this structure, and for a moment, Lisa wondered if this was what all the houses in the older section of town would look like if Artisan's Ridge continued to expand. Her thoughts were interrupted by a hoarse voice from behind her.

"Who the hell are you?"

Lisa turned and saw Frank O'Sullivan standing in the corridor's entrance.

"Mr. O'Sullivan, I'm... we were worried about you. We saw the window and..."

"So you broke into my house?"

"No! I mean, the window... it was..."

Frank moved closer, suddenly recognized her in the light seeping through the window in the bedroom to Lisa's right.

"McCready's daughter again. What do you want from me?"

"I...ah. No, Mr. O'Sullivan... I came back to talk to you, but-"

"You came back with people I didn't want to talk to."

She hadn't considered this; would Misty's presence sour the deal this time, too? Lisa found herself hoping Misty remained outside and silent.

"They're my friends. They didn't want me to go into the woods alone."

"Wonder why, hmmm?"

"Mr. O'Sullivan... did you bring me Onya's turtle? The one with the book inside on the -"

"What book?"

"I don't know its name, but there's a half-moon with a face on the cover."

"Liber Korrupt! What do you know about that, child?"

"Ah, well... someone gave me a flash drive that had it as a PDF file, but my father has the actual book book."

"He does?"

"Yes."

Frank grasped Lisa by both shoulders and began to shake her to emphasize his words.

"Do you know what's in that book? Do you? It's your doom, girl, do you hear me?

"I haven't... I won't... I just... I need to know how everything figures into the murders? How do we stop the killer?"

"You're not gonna like the answer to that one, princess. Thirty years I been chasing kids off that land for their own good. Ever since I saw Betty's sister taken by that... thing."

"What thing?"

"It was Samson Bradley who called it up from the Abyss, from the rotten garbage dump of their souls! A thing made up of their lust for power, for money. He pledged to feed it blood; in return, it grew his family's power for generations. Then Roland Bradley came along. His daddy never did trust him, on account of his birthday..."

"It wasn't the same day as the others, right?"

"He toed the line for a good number of years, but Betty telt him what his family were doing was wrong. He wouldn't have gone along with any of it had Charles not killed her and brought another of those Pit-Wenches over from the Old Country, just like he and his daddy had. See, it's a whole process, procreation..."

Lisa saw a shadow appear in the corridor behind Frank. Silently, Misty slid into the room just behind him. She listened, remaining perfectly still.

"Does that have something to do with why all our moms die during childbirth?"

"That's the first sacrifice! The second is the sibling. All the men in town know. Well, the Bradley's anyway. After Roland turned his back on their ways, the business nearly died. But the book says once a thing like that's summoned, it's tied to the land it has trod upon. When Nancy Walters discovered it, she took over. Started making me do things for her. Horrible things. Now, though, the Bradleys want it back, all for different reasons. No matter which of 'em gets it, they'll have to spill blood to seal the deal."

"I'm not understanding this, Mr. O'Sullivan. How was my Mom a 'sacrifice?' I'm not a Bradley."

"Oh no? You ever looked at your family tree? Hahaha..."

The air around Lisa went cold; spots flickered before her eyes, and a rush of stale, heated air spiked her nostrils.

"What? No, but..."

"You stupid brat! Your father's mother was a Bradley! That's why your mother's dead! You're one of 'em! Hahahaha."

"NO!" Lisa screamed, and Frank let go of her shoulders and moved his grip to her throat.

"You Bradleys are a poison on this land! If one of you retakes control of the Wilhelm Egregore, there's no telling what kind of Horror you'll unleash!"

Frank O'Sullivan's grip tightened quick, and Lisa felt that rush of stale air again. She swung her fists at his face and chest, but she was tiny compared to him, and her blows had no effect. Lisa's vision began to spiral black when Frank dropped her to the floor, her consciousness oscillating on and off, affording her only a segmented view of Misty Bradley as she brought one of the bricks from the living room down again and again on Frank's skull. The last thing Lisa heard before consciousness slipped away was the sound of a large, sloppy watermelon cracking open and divesting its contents onto the carpet before her.

———

"I'm going to need you to tell me exactly what you and Lisa were up to at Peppermill last night, Vic. I'm also going to need you to tell me if she was with you when you killed Craig Walters."

"How many times I gotta say this, bro? I didn't kill Craig fucking Walters, okay? As for Lisa, she told me she was going to Peppermill. I didn't want her to go alone, so Misty and I went with her. You're welcome."

"What happened?"

"Nothing happened.

"I don't believe you."

"Look man, I get that since I sell drugs, everyone thinks I'm some kind of degenerate scumbag, and maybe I am. I mean, I'm a fifth-year Senior, my dad runs a fucking dive bar, and I haven't been sober since... Sophomore year, maybe?"

"What's your point?"

"Just that none of that makes me a killer. Think about it, man. You think I drove out to wherever the fuck Lisa's sister was going to school and killed her, too? Or what about the Fire Pit? You interviewed my alibi yourself - you know that wasn't me."

"Your alibi was your girlfriend, Vic. In my book, she's no better than you. Worse maybe. Lisa's told me she thinks Misty turns tricks at your dad's club."

"Slo Motion ain't his, man. You know this - everything in this town goes back to the freakin' Bradleys."

"Who you also work for."

"Work *with*, man. Seriously, I'm not about to put a fucking target on my head by telling you what kind of work I do for who, but look at me, Matt. I'm a fucking mess," tears leaked from Vic's eyes, and his speech devolved into sobs. "Do you really think I could kill anybody, let alone a guy as big as Craig Walters?"

Matt thought about it. He remembered Lisa telling him about the altercation her father had intervened in the day after she left Mather's - David Bradley and Craig Walters, trading blows outside the Red Lion. Matt was a pretty good judge of character, but also, after making Varsity Wrestling his Junior year and coming close to winning state for Sundown High, he was an even better judge of physical matches. Drunk or not, Walters would have had almost a hundred pounds on Vic, who was scrawny with long, wild hair. Fran McDelmond's Forensics report would take several weeks at the very least, but something as big and obvious as a strand of this kid's hair would have announced itself fairly quickly, especially since Matt had taken it upon himself to do a rudimentary scan of the scene when he'd first arrived.

On top of all of that, Matt had heard Jeff Wilson tell the Sheriff he'd seen Vic's car near the Walters's place last night, but he wasn't inclined to believe him; there was no love lost between the two deputies, and Matt knew for a fact that when Jeff worked overnight, he liked to stop by Slo Motion for a beer or two himself. It was the kind of thing a bad cop thought was okay, and Matt had simply been waiting to catch him in the act before reporting it.

"So who did it then?"

"I don't fucking know, man."

"You know these people, Vic. You travel in their circles. You hear things. Take a guess."

Vic looked from side to side, afraid someone other than Matt might hear.

"We're alone."

"Too bad for you."

The voice startled Matt, and he spun around too far and slammed headfirst into the black-masked figure that had snuck in behind him. Their heads connected, sending both momentarily reeling. Matt recovered a fraction of a second faster than the intruder, and his hand went directly for his holster... which he now realized was empty, his gun sitting in the top drawer of his desk.

"Shit!"

The figure was up and swinging; their fist caught Matt square in the jaw, and he felt the cartilage in his right cheek pop. The pain was immediate and intense, but nothing compared to the follow-up blow across the back of his neck. It was this shot that sent Matt spiraling into a blackened void as his body collapsed onto the cold, concrete floor. The figure assessed the situation from a defensive stance. When it became clear Matt was not getting back up, they relaxed their posture and turned their icy regard to Vic.

"Hey man, I didn't say shit, okay?"

"Mr. Bradley doesn't really care. You're simply more useful to us dead."

The attacker's voice, unexpectedly, sounded female. Vic wanted to talk, to spew nervous nonsense, but something told him to hold his tongue and let the moment evolve. His eyes trained on the black gloves, waiting for them to strike, but for all his anticipation, Vic's stoner reflexes were no match for those gloves when they shot out and grabbed him by the wrists.

Vic screamed, the sound truncated by a hot, wet gurgle when the gloves pulled him forward, face-first into the bars of the cell. One of his front teeth broke in half, and Vic reflexively swallowed it and began to choke. Not understanding what was happening, the figure held onto Vic's arms. After a few moments of his staccato gagging, they began to laugh. It was a cold, hateful sound.

"This is certainly something new. Trouble breathing?"

Vic flailed his arms up and down to shake off the figure's grip, but female or not, they were considerably stronger than him. As panic ate the last of his oxygen, his tormentor let out a startling shriek and dropped to the floor. Vic collapsed backward, his fingers trying in vain to massage the outside of his throat for air.

The intruder lay on their backside, blood spurting from their right leg as Deputy Matt Hartman climbed on top of them. A blood-smeared pocket knife in hand, Matt's next blow aimed directly at the figure's throat. Without hesitation, Matt drove the blade home and the attacker's life left them in a loud, chunky belch.

Realizing Vic was still choking, Matt threw himself at the cell door, struggling through his keys for the one that would open it.

The world began to fade to an omnipotent red; the bursting capillaries behind Vic's eyes preceded all feeling evacuating his extremities.

"Come on! Come on!" Matt screamed as the door swung open but caught on Vic's prone body. Barely able to squeeze through, Matt wasted no time flipping Vic onto his stomach to easier work his arms around his midsection.

"Breathe, damm it! Come on, Vic!"

Matt worked Vic's diaphragm so hard he felt a rib snap, but a moment later, Vic's airway cleared and he vomited a lake of bile onto the floor before them. Like spent lovers, both men collapsed onto their backs.

"Jesus fucking Christ that was close."

Hoarse and barely audible, Vic said, "I hope this means you believe I didn't kill Walters."

"Yeah," Matt said, panting. "I believe you."

———

The entire world hummed with an undercurrent of purple electricity. Lisa could feel herself plugged into it, could feel the power it granted her in the calves, thighs and upper body.

It works both ways, a voice said from somewhere in the distance. The words eked out slowly, gaining proximity as the voice warbled around inside her head.

A threshold of flesh yawned before her. Beyond, she could almost make out a city. Some place she'd never been before.

Is this Seattle? she thought.

"This is the town we will make, a new place for our family to live and breed and carry on the tradition. It works both ways, Lisa. The Flesh...

A faint, familiar aroma tickled her memory. It brought vague images from the past... distant, just beyond reach. A doorway to some Archetypal well; she became aware for the first time of a place inside herself that predated the parameters of what she thought of as 'Lisa.'

"Blood and tissue flex before you. They are a door, now open. Walk through."

The blade moved through the wall of flesh before her, the resistance from muscle and tendon unable to dispel the force. Dissolving, Lisa saw her father's face in the rivulets of gore that trickled toward the floor.

"Well, wouldn't you like it if he didn't have to die like I did?" Lisa heard her mother say as she stepped through the meat partition and it closed behind her. To the left, sunlight poured through the picture window in the front room. The light made her feel exposed, so she stepped into the room and closed the large purple drapes. A noise from behind announced someone descending the staircase. She turned; their shape looked... familiar.

"The only way to save him is to give him to us. Make us flesh, Lisa. Make... us... flesh..."

She turned and saw herself reflected in the dark folds of a broken mirror. Every facet showed a different road. A different Lisa.

"Which will you choose?"

———

When Lisa came to, drool glued her mouth to the filthy shag carpet. She'd been lost in deep, purple dreams that still stained her senses, making it impossible at first to distinguish between reality and the residue from her subconscious. Disoriented, a series of sharp noises pulled her back to herself, intimating danger.

It's Philip's pills - they're poison. They erase the borders of reality.

For a moment, she thought she was in her room, that she'd drifted off after the argument with her father and dreamed Misty and Frank and the entire episode. She'd gone upstairs and found the bottle of pills she'd thrown across the room and taken too many, passed out, overdosed, everything since then a hallucination.

A sound from the room to her left told her this was false.

"Oh, gross."

Lisa recognized the voice instantly.

"Misty?" she croaked, the words caught in her throat.

Everything returned to her then, and Lisa opened her eyes with an urgent sense of dread, as if she could prevent any of what just happened. The sight of Misty struggling to pull Frank O'Sullivan's lifeless corpse into a closet told her this was impossible. What was left of Frank's head trailed a slimy mixture of blood and brains as it dragged across the carpet.

"Help me already! What the fuck, Lisa!"

"You... killed Mr. O'Sullivan?"

"He was strangling you! What was I supposed to do, let him? Help, goddamnit!"

"Okay, okay."

Lisa stood up and immediately went lightheaded. Those black spots returned to eat her peripheral vision; she took a deep breath and, with the exhale, steadied herself against the scene before her. It was, simply put, the most revolting thing she had ever witnessed. Still, the memory of Frank's hands around her throat told her Misty was not lying: his intent had been to squeeze the life from her. What's more, the smell of gas seemed stronger. Did they interrupt him in the middle of some elaborate suicide plot? Had the entire town, Lisa included, lost their minds?

"Does it matter," she said as she tried to pick Frank up by his armpits. Lisa maneuvered as best she could to try and avoid his leaking head, but she got tripped up in his arms, and her left hand slipped directly into his open brain case. She tried to look away and adjust her grip, but the texture of the goo hanging from her fingers made her gag. She turned her head an instant too late and spewed vomit across Frank's chest and legs. Misty dropped his feet and jumped backward, too late to avoid having her shoes covered in bile.

"Eww! Oh my god!"

Now it was Misty's turn; she turned her head into the closet just in time to coat the clothes hanging therein with the contents of her stomach.

A few more dry heaves and the girls finally regained their composure.

"Jesus Christ, Misty!" Lisa said, breathing heavily through her diaphragm.

"You're fucking welcome!"

The moment throbbed with tension. Then, without warning, Lisa burst into full-on laughter. Misty followed a moment later.

"This is, like, the nastiest shit that's ever happened to me!"

"No maid to clean it up, huh?"

They laughed even harder at this.

"We have to get out of here and hope no one comes looking for Frank. Our DNA is all over this place."

"We should just burn this shithole down."

"Misty, that's insane."

"Why? Looks like that's what he was about to do. Besides, you owe me! I'm the one that'll go to jail if anyone finds out."

"We can't just blow up a house in the middle of -"

"In the middle of what? Half the houses on this block are empty. Craig had this whole part of town scheduled to be bought, knocked down and fixed up, Lisa."

'Craig's dead' is what almost popped from Lisa's lips, but she caught the thought and let it pass. No need to hurt Misty's feelings. Also, the girl wasn't wrong...

"This is insane," the idea of burning the O'Sullivan house down gained momentum in Lisa's mind.

"No, *this* is insane," Misty held up her hands, coated in black blood.

They finally got Frank stuffed into the closet and argued all the way back to the front of the house.

"We don't even have to do anything. We can just turn the gas back on and leave. When it gets thick enough and the fridge kicks on, the spark should be enough to ignite the gas."

"How do you know that?"

"I saw it in a movie once."

Internally, Lisa rolled her eyes but was pretty sure she'd seen the same movie. And Misty wasn't wrong; Frank O'Sullivan was a troubled man who had tried to kill her - *would have killed her* if Misty hadn't intervened. Even as she rationalized the idea, Lisa became aware of something else. Something she couldn't believe was right there inside her.

Which will you choose?

She *wanted* to blow the house up *just to do it*. Just to finally take a piece back from this cursed town that had taken so much from her.

Rational Lisa swooped back in at the last second.

"What if someone else comes in right before the explosion?"

"Who's gonna come to see Frank the fucking Hobo? Come on, you owe me BIG TIME, McCready! We'll be doing this town a favor."

Even Rational Lisa had to acknowledge that Misty was

right. Or better yet, why even make a decision? Misty was set to do it all herself - Lisa didn't have to do anything except...

Take another pill.

Lisa walked straight toward the hole in the picture window through which they'd entered. Still mindful of the potential for injury, she stepped through the jagged teeth.

"Come on."

"I'm gonna do it!"

Lisa didn't say anything to that, just hoped Misty would hurry the fuck up.

CHAPTER EIGHTEEN

They left Frank's and parked at the far end of the building. The local teenagers affectionally referred to this spot as "Home Run Inn." This was another of the between places only those on the cusp of adulthood knew about. Once a small, twelve-unit motel, when the Bradleys petitioned the state to build an exit from the Forty that led directly to the old Inner Earth (Peppermill) facility, it completely negated the previous exit, Old Bell Road. The Johnson family had run the Sundown Inn for close to forty years, but it only took six months of the new road to destroy their business and render this entire corner of town a forgotten husk. The family fought, but less than two years later, they joined Old Bell Plaza and Ginger's Bar and Grill as casualties. Based on Misty's comments about Craig Walters' plans to gentrify the area, he must have been the one who purchased all these buildings and the land they resided on, probably for a song. Gentrification takes time, though. In the interim, the local youth had claimed them.

This was the ultimate make-out spot. Not only did the parking lot provide a secluded area, but the locks on most of the motel's rooms could be easily jimmied. The rooms were musty, the beds old and stained, but, as ever, teenage lust finds a way.

It was dark now, and from the Inn's position at the top of Old Bell Road, the girls enjoyed a magnificent view as orange and cherry flames lapped at the sky. Flames they'd instigated.

Misty took a hit off her pipe and offered it to Lisa, not really expecting her to accept. They were both surprised when she did.

Apprehensive at first, Lisa drew the bitter smoke into her lungs and held it for the count of three. When she exhaled, her entire body relaxed into her seat.

"Wow. Have you ever even smoked pot before?"

"Yeah. A couple times, Sophomore year."

"No way. You were such a goody fucking two shoes back then."

"Yeah, well, I saw my best friend was starting to hang out with a rabid pack of druggies and figured I had to do something to keep her around."

"Didn't work, huh?"

"No," Lisa said, disguising the emotion in her voice with a sudden coughing fit.

They sat watching the flames for a long time. Finally, Misty said:

"You think I'm a skank, don't you? For sleeping with Angela's dad?"

"Actually, no. I think... well, I think we all need something different from people, and it's not always convenient or socially fair where we find what we need. I think it would have been really messed up if Angela found out, but that's not the case, so... I guess I understand."

"You do?"

Lisa nodded, then added, "Besides, he was kind of hot."

Misty smiled, and a funny thing happened; she placed her

hand on Lisa's knee. There was no trace of flirtation; instead, it felt warm and friendly. Against all odds, they'd become friends, and with the mystery mounting around them, an expression of that friendship and concern felt right. Lisa thought of Vic again; those feelings of attraction remained, only diluted, no longer an urgent distraction. Was it possible her feelings had simply been born of her animosity toward Misty?

"So what now?"

"I was just wondering that myself."

Since leaving Frank O'Sullivan's house, Lisa felt possessed by equal parts regret, awe and confusion. She needed her father, needed to question him about Frank's accusations. The idea that she might be related to Misty seemed preposterous, but in the last few weeks, what didn't?

Unable to reach Gerald by phone, Lisa realized there was only one other person in town she'd trust to ask this question.

"Start the car, I know where to go."

When they arrived at Mr. Harrison's, Lisa instructed Misty to park her car on the next block so they could approach from behind the house. They cut across Lonnie Stone's property, careful to stay hidden by the thick arbor vitae that lined it until they emerged into Harrison's backyard. The light over the backdoor clicked on as they approached, so that only a few seconds after Lisa pulled open the screen door and knocked, Harrison answered.

"Lisa. Misty. I wasn't expecting to see you girls this evening, especially not together. No offense."

"None taken. Can we come in? It's kind of cold."

"Please."

Harrison ushered them inside with a hospitable flourish that devolved into a particularly nasty coughing fit. After, Lisa pretended not to see the crimson stain on his handkerchief, but it shook her inside.

"Pardon me. Damn cold," he said, shutting the door behind them.

She teared up at this but played it off as a yawn. He wasn't fooling anybody.

Jim waved them through the kitchen, and they emerged into the den.

"Can I offer you girls some coffee?"

"Sure," Lisa said.

"I hope instant is okay?"

"Whatever you have would be nice. Thank you, Mr. Harrison."

Lisa's eyes met Harrison's, and they exchanged a smile.

"How fortunate I am: two visits this month."

"We just... *I* wanted to talk to you."

"Sounds serious. Is everything okay?"

"Honestly? I don't know. I'm trying to figure things out, maybe help my dad. You know, like we talked about?"

As she spoke, Lisa caught a whiff of something familiar but out of place. It smelled like... perfumed lumber?

"That's great, Lisa. I spoke to your father just a little while ago, and frankly, it seems like he can use all the help he can get."

"I know. Look, Mr. Harrison, can I talk to you alone for a minute?"

An odd look passed from Misty to Lisa, then from Harrison to both girls in succession. Everyone seemed to breathe a little easier once he nodded his approval.

"Why don't you help me fix the coffee?"

"Okay."

Once in the kitchen, Lisa felt less awkward talking.

"Ugh. No more instant. Tea will have to do. So, what's on your mind, dear?" Harrison asked, placing a kettle on the stove and lowering the burner.

"Normally, I'd never dream of asking you something like this, but I was snooping around and I found something. Something I can't reconcile."

"Color me intrigued," another brief coughing fit. When it passed, he nodded for Lisa to continue.

"My dad told me that Annie's real mom died during childbirth, just like mine. But here's the thing - so did Misty's, so did Onya's."

Harrison didn't answer at first; he seemed to weigh the facts, considering their value as juxtaposed against some unknown criteria. Finally, he took three mugs from the cabinet above the sink and set them on the counter beside the range.

"Lisa, you know I care for you, but whatever it is you think you've discovered, it sounds like something that can hurt others. Do you understand?"

Lisa's face turned red, and she began to tear up.

"I'm sorry. It's just, well, I found a book. Inside, there's a bunch of girls' names in pairs. When I thought about those names, I realized that Onya O'Sullivan and I are paired the same way Annie and Misty are."

"The commonality is mothers who passed away during childbirth?"

"I think."

"Lisa, you are phenomenally perceptive," Harrison said as he pulled a fresh lemon from a basket on the island. He faced her, a kind of dream-like sadness settling over his features.

"Yes. Annie's real mother, Eleanor, passed away after an agonizing thirteen-hour labor."

"Oh my god."

"Yes. Eleanor was -"

A knock at the front door split the moment into two frozen slabs - inside one was James Harrison; in the other, Lisa.

"Pardon me for a moment, dear," Harrison said as he left the room, placing the knife on the counter next to a small basket of lemons. Lisa breathed a sigh of relief as he disappeared through the door, then poked his head back in for a second.

"Could you cut some lemon for our tea? Water should be done in a few moments."

Harrison smiled before ducking back out.

"Your tea will be ready shortly, Misty dear," she heard him say before the sound of the front door opening brought a new voice into the house.

"Can I talk to you?"

"Outside."

The door closed, and Lisa ducked her head out. Misty sat on the couch, eyes pinned to her phone. Through the picture window in the front of the house, Lisa could see resting Police lights, the kind that adorned the roofs of the department's cruisers.

Deputy Jeff Wilson. That's the smell she recognized; her father's least favorite deputy always smelled like he bathed in old man cologne.

She texted Matt.

Who's on patrol tonight?

When Matt didn't respond right away, Lisa set her phone on the counter, took a clean knife from the dish rack and cut the lemon. The kettle whistled, and Lisa poured equal portions into the three mugs. She found a small charcuterie board and used it as a tray to carry the tea to the den.

"Outta coffee. Tea instead."

"I've never had tea before."

"Really?" Lisa laughed and sat next to Misty. "How have you never drank tea?"

"I'm more of a Latte girl."

They laughed at this, their knees knocking together for a moment, and suddenly Lisa felt like she was here with Annie again, drinking hot chocolate while her dad made grilled cheese in the kitchen. The harmonic resonance of the experience overwhelmed her, and Lisa stood abruptly and began to inspect the bookshelves that lined the far wall. Anything to break the illusion that things were, even for a moment, as they used to be.

After running her fingers over several shelves, she stopped on something she recognized.

"Oh! Check this out."

She pulled the leather-bound volume Harrison had shown her previously. Next to it, Lisa spotted a stapled manuscript slouched against the back of the shelf. She pulled it out and, once open, realized it was a photocopied version of the same book in her father's room and the flash drive.

"What's that?" Misty asked, still glued to her phone.

"*That* is Liber Korrupt, a ledger of all those who have profited from the Wilhelm Egregore and all those who may yet still profit from it, either directly or indirectly."

The girls turned to see Mr. Harrison in the doorway, Deputy Wilson beside him.

"What's he doing here?"

In answer to her question, Jim Harrison raised his hand to Misty's head, and a thunderclap rocked the room. Misty's head exploded like an egg dropped from a roof, blood and brains and bits of face blossoming in every direction, most unrecognizable. Still, a few pieces - a bit of nose, part of an ear - carried with them the sudden, horrifying news that Misty Bradley was dead, and the one man Lisa thought she could rely on was, in reality, a cold-blooded killer.

PART THREE

CHAPTER NINETEEN

Sunday, November 1

"It works both ways, Lisa. Make us flesh!"

Reality returned in an explosion of senses; Lisa's head rang like the aftershock of a hammer blow. Her skin felt covered in sand, and her nose flooded with the cloying stench of mold. Lisa knew she was in trouble but couldn't remember why or how at first, possessed instead by a crippling, ambiguous terror.

Finally, her eyes opened and the world began to spiral into view. Images filtered in, but she'd been immersed in those deep, purple dreams again, and their effects clung to her senses.

"Make us flesh!"

The room was dark and littered with filth. The floor felt damp, the walls covered in black mold. A general sense of decay permeated the air, and broken furniture littered the space. To her left, a modest dresser, the drawers missing, the frame of the attached mirror empty save for several jagged pieces of glass holding fast at the corners. On her right, a stained box spring covered in dust, a simple wire-framed headboard sagging behind it, one of the corners bent backward and pushed through the wall.

Lisa forced herself to her feet. As she did, memories burst like bubbles inside her mind's eye:

Jim Harrison raising a revolver to Misty Bradley's head and pulling the trigger...

A thunderclap so loud reality skips...

Misty's head exploding... blood and brains everywhere, a piece of scalp with a sizzling lock of hair landing on her lap with a wet slap...

Lisa leaping from the couch, running toward the open door. The smell of that cedar cologne, Deputy Wilson's fist swung so hard into her face the world instantly stuttered black...

Stunned into a brutal fugue, Lisa's mind vomited a stream-of-consciousness diatribe of conjecture and regret. Where was she? Why hadn't they killed her, too? She was glad she hadn't stopped Misty from burning down Frank's house because if she couldn't trust Jim Harrison, then the only way to ever be truly safe was to set fire to the entire town. There was an evil in Sundown Hills, some outside influence that had turned everyone in her life into a maniac. This last thought pressed home the realization that Misty was dead, murdered by Annie Harrison's father.

Lisa began to cry. Deep, soul-searing sobs that moved all one-hundred and forty-five pounds of her in slow, staccato ululations. She felt it in her stomach, back, shoulders and chest: her body insisted she cooperate with its desire to eject itself from everything around her. Take the entire bottle of pills and go to sleep, drift off into the Purple and never come back.

It works both ways

A sharp CLACK interrupted her reverie, sidestepping her emotions so the pragmatic problem solver who'd been captain of last year's Varsity Debate Team could slide into the pilot's seat. Lisa held her breath and listened, was rewarded with a familiar sound: footsteps.

Clik-Clop

Clik-Clop

"No, please. Not him. Not now."

Even as she made her pleas, Lisa knew reality would once again refuse to acknowledge her prayers.

She was on the abandoned third floor at Mather's, and Philip was there, too.

———

"So what the fuck do we do?"

"Hold still."

Matt had never field-dressed a wound before, but the gnarly-looking cut running from Vic's right eyebrow up into his hairline was leaking blood into his eyes. His hair was long and unkempt, so the process proved difficult. After a few minutes and several aborted attempts with tangled adhesive, Matt finally closed the wound.

"How do you feel now that you don't have a steady stream of blood in your eyes?"

"Fucked up, but whatever. You got anything to eat in this place, man?"

"How can you possibly be hungry?"

"Well, just before y'all arrested me, I took a pretty strong gummy, so, you know, kinda starving."

Matt went to his desk and tossed Vic two peanut butter granola bars and a bottle of water. He dialed the McCready's home. The phone went straight to their answering machine.

"Shit," that bad feeling he'd had talking to Bridget earlier turned a corner and caught him in its high beams.

Matt's mind spun in a dozen directions, no train of

thought congealing long enough to assuage the fact that he'd just executed a masked killer. A masked killer who worked for David Bradley. The implications were terrifying; there was just no other word - Lisa had been right all along with her conspiracy theories.

"Eat fast. We're heading out," Matt said, pocketing a box of shells.

"Were we going?"

"To talk to Jim Harrison."

———

The footsteps sounded slow and steady, the confident swagger of a psychopath who knows his prey has nowhere to hide. She remained perfectly still and listened.

Clik-Clop

Clik-Clop

Clik-

Philip stopped somewhere in the hall outside. Nearby, a door creaked open.

'He must not know what room I'm in.' That meant Philip was here of his own accord, that Nurse Landing hadn't sent him to kill her.

She had to act fast. Pushing past the pain that still rang behind her eyes, Lisa tiptoed to the door. Terrified, she whispered a prayer, not so much to any god as herself.

"Just get out of here in one piece."

With a trepidatious application of strength, she twisted the knob and slowly inched the door open. The rusted creaking amounted to little more than further sonic ambiance on an entire floor of rooms left to rot for decades.

When she could see into the corridor, a familiar voice echoed from a room further down the hall:

"Lisa Lisa, time for your meds, baby."

Not if you do what I ask, Lisa

Steeling herself, Lisa slipped out into the hall and crept silently toward the door opposite. One room was as good as the other - Philip would locate her eventually - but Lisa hoped she might improve her odds of survival by finding something she could use as a weapon.

The first door she came to, marked 3E, was locked, so she hurried further down the hall. As she did, she heard the voice again.

"Bitch. I'm gonna find you. I'm gonna find you, and then we're gonna have us some fun."

A shiver racked Lisa's entire body as images of the potential assault assailed her. She had to find something to give her an advantage.

The next door she came to opened, revealing a noose hanging from the rafters. Lisa recoiled at first but fought the wave of nausea and was rewarded. Further in, a large pile of handbags and backpacks lay stacked in disarray beside a bed that appeared to have been burned. Unable to believe her luck, Lisa slipped inside, but when she tried to close the door, it wouldn't fit true. Inspired, she left it open a crack, realizing an unsecured door might persuade Philip to move along.

This room was brighter than the previous one. A window against the far wall covered in black, oily grime issued a thin ray of light from outside. She had no idea whether it was sunlight or one of the building's security lamps. How long had she been unconscious? What day was it?

Doesn't matter

Lisa began to open bags. In short order, she found makeup, several wallets devoid of cash or cards, and a small stack of High School textbooks in one backpack. The largest of these was a US History book, outdated and heavy, with a thick cover and even thicker spine. She held on to this and scanned her surroundings, landing again on the noose.

The rope was badly frayed; whoever had used or attempted to use it had been smart but not tall or strong. The length was considerably longer than needed if tied to the ceiling. Instead, its creator had pitched the rope over the rafters and tied it to the inside door handle. Lisa experienced another flash of insight and quickly undid the noose, pulling it from where it hung.

Rope looped around her right shoulder, book in hand, Lisa moved to the window. There existed no discernible method by which to open the aperture. That tracked; this was, after all, an asylum. Seeing the outside, she wondered again how long she'd been here. This was good, in a way, because it squashed any hope that Matt or her father might find her in time to prevent whatever her captors had planned. The last thing Lisa needed right now was hope. Hope had brought her to James Harrison and now Misty was dead. No, Lisa put up her fists and pushed hope straight down the fucking stairs. What trudged to the top after was hate. Exactly what she needed.

They drove by Lisa's first, but as Matt feared, the house was dark. Neither Lisa nor her father were home.

On their way to Harrison's, they circled the block until Vic spotted Misty's Tesla.

"You said they're together, right?"

"Yeah. Why?"

"That's Misty's car."

As soon as he pulled into Jim Harrison's driveway, Matt knew something was wrong. He'd always possessed strong intuition, back to his earliest memories. Talking to Lisa about this recently, she'd suggested the accuracy of Matt's gut might be because he grew up with an alcoholic mother who could turn on a dime, lashing out with verbal, emotional, and sometimes even physical violence. To navigate such a scenario, children learn to watch for subtle, sometimes imperceptible cues in their environment, clues that might trigger such outbursts. This skill often follows them into adulthood, becoming a kind of sixth sense about situations others might overlook. Staring at Harrison's house with all the lights off and the curtains drawn, Matt wasn't sure what felt wrong; he just knew something did.

"Looks like no one's home."

"Maybe. Stay here. I'll be right back."

Matt stepped out of his cruiser and headed toward the house. When he hit the front porch, he washed his flashlight back and forth over the wood, where a dark stain caught his eye. Something on the porch briefly twinkled in the light. He stooped to pick it up, revolted to discover a human tooth. It looked like a front tooth, but not one that belonged to a seventy-something-year-old man of Harrison's size.

"What's that?"

Vic's sudden presence startled Matt, and he nearly lost his balance.

"I thought I told you to stay in the truck?"

"You didn't say that at all, man."

"Well then, I guess I thought it'd be obvious. I mean, you are still supposed to be in a cell and all."

"Yeah, well, we both know it's gonna be front page fucking news that David Bradley sent his secretary to slit my throat. I'm not worried; looks like we've got the killer out of the picture and the mastermind on the run. Time to, like, mop this case up and shit, right?"

"Vic, did you ever think David Bradley is insanely powerful? For that matter, so is Jim Harrison. One of them sent that killer after you, and one of them might have Lisa and Misty."

"David and Harrison? Really..."

"Why? You got something?"

"Well, there was this time when Annie was, like, still alive. We were all hanging out at Misty's. Her dad comes home and gives us this funny look. Two minutes after he leaves the room, Annie's father calls and starts lacing into her to get home."

"Hmmm. I wouldn't have pictured the two of them as friends. I know Harrison tried to get the Sheriff to run for Mayor just so David wouldn't win. Sounds more like the girls stumbled into the middle of some kind of power struggle."

Matt stepped up to Harrison's front door and tried the knob. When it didn't open, he took a step back and spun a roundhouse kick with his right foot; the door splintered near the knob but didn't quite break.

"Whoa! Don't we need a warrant or whatever?"

"Yeah. We do."

Matt let loose another kick and the door broke enough that when he threw his shoulder against it next, the weather-beaten maple collapsed with little say.

The Harrison house yawned in total darkness before them.

"Gross. What's that smell?" Vic asked as they entered, side by side.

———

Lisa waited until she heard Philip enter the room next to her, then darted into the hall and looped one end of the rope around that room's door knob. Next, she tied the other end around the knob across from it. When she had both in place, she pulled hard enough to secure the first. Her stalker must have heard her; an instant before the door clicked into place,

Philip let out an angry howl and the door swung open, completely unimpeded by her knot.

"There you are!"

With the textbook held eye-level in both hands, Lisa pushed off with her right foot and virtually flew across the hall, hitting Philip square in the nose. She heard bone crunch like gravel underfoot. He screamed in pain and staggered backward. Lisa hauled off and kicked him as hard as she could in the nuts, then slammed the door and quickly began to gather the rope's slack, pulling it with her as she backed across the corridor toward the other door. She had to get this secured or Philip would be free and this time, his savagery would be apocalyptic.

Reaching the door, she realized she had to slip the loop off the doorknob and retie it to account for the slack. The rope was longer than she'd thought. She looped it once, twice, and the third time, it flew through her hands, skinning her palms as it went. Lisa caught it at the last minute, but the pain was dizzying as she fought to hold on. Behind the door, Philip grappled viciously for his freedom.

"You fuckin' bitch! I'm gonna skin you alive!"

Lisa pushed past the threats by focusing on the slow-motion image of Misty's head exploding. She held onto the rope for dear life, palms burning like they were on fire. Closing her eyes, she sent Matt the image of Harrison with the gun, realizing that even if she could somehow psychically reach him, there would be no reason on Earth it would lead him back here, to Mather's. At least, not in time to save her.

———

"Someone fired a gun here recently."

Matt's tone betrayed the fear that gripped him. What

little hesitation accompanied busting down the Mayor's door disappeared when he caught the scent of cordite on the air.

"Wait outside, Vic. Do you understand this time?"

"No problem, man. All you."

Matt stepped further inside and could smell what lay beneath the gunpowder: the bitter iron tinge of blood and charred human hair.

Adjacent to the large picture window, Harrison's living room looked straight from *Southern Living* magazine. The couch was a massive, claw-footed beast with a bougainvillea floral print. Tucked into one of the cushions and forgotten, Matt found a small purse. Louie Vuitton.

On either side of the sofa, matching loveseats flanked tall vases filled with fake flowers. Opposite these, an 80s tube television beamed static from an ornate, red cherry cabinet. Atop this, a vintage Victrola completed the tableau with the majesty of its seashell horn. The walls, where they weren't splattered with blood and what looked like brains, sported another, complimentary floral print, and the acorn-shaped light fixtures' patina marked them as priceless antiques.

Someone had died here recently.

He moved around the room slowly, his flashlight revealing ever more gore but no body. Further on, an open doorway led to the kitchen. Crossing through, Matt clocked a wooden knife block, one blade missing. On the stove, a tea kettle still trailed an apparition of steam. Beside that, freshly cut lemon slices glistened on a cutting board.

The unmistakable odor of Deputy Jeff Wilson's bargain-store cedar plank cologne hung in the air.

"I'll kill that fucker."

Matt moved through the door that opened into the dining room. Harrison's house was laid out so that the living room was the tip of a triangle; the kitchen and dining room formed the base, each room tapering slightly as they fed into the front of the house. Tucked into the Southeast corner, he found the staircase leading to the second-story bedrooms. It was to this Matt moved next, flashlight trained on the ground before him, occasionally dashing up along the walls and eventually settling hard on the open stairway. If someone was hiding up there, he wanted them to know he was coming.

"Hello? This is Deputy Matt Hartman from the Sheriff's Department; we had reports of possible gunshots. Is anyone here?"

The story he concocted on the spot was enough reason to be inside the house. Add to that the smell of gunpowder and the splatter pattern he observed downstairs; violence was certainly involved.

"If anyone is here, I need you to identify yourself now. I am armed."

No answer. Matt's pulse crested 115 bpm; everything about this house set his gut in turmoil. Something bad had happened here.

He placed his right foot on the first stair.

"This is your last warning. If you're here, you need to identify yourself now!"

This came out panicked, and he shook his head in disgust. He thought of Sheriff McCready. Until this morning, Matt had never seen the man balk at anything; whether it was losing his oldest daughter or seeing Craig Walters's severed head that finally broke the Sheriff's armor, it was that previously unflappable ideal Matt reached for now. He thought of his grandfather's stories about Vietnam:

"You ain't getting around the fear, boy. That's what the older guys told me. The ones that'd been on two, three tours. They said ya just gotta put one foot in front of the other and pretend that with each step, you're killing whatever lay ahead of you just by facing the fear it starts in your heart. You do that long enough, eventually, you walk

right over that fear. Still might die, but then, you're gonna do that at some point, anyway."

Third stair. Fourth. In his head, Matt heard the mantra Lisa had shared with him:

Just. Breathe.

Two steps from the top.

One.

Matt alighted on the second story proper and moved the flashlight across the hall: two rooms to the right, one on the left and a final door at the far end.

"Sheriff's Department. If anyone is here, I need you to identify yourself."

That was better. His breath flowed, his voice emboldened by it, no cracking this time.

The first door on the right was an office. Jim Harrison's diplomas hung framed on the wall, along with his registration with the Tennessee Bar Association. An outdated computer took up most of a large, antique desk. The screen faced away from him, but in the dark, the intermittent light of moving images flickered on the far wall. Matt circled to the other side, where a fractal screensaver danced its mathematical jig. Cautiously, he tapped the keyboard and the screensaver flickered away, revealing a messenger thread between Harrison and, of all people, one H. Landing:

> I have Gerald's daughter. Misty is dead. Are you equipped to deal with this yet?

> We talked about this. I've had a lot of police activity here lately. What exactly should I do if that deputy shows up looking for her?

> You said Lisa was the one who brought him the last time. Why would he show up without her?

You're putting me in a position I have not
been compensated for.

Ah, there it is. Money - the only thing you
ever think about. Very well. I'll have Inoue
transfer you another ten thousand. How's
that sound?

I'm on my way with an ambulance. If anyone
asks, we say Lisa went nuts and killed Misty
right in front of you.

As he read, Matt unconsciously began to back away from the screen.

"Vic?" he called, his voice cracking again. The world was spinning out of control; reading two town elders' candid, private conversation and finding this... it amounted to a kind of apocalypse. Here was proof of the conspiracy Lisa had insisted upon for months, the same one Matt had denounced as paranoia inspired by recent events. If Lisa was right, if the danger went this deep into the town's socio-political strata, who else might be involved?

"Matt," the voice startled him, and Matt turned so quickly he almost lost his balance. Behind him, Sheriff McCready stood in the doorway, his revolver drawn. "Gonna need you to toss me your weapon and put your hands behind your head."

———

As she struggled with the rope, Lisa's palms continued to bleed, lubricating her grip until the threaded fibers began to slip from her grasp.

"No! No! I will not let you out, you bastard!" She held on until she sensed a lull from the other end, then dropped the rope, wiped her hands on her pants and snatched it back off the floor just in time to catch it as Philip yanked the door open a crack.

"What's the matter, Lisa Lisa?" Philip's reptilian snarl sent shivers down her spine. "You hurt your wittle hands? Hurts bad, I hope. Ain't the least of what you're gonna get when I'm outta here."

"Fuck you!"

Lisa gave the rope an unexpected jerk and the door slammed again, this time directly on Philip's finger. He screamed and fought to pull the digit back through; once he had, Lisa finally cinched the knot on the handle behind her. She tied it good - Gerald had taught her several intricate knots, and she used one of those now, as Philip pounded on the door, howling like a rabid animal. Lisa closed her eyes and took a deep breath, Miss Galdykas's mantra running on repeat inside her head:

Just. Breathe.

She imagined every cell in her body inflating with nourishing oxygen, dozens of strength lights winking on, recharging her batteries. Unfortunately, another voice broke this recharge.

"Hey!" Lisa's eyes opened and she saw two men at the far end of the hallway.

Panic reclaimed her; she took off down the corridor, deeper into the hospital's abandoned third floor. She could hear Philip screaming for release as the new arrivals struggled to free him. This bought her enough time to round the corner at the end of the hall. Unfortunately, there were no more rooms, just a large window at the far end. Lisa didn't break stride, picking up momentum as she heard a single set of steps gaining behind her.

"Where you gonna go, bitch?" her pursuer challenged, but Lisa already knew where she was going to go.

Out.

———

"Sheriff, we have to hurry! Harrison's in on whatever the hell is happening here. I think he killed Misty Bradley and brought Lisa to Mather's. I think Nurse Landing is helping him."

"Matt, I ain't gonna say this again; toss me your weapon."

Matt stared at McCready in disbelief.

"You're in on this, too, aren't you?"

"If you mean stopping David Bradley, then yeah, I'm in on it."

"What about Lisa?"

"Lisa's fine. Deputy, I am losing my patience. I'm not gonna ask again: drop your goddamn weapon. Now!"

———

Lisa leaped directly at the window, twisting midair so her shoulder went through the glass first. The pane shattered into dozens of pieces, breaking away enough that what few cuts she suffered were fleeting, the shards all flowing outward from her momentum.

Once through, however, the world fell away. Lisa dropped at a quick angle and landed on the rough shingles of one of the eaves. She rolled, her momentum working against her, so it was only with sheer luck and a blind grab that she caught a box vent and managed to hold on and not fall three stories to what would surely have been a bone-crushing death.

The roof here was steep. She'd come out one of the dormers that dotted this more ornate, angular section; ten feet to Lisa's right, the surface flattened out above what she assumed was the hallway she'd just run through. If she could reach that, she might have a chance.

Lisa stretched her right hand up toward the bottom of the

pane she'd come through, but just before she let go of the vent supporting her, a slight preparatory shift in her weight broke the rotted wood off in her hand. She caught herself instantly, but the adrenaline pounding in her ears prevented her from focusing on anything but falling. Lisa's left hand clutched dramatically to the vent while her right still grasped the broken piece of window sill.

"Hot damn, you are one lucky bitch, know that?"

Andre the orderly beamed down at her, his upper body halfway out the window. Consumed by hopeless rage, Lisa swung the board up and around, connecting with the left side of Andre's face; there must have been a nail on the side that collided with his flesh because Andre let out a loud, shrill scream and disappeared back inside with the board hanging from his face like the ribbon tail on a paper donkey. Simultaneously, a loud explosion muffled everything but a high-pitched whine. Lisa flinched and felt a sudden searing pain in her right side, even as something slid down the shingles and slammed into her chest. Barely hanging on, she looked down and realized Andre's gun now lay between the roof and her midsection.

Had she been shot?

It seemed impossible, but she could smell gunpowder and blood; with incredible care, Lisa set about crooking her arm to retrieve the gun from where it rested. Meanwhile, the fingers on her right hand were turning numb, the edge of the vent digging so deeply into her flesh, the circulation had expired.

"Come on... come on..."

She retrieved the gun just as Philip stuck his head out the window.

"You're gonna get it now, bi-"

Lisa threw her arm up and squeezed the trigger. She missed, but the shot sent the little coward scurrying back inside amidst a string of curses. She'd bought herself a few seconds but realized as the recoil sent her sliding straight for the edge.

———

"Okay Sheriff, whatever you say."

Matt slowly lowered his handgun to the floor, cursing himself.

"Now kick it over to me. Slowly."

Matt did as he was told. Sheriff McCready bent down to pick up the gun and Vic appeared behind him in the doorway, a rolling pin raised above his head. The floor creaked as Vic's weight shifted into the wind-up, giving away his presence. McCready turned and got off a single shot that hit Vic in the leg and sent him flying backward, the kitchen utensil falling to the floor. As the Sheriff recovered, Matt dove for him, caught the hand with the gun and snapped it over his knee like a piece of kindling. McCready let out a painful scream and, caught in the moment, Matt punched him so hard in the face the Sheriff fell to the floor, unconscious.

Instantly, Matt ran to Vic.

"You're hit!"

"I'm okay. Bullet glanced my leg."

Matt rolled Vic onto his side and checked the accuracy of his diagnosis.

"Jesus H. Christ, you are one lucky motherfucker."

"Guess so. What the fuck's up with your boss, bro?"

In spite of himself, Matt laughed.

"That's what I aim to find out."

Matt took his cuffs, rolled McCready onto his stomach and secured his arms behind his back. Next, he found the Sheriff's cuffs, his knife, and the telescopic baton he carried in a pouch on his belt.

"Can you walk?"

"I can limp."

"Okay then. Grab his legs. I'm taking him to go."

"What about me?"

"I can drop you along the way. Where's your car?"

"Fuck that. Too much time," Vic produced a small, black plastic fob. "I can take Misty's."

"Okay. You know where the State Police HQ is?"

"Out past Exit ten?"

"Yeah. Go there and ask for Roy Ayers. Tell him Matt Hartman said we need as many men as they can spare."

"Where?"

"Mather's. I'm going to get Lisa."

———

Contrary to what she would have guessed, Lisa's body did not pick up speed as it slid toward the edge of the Sanitarium's roof; instead, the sticky, granulated texture of the shingles created such friction that she slowed enough to catch a small hole in the surface and stop herself entirely. Shaking from exertion, it took a moment for Lisa to steady herself enough to lift her chin and peer up toward the window.

No sign of her attackers.

Not necessarily a good thing.

Looking around, she spotted another hole within grasping distance; Lisa caught that with little effort and used it to hoist herself up and over to another box vent. From there, she employed great caution as she scaled up another ten feet or so with the help of make-shift steps created where shingles had pulled away enough to give her a hold. After several minutes of intense physical exertion, she reached the roof's apex. Straddling the divide, Lisa waited. Her calves ached from traversing the steep grade. The night was cold and eerily quiet, and Lisa could hear footsteps in the building below her. Holding the revolver in both shaking hands, Lisa kept her attention focused on the next attack; when would it come?

Minutes ticked by. Lisa thought back to her twelfth birthday, dad taking her to the range, the thought that she might one day have to actually shoot someone never occurring to her. Did one of these scumbags kill Ashley? Were they responsible for murdering Bill and the others at the fire pit? She thought about the intruder she had killed in her home; the feeling was empowering, made her want to do the same to these three pukes.

The sound of a window opening broke her introspection; the chill night air made goose flesh of her arms. The mounting terror of the inevitable attack ravaged her brain and her eyes began to water with terrible expectations. She leveled the gun at the edge of the roof before her and waited. Where were they? Why didn't they just show themselves? The waiting proved almost unbearable. She began to move a bit, relinquishing the apex by sliding across the shingles on her ass, feet, and the palms of her hands. A shuffle, really, as she tried to squeeze a little more of a vantage point from her position. Closer and closer until the shingle under her left foot came loose. Lisa lost her balance and her leg slid out from under her, but again, she recovered quickly. Shaken, she realized she would receive no respite as Philip's tattooed hands appeared over the apex of the roof.

"Come on, you bastard!"

"How 'bout me, bitch!"

The voice came from her left, and Lisa turned to see another orderly had somehow snuck up behind her. She stood and tried to raise the gun in his direction, but she moved too fast and there wasn't enough clearance between her and the roof; the barrel of the gun bounced off the shingles and slipped from Lisa's hand. It hit the roof at a slide that Lisa stopped by hooking her left leg out and catching the weapon against her shin. Only now, her attacker's hands were closer to the gun than she was. There was a moment when their eyes met just before the orderly pulled a total Hail Mary and dove for Lisa's leg. At the same time, Lisa kicked up and out; the gun flew backward, hitting her in the shoulder and once again coming to rest between her chest and the roof; simultaneously, she caught the bastard under the chin, disrupting his balance and sending him careening over the edge.

No sooner had he fallen than Lisa turned to see Philip nearly on top of her.

"I'm gonna kill the fuck outta you!"

"You think?"

She was up by two and feeling cocky because of it.

Philip didn't respond; he simply continued climbing toward her. Behind him, another hand came into view, reaching through the window and gripping the roof's edge.

Lisa freed one hand, rocked to the right and, although nearing the end of her strength, was able to snatch the gun and lift it enough to put Philip even with the business end. Bracing herself, Lisa pulled the trigger.

Nothing happened.

"Stupid bitch! Got you now!"

Philip's excitement got the better of him; he'd crab-walked down and now windmilled his arms past his head one at a time, planting his palms so that once he brought his torso around, his face was less than a foot from Lisa's.

"Got you!" he said triumphantly, grasping for her. Lisa reared her head back just enough at the last minute that Philip missed, leaving him off balance and unprepared when she whipped the revolver directly at his face. It connected with a sharp CRACK. A moment later, he lost his balance and fell face-first onto the shingles. Lisa turned back toward the edge and carefully made her way down, hoping she could use the gutters to lower herself to a second-floor window. Once at the edge, however, she was too rushed to safely discern how to lower herself. She planted her bottom, used her hands and feet to begin slowly lowering herself. She was almost there when a sound behind her caused her to snap her neck around just in time to see Philip reaching for her. This time, he succeeded; Lisa struggled but couldn't shake him. Desperate beyond measure, she whipped her head from right to left as hard as she could; Philip instantly lost his balance and fell sprawling toward her. He slammed into her legs, still holding her hair, and an instant later, Lisa felt herself slide out into the open air.

———

They were five minutes out from Mather's when Sheriff McCready regained consciousness.

"You really fucked up this time, Deputy."

"Good morning to you, too, sunshine."

"You outta your goddamned mind, Matt?

"I could ask you the same, Sheriff. My big question, though, is why you don't think Jim Harrison would harm your daughter if he killed Misty Bradley."

"You don't understand what you're getting yourself into, Deputy. I know you care for Lisa; that's the only reason I didn't shoot you back at Jim's. You're not even on the goddamn clock!"

"Yeah, well, can't punch out while someone's in danger. Pretty sure you told me that once upon a time."

"She is not in danger! How many times do I have to say it?"

"How many times do I have to ask you why you're so sure?"

For a moment, it seemed like McCready was about to

spill, but he kept his mouth shut, staring past Matt and out the windshield as the cruiser pulled onto the long driveway that led up to Mather's gates.

Matt stopped at the talk box, rolled down his window and pressed the buzzer.

"They're not going to buzz you in."

"We're in your truck, not mine."

Almost three minutes passed before Matt saw the camera mounted to the top of the gate swivel toward them. He put up the window just in time to make sure whoever was observing them would see the Sheriff's truck but not who was driving. A moment later, the gates lurched open.

"Bingo."

"Matt, I'm telling you again, do not do this. You're getting involved with things you don't understand."

"Look Sheriff, I know that I love your daughter, okay? I have since High School. And I know she's in trouble."

"For the last goddamn time, she is not in trouble! I told Jim to bring her here! They're protecting her from David Bradley's people!"

The cruiser came around the final bend in the massive, winding drive just as two people fell from the roof, landing on the overgrown grass to their right.

"What the hell was that?"

"Oh my god! That was Lisa!"

Matt rushed to where Lisa lay sprawled across the broken body of a man covered in tattoos.

"Lisa!"

She didn't answer. From the truck, Sheriff McCready screamed for an update, the raw fury in his voice echoing across the otherwise quiet grounds. Within moments, the front doors opened and several staff members came out, batons and tasers ready to go.

"What happened here?" a tall woman with long, raven-black hair demanded. Matt recognized the voice, but it took him a minute to realize he was looking at Helen Landing, dressed in tall leather riding boots, black jeans and a torn t-shirt that sported a bright red pentagram. Her hair was down, her face painted with flourishes of makeup: equally red lipstick, eyeliner, rouge. The look was pure cringe - an older, slightly haggard woman trying to look twenty.

Behind them, the Sheriff began screaming Helen's name, howling in anger. She ignored him the same as Matt.

"I asked you a question!" Matt turned to engage and realized Helen wasn't talking to him; instead, she bullied an orderly he'd seen on a previous visit to the facility. The man, probably ten years Matt's senior, had a gaping hole in the side of his face that oozed blood continuously despite his attempts to staunch the flow with a dirty white rag.

"Philip said we was just gonna scare her. We didn't think..."

Matt turned back toward Lisa; as soon as he did, a gunshot shook the world. Instinctively, he grabbed for his gun, but someone planted a heavy boot in his lower back and sent him sprawling across the lawn. He rolled over to see the orderly on his back, bleeding from a gut shot Nurse Landing had administered with a snub-nosed .38.

"Let that be a lesson to the rest of you. Now help me get this mess inside."

Matt opened his mouth to respond, to take charge of the situation. As he did, something collided with the side of his head and the world drained into a black, featureless swamp.

CHAPTER TWENTY

He lay in the shallows of consciousness on the cruiser's back seat. Voices filtered through the windows, and despite the opaque, hollow sound the glass added, Matt recognized the two men and could easily discern the woman.

"Why are you here? You're supposed to be preparing your victory speech."

"I never said I would run."

"Yes you did. Yes he did."

"No, I didn't, Jim."

"Then why are you here?"

"I'm here, Helen, because my Deputy knocked me cold, handcuffed me and brought me along in a frenzy, thinking he had to save my daughter from the likes of you."

"You know I would never hurt Lisa, Gerald."

"Do I, Jim? Which one of you blew Misty Bradley's face off? Or was it the overly ambitious Deputy Wilson?"

"You really have some trouble controlling your staff, don't you, Sheriff?"

"No more than you apparently do, Helen. That was one of

yours who broke my girl's fall, right? That the same scumbag that's been molesting patients? I told you to get a goddamn handle on that."

"Problem appears solved from here."

"Is it? Who's gonna clean up Jim's house before someone finds it?"

"Oh relax. No one comes to see me. At this point, I'm little more than the town's pity case. People just want to forget I exist until the funeral."

"Way I see it, Sheriff, Jim did you a favor."

"How so?"

"With David ineligible to run, you're a shoo-in for Mayor."

"How can I say this more plainly, folks? I'm. Not. Running. By the look of things, I'm thinking of just taking Lisa and -"

"Take her where? You going to run away, Gerald? Didn't your childhood teach you anything?"

"What the hell's that supposed to mean, Jim?"

Matt could hear every word. They didn't seem too concerned talking in front of him, which probably meant they were planning to kill him. He thought of the woman lying dead at the station, how if the Sheriff knew about her, it might give him a bargaining chip. Then he realized the Sheriff no longer deserved his help. Whatever was transpiring here, he marked McCready as much a problem as the others.

How do you wipe the slate on a community's leaders and start over?

You don't. They wipe the slate of you.

"Do you know how easy it was to find you? There's nowhere you can go on this Earth that we can't track you. Geist-Wihelm is global."

"So that's who's really pulling the strings here then, eh?"

"Not in the way you think. Samson Bradley tapped into something others already knew about. There's a network that spans the globe."

"A Satanic Underground, eh?"

"Underground? Gerald, we run *everything*. This is the way of the world, so unless you're planning on hiring a shuttle to Mars, you better fall in line. Capiche?"

A global Satanic conspiracy? Lisa had been right from the jump and he'd dismissed her. She had even downplayed things, but here it was, larger than life. A chill passed over Matt as he pondered meeting a violent end before ever really knowing the world for its true self. If all this was real, what else? UFOs? Atlantis? God? The thoughts proved staggering.

"You think because you're six months out from a pine box I won't arrest you for murder? Two murders? Think again."

Two murders?

"Careful, Gerald. We're your only friends now. I can easily turn the people of this town against you *and* your daughter."

"Where is my daughter? Your orderly threw her off the goddamn roof-"

"Oh please. It looked to me like your daughter was the one who sent two members of my staff plunging to their deaths, not the other way around."

"Good for her."

Matt could hear the smile in McCready's voice.

"It's all water under the bridge now, Gerald. Or at least, it can be."

"So what do you suggest I do?"

"Accept your fate, seize the election and take control of the company. I'll kill David myself."

"What the hell do I know about oil, Jim? I'm not even a full-blooded Bradley."

"You have the paternal blood; that's all that matters. I

tried years ago, all for nothing! Our family made the same pact as Samson, but we get nothing!"

"Boo-fucking hoo."

"Your mother-"

"Stop! Don't say it. Don't sully my mother's name, goddamnit."

"You're looking at it backward, Gerald. This wasn't some untoward act. Roland was removed from power as both CEO and Mayor. I took over, had him sequestered at Mather's. He was only the third Patriarch since Samson enacted the bargain that created the Egregore, and already the spell was broken in him? We didn't know what we were dealing with. There were requests the creature made that we were... uncomfortable with; did it renege on the deal because of our aspirations? I tried to align my family, my blood, but it didn't work. The fucking Egregore took Nancy Walters' blood but not mine! But you, Gerald, you're my ace."

"Fuck you, Jim. I'm nobody's goddamn ace!"

Matt heard the unmistakable sound of a revolver cock.

"Oh, but you are. It's what I brought you here for; to help me pull off the greatest coup since Samson Bradley turned a barren farm into a billion dollars almost overnight."

"You're wasting our time. Whether you know it or not, you will cooperate by night's end. Lisa's already being prepped for transport."

"Bastards..."

"We're all bastards, Gerald. The entire human race. Our creator skipped town, so we side with the powers that can grant us a modicum of solace in an otherwise heinous existence."

"We still have a piece of unfinished business here, boys," Helen's voice suddenly sounded so close to Matt's ear that he flinched and rolled over only to come face to face with her homely countenance.

"I knew you were playing possum! Doesn't matter now. Nighty nite, pretty."

The impact as Helen drove the syringe into the soft flesh of Matt's neck nearly short-circuited his brain; he felt the plunger go in, and seconds later, Lisa's name spiraled with him down into the realms of the unconscious.

CHAPTER TWENTY-ONE

Helen Landing had known the Bradley brothers since High School. She hated them both, hated the entire Bradley family.

First, Helen resented that no one would ever mistake her for being roughly the same age as David or Michael, both of who appeared to have stopped aging at thirty. Helen looked ten years older, *at least*. There'd been the cancer, which she beat but which took a piece of her in the process. Nearly three decades at Mather's had done the most damage, but what else could be expected, spending day after day in a place where pain, frustration and sadness were full-time occupants? And while these emotions were little more than hor d'oeuvres to the entities the Bradleys did business with, to everyone else, they were toxic. Despite all this, or maybe because of it, Helen's abilities to compartmentalize and persevere impressed David. In exchange for her assistance with certain matters, he'd introduced her to the healing powers of bathing in the blood of teenage girls.

How many had the health system brought her over the last year? As the only State-subsidized mental Hospital in three counties, there proved a nearly constant influx, especially as marijuana use became normalized and the grass got more and more powerful. Stupid little fools smoked themselves into oblivion, some of them unable to come down. Court-assigned to Helen's care, it proved startlingly easy to disappear the occasional patient. They came in as runaways and Jane Does, black sheep and castoffs. Helen diagnosed them as dangerous and sent them straight to her little shop of horrors on the third floor. From there, some simply never returned.

Unfortunately, like any other medicine, she'd accrued something of a tolerance, and supply no longer met Helen's demand. When confronted about this, David promised her power, wealth and renewed vitality once he was back in charge of the Egregore.

That was three years ago. Helen grew tired of empty promises and, sensing greener pastures, had helped Jim Harrison see to it that David's ship had sailed.

Sitting in the passenger seat of the hospital's dirty black in-take van, Helen watched dark grey thunderheads roll in across the sky. With them came a balmy breeze uncharacteristic for early November. A positive omen, no doubt and Helen took a final deep breath of ionized air before rolling up her window. Even with the cover of night Helen's skin crawled at the possibility of being seen riding in such a utilitarian vehicle. Hence the windows' heavy custom tint.

In her own mind, Helen ranked higher than her social status dictated. The town itself held her down, as despite nearly ten years as Hospital Director, Helen remained an undesirable among the local glitterati, demonstrated time and again by everyone from the hospital board to her patients' refusal to extricate the word "Nurse" from its union to her name.

"Nurse Landing, you're over budget." "Nurse Landing,

Philip touched me." "Nurse Landing, why are you covered in blood?"

Helen longed to show the world who she really was, to let her hair down, fuck half the men in town, and pull up to City Hall in a brand new Tesla Model X just like the one that spoiled brat Misty Bradley drove.

'Hell,' she thought. 'Maybe I can just take her car. She certainly won't be needing it anymore.'

Wealth, power and renewed vitality. These were the things promised to Helen, and tonight, finally, she would collect.

Only, if she was being honest, the night slipped increasingly 'off script,' a fact that did not bode well. If tonight went tits up, the cancer would end Jim's misery within a few weeks. Helen, on the other hand, would be stranded in this life she hated; she'd never own a Tesla, never buy a house in Artisan's Ridge, never be granted the vestigial youth she deserved. The more she thought about it, how could she bank anything on a man who had six months to live at most?

Good thing, then, that Helen had made other plans.

CHAPTER TWENTY-TWO

When she woke, Lisa knew right away she was at Peppermill. The smell of marijuana felt overpowering, further fogging the memories that washed over her like a lazy current over sand. She'd landed on Philip and felt his body break upon impact. She thought she remembered hearing Matt's voice before cold, uncaring hands picked her up and moved her back into the hospital. As if all her fears during her stay here were realized.

"Once you're here, you can never leave, Lisa Lisa."

The memory of Philip's hands on her felt so close, so fresh, that Lisa jerked from her stupor and nearly fell from the cold steel table upon which she'd been placed. She calmed as the memory receded, replaced by vague images of being zipped inside a translucent bag and transported in a van. Which brought her back to the here and now.

"Why did they bring me here?"

Lisa began to assess her surroundings. She was in a small room with metal walls and overhead lights that emanated heat. A grow room, perhaps?

A small panel with knobs and buttons on the wall by the

only door caught her attention. She tried to sit up but received a further shock when she found she couldn't feel anything below her waist.

"Oh god, no. No, please..."

She tried lifting her legs with her hands, but neither responded as she pulled one after the other free. They were dead.

Lisa began to scream.

———

When Matt opened his eyes, he lay against the wall in a dark room. A chill nipped the air; it rose through his backside, ran the length of his spine and emanated out into his arms, turning his fingertips numb, like icicles forming beneath his nails. He felt hung-over, his tongue a foreign object forcefully inserted into his mouth. His disorientation disappeared behind the image of Lisa lying broken on the grass as his memory returned to him.

Matt steeled himself, tried to will his eyes to acclimate to the dim light. Eventually, he could almost make sense of his surroundings.

The floor was filthy cement and slightly canted toward the center of the room, which, from what he could see, couldn't have been more than 10' x 10.' A shape directly to his left startled him. A closer look revealed a pair of damp coveralls hanging from a hook on the wall. There were more of these, too, hanging at odd intervals. Piles of blankets or rags dotted the area at his feet. Large, moldering cardboard boxes lined one wall. Further on, a bike rack held several 80s-style BMX bikes upright.

As he found his bearings, Matt saw the room proved larger than he first estimated; a fuzzy blue light in the distance showed where the walls narrowed to a long, open corridor. This was a basement or cellar, someplace people did not frequent. A room beneath the world where he had been left for dead.

The events that landed him here returned, rearranged by trauma. The iron taste of blood filled his mouth, intertwined with the memory of seeing Lisa fall from the roof, her body twisted as he pleaded with whatever sorry excuse he still had for a god to please let her be okay. Then Helen Landing, her flunkies, the Sheriff, all before the world dipped into darkness. Matt swished his tongue over his teeth and realized part of the soft, squishy organ was missing. He'd bitten it off.

Disfigured

He retched, his late lunch pooling around fingers pressed flat on the cool cement floor. Bloody drool hanging from his chin, Matt felt close to collapse when the sound of crying jumpstarted his sense of purpose.

Matt was one of those Police Officers who wholeheartedly believed in the "To Protect and Serve" motto.

"Hello? Ish shomeone there?"

Matt did not recognize his own voice, which came out with an intense lisp, the result of his damaged tongue.

"Thish ish Deputy Matt Hartman with the Shheriff's Department. Are you okay?"

Matt's only reply was a wet, gurgling sound; hearing it produced a visible tremor of disgust.

"If you can, shtate your name."

A pause induced by effort, from the sound of it. Then: "Please..."

Matt didn't recognize the voice, strained as it was by the sounds of distress; the owner must be injured, choking on blood, fighting for every breath. Something vile bubbled up in the back of his brain, something he'd been fighting his entire life. Something working for the Sheriff's department was supposed to alleviate.

Disfigured, discarded, disaster of a person.

Sundown Hills' happy facade hid a terrible evil because this was the reality of not just the world but all humanity. The conversation he'd heard earlier proved this without a doubt. The man who'd shot Matt's father hadn't been a gangbanger or murderer but a white-collar stockbroker high on crystal meth and disgruntled at whatever rich people found to be disgruntled about. Worse, Matt knew his family's tragedy was nothing new or extraordinary. The evil was indicative of the nasty wound where civilization used to stand, now just a facade, a pretense to move undetected among the sheep. Matt was starting to believe that the evil was wealth itself.

These thoughts triggered his anger, seething like a cigarette smoked to the filter. It pushed out the final dregs of his disorientation; he dragged himself toward the voice and saw a mangled human form against the far wall, a shattered bag of bones. Stooping, Matt was not prepared for what he found, and he fell back onto his ass in the throes of absolute repulsion.

The kid was Freddy Snow, one of Vic's cohorts. His right eye was missing, the socket open and leaking dark fluid down the right side of his face where the hollow of Freddy's cheek had been torn open to expose the rear of his bite like a skull or particularly nasty Jack O' Lantern. More wounds covered his neck and shoulders, and three fingers sprouted jagged flesh and bone where they'd been crudely severed. Scattered around him were the half-chewed corpses of rats, one the size of a small dog.

"Freddy. Freddy, pleashe, talk to me."

"..."

"Lishen to me. You're going to be okay. I'm gonna getsh you outta here."

Freddy didn't respond, didn't even move. Matt couldn't tell if he was alive or dead.

Chills ran through Matt as he turned and grabbed the coveralls he'd spotted earlier, began to tear the legs into strips.

"Shay shomething. Pshease, shay something."

Matt cradled the kid's head in the crook of his left arm to work the first strip over the wound, wrapping it around his shaggy head to cover the hole completely. As he did, he jumped when a cockroach crawled out of the empty socket where Freddy's eye had previously resided.

"Jeshush Chrish!"

Freddy began to convulse. For a second, Matt was sure the kid *was laughing*, a dry, sick sound punctuated by regular hacking stabs that led directly into a seizure.

"Hold on, dammit!"

Matt tried to work his arm around him again, but the hacking fit became so violent that harnessing it proved impossible. A moment later, it stopped and whatever was left of Freddy Snow went with it.

"Fuck," he screamed at the darkness while pounding on Freddy's chest.

"You're wasting your time, dickhead. Wouldn't you wanna die if you looked like that?"

Matt turned to see Burke Lamb standing before him, holding a mini chainsaw. His black T-shirt sopped with dark stains of ichor.

"C'mon deputy. Don't choo think it's about time to drop all this hero bullshit?"

CHAPTER TWENTY-THREE

Staring down at her lifeless legs, Lisa flashed on something Mr. Harrison had said:

"I hit what some call rock bottom. I remember one night, I actually contemplated whether your father would adopt Annie if I killed myself."

Had everything that man told her been a lie? Either way, Lisa understood this particular sentiment because, nestled within the realization she'd been crippled in the fall, she very much wanted to die.

After an indiscernible amount of time, two men in camouflage masks entered. They pushed a rickety wooden wheelchair, the type that hadn't been used in hospitals since the early Twentieth Century. The stockier of the two strung a filthy pillow case over Lisa's head and tied it with a cord, while the other stuck a syringe in her neck. She flinched as the needle emptied its viscous load into her vein.

"Hurts, huh?" the administer growled, snapping the needle off inside her.

Lisa shrieked.

They lifted her onto the wheelchair and tied her ankles and wrists to the wood with knots so tight they cut off her circulation. Her fight gone, Lisa gagged on foul cigarette breathe as one of them hissed directly into her face:

"Too tight? Too bad. This is for killing my friends, you fucking bitch."

The sound of the metal door scraping against the rocky floor as it opened was followed by an inrush of cool air and the unmistakable stench of pot plants. Time lapsed as they began to move, Lisa's consciousness wavering on the precipice of some unknown event. Purple flooded her, Lisa's body dumping what remained of the drug in her system, a triggered response to her fear. She felt waves of caustic energy in her fingertips, eyelids, and teeth. She swam in it, a literal sea of black marbled by purple waves that lapped at the shores of Lisa's unconscious mind.

She wasn't sure how long she surged with those waves, but eventually, she fought her way ashore. A tall, spindly figure with mismatched limbs waited for her there. Lisa could not make out the figure's face.

You are stronger than any who have come before you. You are perfect

I don't understand

Then listen and take heed: it works both ways, Lisa McCready-Bradley. Give me what I want and you will be more powerful than all those before you.

———

Bathed in the blue light of the narrow corridor, Matt let Freddy Snow's body slip from his grasp. The corpse crumpled like a sack of rags against the concrete wall. Casting a person off like dead weight bothered Matt, but there was no time for such sensitivities; he had to invoke the badass he'd briefly summoned in the Harrison house earlier - and then some.

Matt straightened to his full height, which was still five inches or so shorter than Burke Lamb, one-time regional High School Wrestling champion. The pictures of him with his medals still adorned Sundown High's Health and Athletics Department office; Matt had seen them every day during his senior year when he'd helped his school bring in a first-place trophy. He raised his right hand and realized he still clutched the torn coveralls, the only thing he possessed for the stand he was about to make.

"You can't fucking do thish to people. I'm not going to let you get away with thish."

"Oh yeah? Maybe if you could see yourself, you'd stop talkin' so brave. Only thing you're gonna do is die, same as that boy right there."

Burke raised the small chainsaw and ripped once at the starter cord.

"Cheap piece'a foreign bullshit!"

Matt stole a deep breath, pushed his fear into a tiny ball and took off straight at Lamb. The older man ripped the cord again and reared back as the chainsaw roared to life.

"Come ta poppa, bitch!"

Matt slowed his charge, waited until Burke's shoulders shifted right, stopped shy and let the older man's downward swing fall short. Before Burke could bring the saw up again, Matt snapped the coveralls at the blade and the gnarled fabric caught in the teeth. Even as the thick material shredded, the motor faltered from the resistance. The saw's whine pitch-shifted an octave higher, the motor working overtime to untangle itself. This threw Burke off balance, and when he tried to pivot to accommodate the stalling saw, Matt went straight for the man's crotch, catching Burke's genitals in both hands before tearing out and away in opposite directions.

Burke Lamb unleashed a sound unlike any Matt had ever heard.

Not about to waste the advantage, Matt drove a fist upward into Burke's chin, sending him stumbling backward against the wall. The saw clattered to the floor, spinning and kicking as the denim continued to choke and tangle the chain.

Burke met Matt's eyes just long enough to see his attention land on the out-of-control weapon. Pushing up from his left side, Burke threw himself toward the tool, landing on his belly with his left hand extended. He missed the handle by less than an inch, and Matt cinched his victory by kicking the saw toward his opponent, who caught its slow but still spinning blade in the face. Burke's momentary surprise delayed his screams, but before Matt was steady on his feet again, the maniac's voice turned to inhuman squelches and gurgles. These didn't last long; the saw tore through Burke's flesh and shattered the skull beneath into dozens of pieces, reducing his once surly visage to a steaming stew of muscle and sinew left to puddle at Matt's feet.

What do you want?

A body, Lisa McCready-Bradley

The shoreline figure felt closer now, almost transposed on top of her. Lisa closed her eyes and scanned past the glowing purple eyes and swirling darkness that obscured its features. Something so familiar about the shape of its shoulders, head and hair...

It works both ways, the voice said again. This vast interiority within began to blossom, taking on the shape of the house she'd grown up in as modified by her recent dreams.

To her left, sunlight poured through the picture window in the front room. The light made Lisa feel exposed, so she stepped inside and closed the large purple drapes. A noise behind her announced someone descending the staircase. She turned; their shape looked... familiar.

Blood and tissue flex before you. They are a door, now open. You need only walk through...

"Lisa? Lisa honey?"

The voice snapped the vision and immediately brought Lisa screaming back to the present. Even with the bag on her head, she knew who now stood before her; she'd heard his voice every day for nearly eighteen years.

"Dad?"

"I'm here, honey. Please, settle down. Everything's going to be all right. Those look awful tight."

She felt him loosen the straps restricting her arms and legs. Loosen, but not undo. Her own father!

Lisa's blood ignited, and she began to thrash in anger.

"Take this fucking bag off my head, you bastard!"

"Now Lisa, please, hear me out..."

The broken needle still lodged inside her pushed and pulled against the tender flesh of Lisa's neck while her head lolled back and forth in a rejoinder of anger that pulverized great chunks of the girl created over the last eighteen years. In that girl's place, something new began to emerge.

"Take this fucking bag off my head!" she screamed again, but she knew her demands would go unanswered.

"Are you okay? Have they hurt you?"

Lisa's incredulity at the question made her voice sharp and broken.

"You saw, didn't you? You must have."

"I saw you fall..."

"You saw them throw me off the fucking roof!" The last four words climbed to a shrieking crescendo of fury that made Gerald visibly flinch.

"Lisa..."

"Don't! Get away from me, you fucking piece of shit!"

"Watch your goddamn mouth-"

"You've been involved in this from the beginning! From the fucking beginning! What is this Horror-show world you brought me into?"

"James was supposed to keep you safe while -"

"Oh, give me a fucking break! I know we're related to the Bradleys and that this entire ordeal is centered around a power struggle for control of whatever terrifying *thing* Samson Bradley conjured from Hell and used to build his empire!"

For once, Gerald McCready stood speechless. He didn't know how Lisa had discovered the things she accused him of, but he knew better than to lie in the face of such bold truth. Instead, she heard him choke back a sob as he turned to leave.

"Coward!" Lisa screamed when she heard the heavy iron door opening. "I hope you fucking die! I hope someone cuts out your fucking coward's heart! I'd take it as a trophy if I could!"

In the aftermath of the encounter, Lisa sat shaking. After a few moments, she heard her father's voice again, this time just outside the door.

"Fuck you."

"Gerald, you have to believe me. Those men were acting on their own, I would never-"

Lisa recognized the voice instantly: James Harrison.

"You sick fuck. What did I tell you? This is exactly why I didn't want to have any part in this. You killed your own daughter; expect me to-"

Lisa's brain crashed. Jim Harrison murdered Annie? Her heart burst into flames. Truly, the world as she knew it was a lie, a mask to cover the putrefaction that festered at the center of reality.

Blood and tissue flex before you. They are a door, now open. You need only walk through...

It works both ways...

Suddenly, Lisa understood exactly what it was that worked both ways.

CHAPTER TWENTY-FOUR

Once Matt left the room where Freddy Snow had died behind, he found himself impossibly lost. The door opened onto a corridor lit by intermittent brackets of HID lights fixed to the natural seam separating the rough-hewn ceiling and wall. The air stank of pot plants, thus confirming Harrison had indeed moved the party to Peppermill. Standing outside the room, Matt saw the corridor snaked off into darkness in either direction. Which way and, more importantly, how far? He'd been down here once before when the Sheriff attempted to close down the tunnels he suspected Vic and Burke used to move drugs around town. As far as he knew, they ran beneath most of Sundown Hills.

Matt didn't have time for that; he couldn't move past the feeling that with every second he wasted, Lisa's death loomed larger on the horizon. Then, something occurred to him, and he stepped back into the room that smelled like an abattoir. He'd almost forgotten the bikes racked against one wall. Five total, but two had flat tires. Of the remaining three, Matt was surprised to find a Raleigh MK1 almost identical to the one he'd rode as a kid.

"No way!"

He attempted to remove the bike from the rack and realized all five were locked together with an industrial-strength chain. Turning back toward where Burke lay in a veritable sea of gore, Matt realized this would not present a problem.

After making short work of his obstacle, Matt wheeled the bike past the corpses and out into the corridor. He mentally flipped a coin, then hopped on and began to pedal with fury to the left, his knuckles white from his grip on the handlebars. He just hoped he wasn't too late.

————

When Lisa emerged from her inner space, she did so with a new-found calm. The bag still on her head, she held her breath and listened intently. The only sound was a constant lush dripping.

'Underground,' she thought. Likely, she was inside whatever Sanctum Sanctorum Samson Bradley built for his kin to continue the legacy of evil he'd begun in 1866. Was this where Frank O'Sullivan had tried to take her that night in the drainage tunnel? Had he been trying to lead her to this fate, too? Was everyone in town gunning for her?

Aren't you glad you helped burn down his fucking house?

She was, she thought, and remembered a line from the strange book Harrison called Liber Korrupt:

What is the cost of one life in the pursuit of such power? In what will become the tradition of my ancestors, my Daisy will die so that our family's reign is sealed...

No longer disembodied, the voice dropped the ruse of the

calming purple friend and instead took on a tone darkened by longing and decay. Now was not the time to breathe and accept. Now was the time to plot and destroy. As if in answer to this, Lisa heard the massive iron door scrape open against the uneven floor.

Someone new entered the room, and Lisa remained perfectly still until she felt them take the handles on the back of the chair. Relying on the element of surprise, Lisa pushed herself as far up off the seat as she could in her restraints and thrust her head backward. The resultant CRACK and yowl brought her great satisfaction.

"What the hell, man?"

Vic?

"C'mon, Leese, I'm trying to help you."

"Vic?"

"Who else, huh?"

"Can you take this fucking bag off my head!?"

Vic did as asked and met Lisa's suspicions with his charming stoner smile.

"I suppose it'd be naive to think you infiltrated this place and arrived just in time to save me."

"Guilty as charged, babe."

Lisa chewed on this for a moment.

"How did you even get here? I thought you were at the station? Matt said they arrested you for Craig Walter's murder."

"I was until David Bradley sent a fucking Amazonian to kill me in my cell. Your boyfriend saved my ass."

"Matt saved you?"

"Yeah. We went to Harrison's looking for you, must have got there, like, right after... there were brains and blood and shit all over the walls."

There was an unnatural pause; it sounded to Lisa like Vic was fighting back a sob.

"It was Misty, wasn't it? They killed her."

Lisa softened in the face of Vic's grief.

"Yeah."

"She... didn't suffer, did she?"

"No. It... it happened so fast... there was nothing I could do."

"I loved her, ya know? I mean, she drove me fucking crazy, and she fucked, like, everyone else in town, but that wasn't really her, ya know? She had a good soul, it was just fucked up from money and drugs and–"

"Having a piece of shit like David Bradley as a dad?"

"Yeah. Exactly. Now come on, we have to fucking go right now."

Vic moved toward her with the bag.

"What are you doing?"

"Look, I need to put this back on you."

"No fucking way!"

Something about Vic's story seemed off, but it didn't matter. Lisa was crippled and tired and helpless. She had to believe in *someone* or give up.

"Trust me, Leese. Please just trust me."

"Vic... I can't walk. I'm paralyzed from the waist down."

"What? Oh fuah– no! We have to get past this part first, then we can worry about that. I'm just amazed you're still alive. If I'd been a little faster I might have been able to–"

"Vic, I don't know what I'm going to do..."

Lisa started to sob, and the sound rallied something in Vic.

"Take it easy, okay? You don't know if it's permanent. Just chill so I can get you outta here. But Leese... I gotta put this back over your head. We don't have a lot of time and I need them to think I'm one of them."

"All right, Vic. Get me out of here."

Vic held the bag up in front of her, and Lisa reluctantly bowed at the neck and accepted it over her head.

"Don't worry, babe. I got you."

They began to move, the rocky, uneven floor tossing her around in the chair as they went. Still no sensations below her belt line.

They went on for a few moments, the ground evening out. Soon, Lisa could hear distant voices. Not chanting, but conversation.

"Where are we?"

"Shh. People ahead. Stay cool."

The voices grew louder: a crowd. Beneath that, an eerie howling blanketed everything.

"Okay, brace yourself. We're about to pass through what my dad calls the membrane. Might make you puke."

"The membrane?"

"Remember that stuff my Uncle Layne told me about Peppermill actually being in hell? Turns out, it's all true."

A shimmer of light slipped through the mask's darkness, and somewhere far off, Lisa heard screaming. Something ice cold pressed against the exposed flesh of her neck and arms, a brief resistance that broke with an audible POP. An explosion of echoes marked their entrance into a larger space. The voices were right here before her. A lot of them, and to her absolute disgust, they began *touching her*, brushing greedy fingers across her body.

"Ugh! Stop touching me!" she shrieked.

"Take it easy. Almost there."

"You! Stop!" A new voice called out, and Lisa could tell the words were directed at them.

"Uh oh..." she heard Vic say under his breath.

"What the hell are you doing?" Lisa realized she recognized the voice from hearing it on the news day in, day out: David Bradley.

"Ah, just bringing the girl to the, ah…"

Quick, decisive footsteps approached, followed by the sound of tearing fabric.

"Vic? What fuck are you doing…"

"Ah, well, ya see, Mr. Bradley…"

Someone snatched the sack off Lisa's head and took a clump of hair with it. Her sight returned for the first time in hours; they were in some kind of underground cave that had been augmented to resemble a cross between a military bunker and an amphitheater. The impossibly black, earthen walls were adorned with dozens of masks - oblong blasphemies of the human countenance that instantly reminded her of the final moments from an old movie she'd seen once, where a congregation of Satan Worshippers melted. Only these masks were moving. They appeared *alive*. Mouths opening and closing, repeating one word over and over:

"Mammon."

Ahead of them, to either side, dozens of people gathered, all robed and wearing masks similar to those lining the walls. Beyond that, a raised dais loomed like the stage at a concert. In its center, a crimson-red inverted cross adorned a large, black altar. In front of her, David Bradley stood dressed in the same ritualistic attire, only sans the mask.

"What the fuck is this?"

"You should stop worrying about him, David."

David turned as Jim Harrison approached, flanked by two goons.

"Oh yeah, Jim? Who should I be worried about? Your old ass?"

"Here's how it is. You're out."

"What the fuck do you mean, I'm out?"

"I'm afraid Misty is quite dead. I saw to it myself," James Harrison sported a fat, shit-eating grin as he stopped just out of David's reach.

"What?"

"You heard me."

"You fucking bastard! I'll-"

"You'll do nothing, you ineffectual little ponce! I told you this was coming, David. When you stood laughing at me outside my Annie's funeral, I told you I'd win in the end. Now, here we are: I'm going to run you out of town and take both Inner Earth and the Egregore. There's nothing you or anyone else can do to stop us."

David's fury peaked; he turned toward Lisa and withdrew a large knife from beneath his cloak.

"We'll just see about that!"

David drove the knife directly at Lisa's head, but Vic threw himself in front of the blade. It pierced him through the back of his neck.

"Vic!" Lisa screamed.

Vic's blood exploded from his body, splashing Lisa in the face as he went into his death throes. Lisa watched as Vic wound down, death settling over him like fog on a lake.

"You stupid fucking stoner. You worked for me!"

One of Harrison's goons caught David by the arm and pinned it behind his back.

"One more outburst like that, David, and you'll follow him into non-existence, understood?"

"Fuck you, Jim!"

"You may disagree with how I've handled things, but there are rules, and you don't exactly play fair, either. Your daughter is dead, so your sacrifice is void. You are out, David. O.U.T. Got it?"

David Bradley regarded Jim Harrison with palpable hatred, but he did not say a word.

"Right. Let's get her up to the altar. We've wasted enough time on temper tantrums."

———

As the men picked her up in the wheelchair and carried her up the steps, the reality of her impending death pushed Lisa's mind into a frenzy.

You are stronger than any who have come before you - You are perfect.

I don't understand

Then listen and take heed: it works both ways, Lisa - Give me what I want and you will be more powerful than all those before you

What do you want?

A body

The vision dissolved when Lisa felt a hand on her shoulder. Jim Harrison.

"I'm sorry, Lisa. I truly am. If it's any consolation, I carry genuine affection for you. You were Annie's best friend."

Lisa realized her hatred for David Bradley did not come anywhere near the malice she'd accrued for this man in the last several hours. She held James Harrison in a gaze that commanded the universe ignite his body in flames.

"It makes me sick to hear you say her name, knowing that you killed her. All the lies... How could you even look at yourself in the mirror?"

"Power, plain and simple. Samson Bradley's pact with the realms infernal locked his descendants' genetics into place so there would always be someone to inherit power over the Egregore. In all the years since, only two Bradley heirs have deviated from the sacred path: Roland and Michael. If not for you, the history of Sundown Hills would be over before the decade's end. In a way, you're a hero, Lisa."

"Fucking save it! You don't even care that you killed Annie - it's not her death but the fact that the Egregore didn't want you! I hope your cancer makes the rest of your life as painful as humanly possible!"

Harrison flinched as though slapped.

"Your words sting, but it doesn't matter. In moments, you will be dead."

"You killed her for nothing!"

"The greatest regret of my life. Still, someone has to take control, and Michael made it clear that would not be him. Honestly, I've always been grateful for that. Too much of a conscience on that one. But then, like I said, the genes skipped him, just like they did his father."

The crowd grew restless; they were eager for blood.

"It's nearly time. I implore you, lie back and accept your destiny."

Harrison motioned, and another robed figure pinned Lisa's left arm behind her back and tried to pull her to her feet.

"I can't walk," she screamed, anger at having spoken the curse aloud driving the tears that streaked her face. Lisa felt power in those tears.

"A tragedy that will only inconvenience you for a few moments longer. Pick her up! Time to get on with it!"

Power in her hatred. Inside, the passenger's face lit up with a thousand-watt smile limned in Purple.

Letmeinletmeinletmeinletmeinletmein

With her right arm pulled tight around his shoulders, Harrison's goon jerked Lisa up out of her chair and caught her around the waist. She bounced against him and caught the scent of elegant lumber. Deputy Jeff Wilson: chosen to lead Lisa to her fate.

Fuck that!

Lisa's fingers slipped around to the small of Jeff's back and found the gun snugged there. She worked her hand through the open slit that ran up the side of his vestment. When he switched his balance to release her, she seized the opportunity and pulled the weapon free. It was a gamble, but what did she have to lose?

Tossed like a doll, Lisa barely managed to slip the firearm beneath her as she hit the stone slab. The stars were with her this once - the gun didn't go off, and its owner hadn't noticed her thievery.

From this vantage, Lisa could see the altar was made of shining black obsidian. An octagonal table covered by black cloth lay to her right. Before it, a viscous red liquid lapped at the lip of a small aperture in the floor. It looked... alive. Through its movement, Lisa heard whispers buried softly within the wet susurrations, the same chant she had learned from the masks:

"Mammon. Mammon. Mammon."

Time came undone; music drifted in from a distance; bathed in echoes, the sound grew steadily louder as though approaching from deeper inside the outlying catacombs. Comprised of percussive or woodwind instruments, the melody sounded *wrong*, a collection of notes unfamiliar to the human ear.

"Welcome!" a deep voice boomed across the space, the echoes fluttering away in all directions, dissolving the scattered racket of the crowd.

"Tonight, we summon the Wilhelm Egregore back into our service and move Sundown Hills into the future! Tonight, we spill sacred blood in the name of renewal and strength!"

The crowd's voice picked up the chorus, raising it to a fever pitch. How many of her neighbors were here to bear witness to her sacrifice? Town elders, teachers, politicians?

Lisa closed her eyes to seek counsel from her passenger.

You want a body? Let's talk about what I get in exchange.

———

As the flame of ritual caught fire around her, Lisa felt something alien push into her thoughts. Images that harkened back to her birth assailed her, assuring Lisa that this night had lain in wait for her since the moment she took her first breath.

The entity's filth-ridden gaze breathed new life into Lisa's dreary lungs. The scene inside her took on characteristics of the corruption she felt; a charred vista of hooks and chains dissolved to reveal rivers of blood, years of darkness. Somewhere far off, she could hear something step across a threshold and begin walking toward her, its slow, methodical footsteps issuing from between dunes of ground bone, piles of dissected tissue stained with the forgotten semen of monsters, a breeze that carried the horrors of contagion upon it...

Clik-Clop

Clik-Clop

Lisa instantaneously gained knowledge of things she couldn't possibly have been privy to. The view from the woods as Samson Bradley and a small congregation of others took instruction to raise the Egregore into existence. The understanding that part of its consciousness came from each of the people present that night, their frustration at failed crops, starvation, children lost to pestilence because they lived weak from hunger; how all of that combined with their Will to shape a small portion of the world into something *they* could control. How it was so much easier to do this in Samson's time because there were so few people inhabiting the land, and the basic tenants of this fledgling civilization called America were still in the most primitive, malleable stages.

Realization at how the power vested into this Thought Form grew, and as it did, how it carved a strong base for itself in the economic scaffolding of the new country whose land it walked upon. Developing as it grew, the Egregore changed with the world. It received a huge boost when the Industrial Revolution kicked off the "American Century." Lisa heard the entity's voice as a sensation inside her brain, neurological impulses that carried with it the story of the Santa Clara v. Southern Pacific Railroad, when Chief Justice Waite - relative of famed Magician A.E. Waite - declared that under the United States's Constitution's Fourteenth Amendment, Corporations would henceforth be recognized as people and granted the same rights as human beings. This event changed the planet's entire ecosystem, as once passed, Humanity ceded its place as the dominant form of life and became cells inside the larger, Corporate organisms that had taken over. The Egregore that Samson Bradley and his community raised functioned in a similar manner; a psychic Corporation that solidified itself on a plane above the natural world, but with the ability to create bodies out of a myriad of natural substances, its favorite being recently deceased flesh.

As if on cue, a blade pressed to her throat pulled Lisa from her visions and back into the present. At the altar before her, Jim Harrison addressed the crowd:

"Hail Hail! Mammon Ousschaken!!"

"Hail! Hai!" the congregation echoed.

"We begin with a reading from the journal of Samson Bradley, June 6th, 1866," the voice boomed across the space. "May we remember the importance of tradition in the dark business at hand."

"Unable still to make good with the crops others in this land grow so freely. My family starves, my mind conjures demons of frustration and anger. A feeling as black as pitch has come unto me, and t'was in the thrall of this Horror, she with the blackest eyes came to me from out the wood. A woman, or something that played at being a woman, mayhap..."

As Harrison read, his voice took on unearthly characteristics.

"A sight that surely belongeth not to the wilds. Society dress, locks of stormy darkness. She knew things... things about me, about the old world and the family there from which I took my wife. Crude in the Earth, she said, that's why nothing here grows. Yet, she telt me how I might use this to make my name."

By the end of the first passage, it no longer sounded like Harrison reading. Drawn to his fervor, something *else* had slipped in on top of him.

"It is to that voice and void we call unto now, the great elated Egregore conjured and conjoined to the Seventh Black Circle of Hell: the rim of understanding, the dark bastion of forbidden fruit, the path to the inside of this short-term world, a means by which to use it against he who would keep us blind."

"Eiah Eiah!" the crowd chanted.

"Oh Spirit of Knowledge, Martyr of Dark Desire Unmasked. Hear our voices rise in unison and part the sea of death so that you might join us once more, here in our Earthly pastures of pestilence and pain."

"Eiah Eiah Olumtwoo Hollum! Eiah Eiah! Eiah Eiah!"

"Eiah! Eiah!" the chant continued as Harrison began to punctuate the ritual with what sounded like a goat's bleating.

"Come to us, oh keeper of knowledge unholy! Come through our unclean brethren, through the meat they have left behind after the blood we have spilled in your name!"

"Eiah! Eiah! Olumtwoo Hollum! Eiah! Eiah!"

From behind her, Wilson grasped her by the shoulders and pushed Lisa prone on her back. From this vantage, a new figure stepped forward, upside down. Draped in a black flowing robe, the newcomer's head was that of a fully mature black goat, complete with curved horns and glowing eyes. Lisa screamed.

The figure to Harrison's left unsheathed a large, polished blade that reflected the light in a dizzying array. As they raised the weapon, the Goat-Man turned both hands palms up and, with an almost sensual motion, cupped them around the steel so that when the wielder withdrew it, the weapon came away damp with crimson stains.

"This is not fair!" Beside Harrison, David Bradley balled like a spoiled child.

"One more outburst, David, and your blood will also stain this altar tonight."

Like a scene from a nightmare, the Goat-Man accepted the blade and turned its attention to Lisa, blood from its lacerated hands trailing in its wake. As it approached, a new voice rang out an impassioned cry.

"Stop!!"

Jeff's hands left her suddenly, and Lisa knew he was about to discover his pistol missing. Flailing with his robe, the Deputy took several steps toward where Michael Bradley now stood at the base of the altar. Beside him, Helen Landing pushed another ancient wheelchair upon which a petite figure sat hunched over, a dirty pillowcase over their head.

"Blasphemy! You have no voice here, Michael. You have no sacrifice."

"That's where you're wrong, Jimmy Cakes."

Nurse Landing plucked the sack from her captive's head and Lisa's mind recoiled at the sight of Onya O'Sullivan, drugged and drooling, her hair sopping wet with sweat, large black circles rimming eyes as white as cloudy mirrors.

Anxious whispers from the crowd crescendoed. How many people had come to see her die? However many it proved to be, Lisa would see they all paid with their lives.

"My brother David may no longer have a daughter to sacrifice, but I do."

"Are you mad?"

"Let me tell you a story, Uncle Jim. I never particularly cared for how my family did things. I saw that, even after my grandfather's death, he manipulated my father's life. As the oldest brother, I knew I would be next in line. I wanted the money, oh yes, but not at the cost of being held at someone else's behest. When you removed my father, I already had an escape plan set. See, my desires just don't match up with your antiquated ideas of power. So, I set out to build my own empire. Before I did, though, I worked up a little secret. Onya here was the product of a carefully enacted business transaction with the O'Sullivan's."

"Frank knew about this?"

"You're goddamn right he knew! I paid him over a million dollars to let me knock up his wife and have him raise the result, watching over her until it was time for me to come collect."

"He killed her. Killed my mother, now he wants to kill you..." Onya had been talking about *her father* all along - Michael Bradley!

"You bastard," David threw off his hood, eyes wet with tears of betrayal. "How could you feed me all that bullshit?"

"Oh fuck you, David. You're just as bad as Grandfather. You can't see past your little empire. Once I reclaim our family's power, I'll use it to change the entire world, not just posh myself out in this backwater shit hole."

Michael's words drove David to charge, his arm drawn back for what would have been a mighty swing had Michael not reacted faster and caught him in the face with a perfect left hook. The younger brother dropped and Michael dove on top of him, the two rolling on the floor like adolescents on a playground. Seizing the distraction, Lisa brought the handgun up from beneath her and put a round in the back of Deputy Wilson's head. The gunshot sounded like an explosion in the vast space; everyone stopped cold except Lisa, who swung the gun toward the Bradleys. She hesitated, trying to decide which one to shoot.

It works both ways

Something clicked inside her, and Lisa turned to her right and squeezed the trigger. An instant later, Onya O'Sullivan-cum-Bradley's forehead exploded in a mandala of blood and brain.

The room erupted in hysteria.

"What the hell did you do?" Michael screamed, tears streaming down his cheeks as he rolled from his brother's grasp and regained his feet. "You've destroyed me! You've destroyed everything!"

"Guess I won't be taking that job in your Seattle office, Mike."

With his attention shifted to Lisa, David shoved his brother from behind, sending him flailing from the dais to the stone floor below, where his head caught the corner of a sharp rock outcropping. The impact twisted Michael's head and body in opposite directions, the SNAP of his neck audible as it reverberated off the cavern's walls like a brief, staccato snare drum hit.

"For the love of all that is unholy! David!" James Harrison's voice cut short when the Goat-Man shoved him aside and used both hands to drive the ceremonial dagger into David's neck. The younger Bradley let out a truncated shriek as his life achieved escape velocity.

"Blasphemy!" someone screamed. Goat-Man lifted his right leg and planted a steel toe boot on David's chest, kicking him free of the blade to fall lifeless beside his brother. The resulting geyser of blood that arced from the corpse splashed the wall with the masks. Lisa gasped at the sight of them licking the foul effluent, some hellish thirst driving them to frenzy.

Another shot rang out, and a piece of the wall behind the

altar ricocheted into the darkness. The Goat-Man turned on Harrison before he could fire a second time and drove the blade straight through the old man's midsection. Harrison howled in pain and fury, the hood slipping free to reveal the saucers disbelief made of his eyes.

Panicked voices engulfed them as the Goat-Man stopped before Lisa and removed what Lisa now saw was a hollowed out goat's head. Gerald McCready stood before her.

"Lisa."

Terror, surprise, betrayal - all of these feelings collided in Lisa as she raised the handgun and fired point blank into her father's chest. A cloud of red mist, bone and seared cartilage bloomed in the air before her slow-motion style, like the special effects in an action movie.

Chaos turned to cacophony around them. Lisa could hear it but couldn't see anything other than her father, whose eyes locked on hers in their final moments of lucidity. In his gaze, Lisa saw what she could only describe as frightened gratitude.

Gerald dropped to his knees; his mouth opened and closed for a moment before he flopped forward onto the stone floor. Amid the bedlam around her, Lisa began to fire indiscriminately at the robed figures. The first shot caught one target in the chest, blood exploding in all directions. There was an animal-like shriek as the figure's hood fell backward to reveal David Bradley's attorney, Ben Inoue. Ben hit the ground just inches from her and, an instant later, disappeared as the cave's floor turned to transparent smoke.

"The Doorway is open! The Egregore has arrived!" someone screamed, prompting Lisa to fire two more shots into the crowd now swelling in from beyond the lights. The congregation wasn't running at her; they were running past her, no doubt scrambling to save themselves from whatever encroaching nightmare issued directly from the abyss before her. Lisa braced herself when, just as in her vision, purple eyes emerged from the swirling vapor that had replaced the cavern floor.

"Hey, kiddo..."

Lisa fell to her knees as her older sister Ashley stood before her once more.

CHAPTER TWENTY-FIVE

Throughout his life, Gerald McCready had fought a tireless darkness. This void lapped against his staunch American upbringing, a violent, eroding tide. Gerald's battle proved unceasing, and he understood from a young age that it would be his burden to bear until he closed his eyes the final time.

"Your mother's people aren't like others. They trafficked in bad shit, and because of it, son, you're gonna have to fight against it your entire life."

Gerald's father, Powers McCready, told him this on his seventh birthday. Gerald never forgot those words. It was nice because regardless of how far into the past that moment moved, Gerald could always hear his father's voice clear as day. If he closed his eyes, he could almost see him standing before him, wide-brimmed stetson worn low on his forehead to hide his receding hairline, his broad jaw and sharp nose creating the perfect profile for the hero in a cowboy film.

Through the years, Gerald managed to successfully navigate his dark urges with the help of his father's lessons. The secret came in the understanding that the man he presented to the world was, in fact, a work of fiction. That the dark, bitter creature inside constituted Gerald's true self.

"For that, son, you can thank your great, great grandfather."

Samson Bradley sold the souls of his family's future generations in exchange for success on a scale most people do not see in this life. As promised, each successive patriarch in the family enjoyed this same level of wealth and power; for the few who attempted to break free of the Bradley Family Pact, life held only suffering.

Roland Bradley had been the first to renounce his Grandfather's infernal associations, and he suffered exorbitantly for that choice. Roland balked at killing his daughter, and Linda Bradley's subsequent flight from Sundown Hills spurred her father to renege on the pact, selling the family land and renouncing the Egregore.

Gerald remembered the day Powers explained his mother's complicated family history to him, every lurid detail. It sounded like a movie. After fleeing, Linda moved around the country, changing her name until the day she met Powers McCready. A tough-as-nails Sheriff in Wallace, Idaho, Powers was nearly twenty years Linda's senior. He took her in when he discovered her squatting in an abandoned house on the edge of town and, eventually, coaxed her into telling her story. Her escape; how no matter where she went, who she became, Linda's past always caught up with her. Powers spent much of his younger years in the Pinkerton organization. He knew the signs of professional work. He leaned on old contacts, discovered what they were up against, and swore to protect the girl.

Eventually, Powers and Linda fell in love. Tragically, on the day Gerald was born of that love, Linda took her final breath. Afterward, the threat seemed to fall away and Powers raised Gerald according to his personal code. John Wayne tough-guy aesthetics as applied to a rigid sense of justice and honor. At eighteen, Gerald became his father's Deputy. Wallace was a small town, barely two thousand people in 1985. Mature beyond his days, Powers hoped his son would one day replace him. On the surface, the boy made his father proud. Inside, however, something else began to affect the youngest officer in Idaho.

The tide.

Gerald sensed a gathering darkness. He was drawn to violence, developed an insatiable sexual appetite and an interest in the Occult. Powers was a small-town man all the way but never a Church-goer; he viewed religion as a tool for those too weak to develop their own sense of morality. Perhaps because of this, Gerald grew up harboring a degree of cynicism when it came to the story of his heritage, bathed as it was in Christian imagery.

Shortly after Powers passed, Gerald met Hope. Much like the story of his own mother, Hope Lange came to Wallace on the run. A recovered drug addict and criminal, what started as pity on Gerald's part soon turned to affection. He hid her, helped her put her life back together and eventually put a ring on her finger. The wedding was small, even by Wallace standards, but one attendee stuck out like a sore thumb. At the reception, James Harrison introduced himself to the couple under the guise of a 'long-lost friend' of Gerald's Mother. Over the course of the conversation, Harrison mentioned an opening for Sheriff in Sundown Hills, his mother's hometown. Gerald politely declined the offer but liked Harrison, and the two kept in touch. Less than a year later, Ashely was born.

Five years passed before Ashley's baby sister, Lisa, took her first breath and Hope took her last. Gerald fought to keep his head above water, but his grief proved so great he eventually gave in to his darkness. The result saw him removed from office and reduced to a pariah. It was at this exact moment that James Harrison returned. With no prospects and little money, Sundown Hills proved Gerald's only option. Fortuitously, the Sheriff's position had recently opened once again.

"You won't be the only person in town with a few skeletons in the closet."

For a time, the family achieved a level of normalcy. Then Michael Bradley absconded from town and his position as CEO, and the newly elected Mayor Harrison approached Gerald with the idea of a coup. Harrison revealed he had brought Gerald to Sundown Hills as a strategic move; his own ancestors may have fallen in line with Samson's ambitions, but entering into the pact was restricted to Bradley blood.

"My great grandfather sacrificed just as much as Samson, but we're excluded from the deal, left to accept whatever scraps the Bradleys throw us."

Gerald refused, horrified that his family's stability proved nothing more than a chess maneuver. Things soured between the two men quickly after that. When Annie Harrison died, Gerald knew who killed her, and when Angela Walters and her friends were murdered in the Peppermill Massacre, Gerald approached Harrison in the interest of stopping whatever he'd set in motion.

The day before Gerald picked Lisa up from Mather's Sanitarium, Harrison sauntered into his office and reminded Gerald that everything he had was because of his help.

"You owe me."

Not even a week later, Ashley was dead and Lisa attacked. It was at that moment Gerald's course became clear to him. He would play the cards he'd been dealt, maneuvering everyone into a position where he could finally end his family's haunted legacy once and for all. Never did he dream it would be Lisa who dealt the killing blow.

When Gerald turned the blade on Harrison, he moved

with no thought, only intention. It happened so fast that he wasn't even sure he'd connected until the older man's blood doused him. In the next moment, a bolder hit him in the chest, and it was not until he locked eyes with his daughter that he understood what had happened. The horror that had cast a pall over Gerald for as long as he could remember drained away, and for the first time since he was a child, that dark tide broke and rolled back, leaving only love in its wake.

Gerald died with love and admiration for his daughter. She had finally freed him from this world to move into the peace he craved.

As their eyes locked, he tried to communicate his gratitude. He did, too, or at least he hoped so. Everything turned cloudy as the floor fell away and two purple eyes appeared inside the rising tendrils of smoke. Eyes that stared up at Lisa with a lust heretofore unknown. Gerald's joy turned to fear; he tried to fight through his encroaching death, tried to pull himself back long enough to warn her, but it was too late. As the Egregore began to take shape - a shimmering apparition constructed more of Intent and Force than actual flesh and blood, it took a moment to push itself into Gerald's brain, tearing Gerald's mind in two as the red wasps of madness poured through his eyes, his final earthly thought terror at what his daughter had now bound herself to.

———

People ran in all directions, and to her horror, Lisa realized that her previous estimate of attendees had been way off.

There were hundreds of people, possibly the entire town.

"Damn near it," Ashley said, reading her mind. She snapped her finger and everything stopped on a dime. There was Adele Johnson, tripping on her cloak, the hood three-quarters down the back of her head, gravity denied. To their left, Principal Severin, flat on his back, legs crushed beneath three hooded figures frozen in mid-flight, two of whom might have been Beth Grobe's parents, Phylis and Albert.

Lisa wasn't sure if it was her surprise - mixed with joy, horror and fantasy - that drew the world to a standstill or if she had finally snapped, her senses never to be trusted again.

She shook these thoughts off, tried to firmly reestablish reality. Problem was, the madness proved far more desirable than the world as it had become in recent months.

"You are *not* my sister."

"No? You don't sound so sure of yourself there, kiddo. They told you I was dead, but did you ever actually see the body?"

Gerald had kept Lisa from viewing Ashley's remains on the grounds they were so mutilated that seeing them would provide anything but closure.

"I can see you running the numbers, Leese. He lied to you about pretty much everything else, so..."

They locked eyes, Ashley's gaze burrowing into her. The look was one Lisa had only ever seen her big sister use on their father, a penetrating gaze that carried with it an ultimatum: are you with me or against me?

"Ash? Is it really you?"

Even as she asked, Lisa knew the impossibility of the situation. Yet, the tiny gold flakes in Ashley's left iris, the way the entire eye floated in its orbit ever since the attack under the bleachers her Senior year. Seeing this, that voice inside her changed, and Lisa realized the drug Landing had made sure she'd developed a taste for during her stay at Mather's hadn't just allowed her to be manipulated by this secret cabal, but by this thing they'd called up from Hell.

"What... is this?" Lisa asked, indicating the frozen townsfolk around them.

"This?" Ashley said, her inflection and cadence exactly

how Lisa remembered. "This is a one-time-only deal, sis. Take it or leave it."

Ashley snickered, and the mask slipped for a moment. Then she blew a bubble with that florescent green gum she chewed day and night, and the illusion resumed, strong enough to win Lisa over once and for all.

"What are my choices?"

"You accept me. I can stay in this form, or I can take another. Doesn't matter to me."

"What do you get out of it?"

"Every generation of Bradley I've been affiliated with has fucked me over. See, the oil was only a byproduct of what we really want."

"Which is?"

"Tunnels."

"Tunnels?"

"Samson was supposed to provide us direct access to this plane."

"You mean from what, Hell?"

"Yup," Ashley emphasized this by popping her bubble, and Lisa remembered the cold sensation and icy POP as Vic wheeled her into this chamber.

"Yeah, well, you know that stuff my Uncle Layne told me about Peppermill actually being in Hell? Turns out, it's all true."

"So howz'about it, kiddo?"

"So, you want me to build a tunnel to Hell?"

"Think of it as a highway straight to the Burning Lands. Hell isn't the place where humans go when they die. It's a place where Demons and Monsters live, and just like up here on the surface, technology and time have brought on a population explosion that is very nearly at critical mass. They need somewhere else to go."

"You want me to bring about Hell on Earth?"

"Hell is such a boring concept. You have to stop thinking in terms of how you've been taught."

"Oh yeah? Where else would my sister's evil doppelgänger come from?"

Ashley laughed.

"Okay, well, you couch things in whatever words make you comfortable, kiddo. The fact of the matter is, you stand on the precipice of unimaginable power."

"Can you give me my legs back?"

"Yup."

A chill passed through Lisa's spine.

"Really?"

"If I can freeze a couple hundred people mid-panic, getting another one moving again shouldn't be a problem."

Her legs. How could she turn that down?

"Lisha!"

Lisa turned to see Matt at the base of the dais. His uniform was covered in dried, black blood. His voice sounded... off. When he realized who she was talking to, Matt took an instinctual step backward.

"Don't lishten to it! That thing ish *not* your shishter!"

"I know, but-"

"Your shishter is dead. You can't let it do thish to her!"

The rage she'd felt at her father returned. The body of one controlling man in her life had barely cooled, and now here was another trying to tell her what to do.

"Who the fuck are you to tell me what I can or can't do? You're just like every other man in my fucking life. You all just want to control me!"

"What? No, leeshe... it's jusht that.. *Thing*..."

Lisa turned back to Ashely - the thing that had taken Ashley's form - and her eyes pleaded with it. They said, "Make the decision for me."

"Really? This is the guy you're into? I would'a stuck with the bad boy."

Matt's confusion at the conversation stalled him for a moment.

"So, Tick Tock, Kiddo. What's it gonna be? You in or out? Down with OPP or no?"

"Yes. But Matt's right. As much as I miss her, I don't want you in Ashley's form."

"I'm inchoate, so I can take whatever form you want. Ashley's dead and buried, her body destroyed by her attacker. I would prefer fresh flesh."

"Lisha! We can fixsh this!"

In that moment, Lisa knew that she loved Matt, but she also knew he would never love her if she did what the entity asked of her. She'd lost everyone else in her life - she wouldn't survive losing Matt now that she knew he was alive.

"Then I know exactly who I want you to be."

Matt reached the top of the steps and Lisa turned and leveled the gun at his brow.

EPILOGUE

On the TV at the room's far end, acting Sheriff Matt Hartman gave a thumbs up from his hospital bed. From off camera, Ted Owens' carefully rehearsed newscaster tone told of triumph and tragedy - one man's battle to save his town.

"Despite sustaining nearly fatal injuries at the attacker's hands, Matt Hartman saved the day by overpowering the madman and saving Sundown Hills."

The screen blipped to Lisa lying on a stretcher, an IV bag trailing behind her as paramedics rushed her into the hospital.

"Sheriff McCready's daughter was among those Deputy Hartman saved. Sadly, the Sheriff himself perished, along with nearly a dozen of our city's most beloved residents."

Lisa sat in her wheelchair in the corner of the room, staring at the television, drinking in the world she had helped create.

"With his unparalleled act of heroism and the town's sudden loss of its Sheriff *and* both its Mayoral candidates, there's already talk that the Deputy may be the man for the job."

A nurse knocked gently at the door.

"How're you feeling, honey?"

"I'm... okay. Sore."

"Here, I've got your next round of meds," the nurse walked to her and offered a small paper pill cup. Lisa took it; inside the two purple pills looked like beetles dead on their back.

"Take those and I'll be back to check on you later."

Lisa nodded. As soon as the nurse left the room, she tossed the cup in the trash.

"You've come a long way, babe."

Lisa looked up; Matt stood in the doorway, his smile as radiant as a post-thunderstorm rainbow.

"Hey, I, ah..."

Matt crossed to her but stopped a couple feet out.

"You look better."

"You look great, considering, ya know..."

"You shot me in the head? Hahaha. Yeah, the devil doesn't welch on his promises. A deal's a deal, right?"

"Right. Here..." Lisa offered the tablet she'd been journaling in since arriving at the hospital.

"What's that?"

"I've been researching the best digging machines currently in production. I thought we'd go with the..."

She offered the tablet again, but Matt stayed where he was.

"Don't you want to see?"

He nodded, "I do. Why don't you bring it to me?"

Lisa looked momentarily unsure, then a smile spread across her face.

"Really?"

Matt nodded again, and Lisa planted both hands on her chair's arms, pushing herself up and onto her feet.

"See? A deal's a deal, babe."

Crying, Lisa walked to the love of her life and wrapped her arms around him.

PLAYLIST

As usual, I'd like to pay tribute to the music that proved a mainstay on this project. This isn't all I listened to, but it's what I probably listened to the most, and thus it directly informed the tone:

Type O Negative - All albums always
Godflesh - Purge
Fvnerals - Let The Earth Be Silent
Jim Williams - Possessor OST
Blackbraid II
Forhist - Eponymous
Blut Aus Nord - Memoria Vetusta II
Lustmord - Berlin/Hobart
Justin Hamline - House w/ Dead Leaves
Steve Moore - Bliss OST